THE
MUSEUM OF
UNCONDITIONAL
SURRENDER

Photograph of unknown swimmers. Taken on the Pakra river (Northern Croatia) at the beginning of the century. Photographer unknown.

THE MUSEUM OF UNCONDITIONAL SURRENDER

DUBRAVKA UGREŠIĆ

TRANSLATED BY CELIA HAWKESWORTH

A NEW DIRECTIONS BOOK

The Publisher wishes to thank Damion Searls and Greg Carter for their assistance in publishing *The Museum of Unconditional Surrender.*

Book design by Sylvia Frezzolini Severance
Manufactured in the United States of America
New Directions books are printed on acid-free paper.
First published clothbound by New Directions in 1999

Library of Congress Cataloging-in-Publication Data

Ugresic, Dubravka.
    [Muzej bezuvjetne predaje. English]
    The museum of unconditional surrender / Dubravka Ugresic ;
    translated from the Croatian by Celia Hawkesworth.
        p.   cm.
    "A New directions book."
        ISBN 0-8112-1421-4
    I. Title.
    PG1619.31.G7M8913   1999
    891.8'2354—dc21   99-33134
                                                        CIP

New Directions Books are published for James Laughlin
by New Directions Publishing Corporation,
80 Eighth Avenue, New York 10011

SECOND PRINTING

CONTENTS

PART ONE   *Ich bin müde*   1

PART TWO   Family museum   11

PART THREE   *Guten Tag*   93

PART FOUR   Archive: six stories with the discreet motif
of a departing angel   109

PART FIVE   *Was ist Kunst?*   157

PART SIX   Group photograph   171

PART SEVEN   *Wo bin ich?*   219

THE
MUSEUM OF
UNCONDITIONAL
SURRENDER

n the Berlin zoo, beside the pool containing the live walrus, there is an unusual display. In a glass case are all the things found in the stomach of Roland the walrus, who died on 21 August 1961. Or to be precise:

> a pink cigarette lighter, four ice-lolly sticks (wooden), a metal brooch in the form of a poodle, a beer-bottle opener, a woman's bracelet (probably silver), a hair grip, a wooden pencil, a child's plastic water pistol, a plastic knife, sunglasses, a little chain, a spring (small), a rubber ring, a parachute (child's toy), a steel chain about 18 ins in length, four nails (large), a green plastic car, a metal comb, a plastic badge, a small doll, a beer can (Pilsner, half-pint), a box of matches, a baby's shoe, a compass, a small car key, four coins, a knife with a wooden handle, a baby's dummy, a bunch of keys (5), a padlock, a little plastic bag containing needles and thread.

The visitor stands in front of the unusual display, more enchanted than horrified, as before archaeological exhibits. The visitor knows that their museum-display fate has been determined by chance (Roland's whimsical appetite) but still cannot resist the poetic thought that with time the objects have acquired some subtler, secret connections. Caught up in this thought, the visitor then tries to establish semantic coordinates, to reconstruct the historical context (it occurs to him, for instance, that Roland died one week after the Berlin Wall was erected), and so on and so forth.

The chapters and fragments which follow should be read in a similar way. If the reader feels that there are no meaningful or firm connections between them, let him be patient: the connections will establish themselves of their own accord. And one more thing: the question as to whether this novel is autobiographical might at some hypothetical moment be of concern to the police, but not to the reader.

PART ONE

Ich bin müde

1. *'Ich bin müde,'* I say to Fred. His sorrowful, pale face stretches into a grin. *Ich bin müde* is the only German sentence I know at the moment. And right now I don't want to learn any more. Learning more means opening up. And I want to stay closed for a while longer.

2. Fred's face reminds one of an old photograph. Fred looks like a young officer driven by unhappy love to play Russian roulette. I imagine him some hundred years ago spending whole nights in Budapest restaurants. The mournful scraping of Gypsy violins doesn't provoke so much as a quiver on his pale face. Just occasionally his eyes shine with the gleam of the metal buttons on his uniform.

3. The view from my room, my temporary exile, is filled with tall pine trees. In the morning I open the curtains to reveal a romantic stage set. The pines are at first shrouded in mist like ghosts, then the mist disperses in wisps, and the sun breaks through. Towards the end of the day the pines grow dark. In the left-hand corner of the window a lake can just be seen. In the evening I close the curtains. The stage set is the same each day, the stillness of the scene is broken occasionally by a bird, but all that ever really changes is the light.

4. My room is filled with a silence as thick as cotton wool. If I open the window, the silence is shattered by the twittering of birds. In the evening, if I go out of my room into the hall, I hear the sound of a television (from Kira's room on my floor) and the sound of a typewriter (the Russian writer on the floor below me). A little later I hear the uneven tapping of a stick and the scrape of the invisible German writer's small footsteps. I often see the artists, a Romanian married couple (from the floor below me), they pass silently like shadows. The silence is sometimes disturbed by Fred, our caretaker. Fred cuts the grass in the park, driving the pain of his love away with the noisy electric mower. His wife has recently left him. 'Zy vife ist crazy,' Fred explained. That's the only English sentence he knows.

5. In the nearby town of Murnau there is a museum, the house of Gabriele Münter and Wassily Kandinsky. I am always a little troubled by the traces of other people's lives, they are at once so personal and yet impersonal. When I was there I bought a postcard showing a painting of the house, *Das Russen-Haus*. I often look at this postcard. I sometimes feel that the tiny human form at the window, that dark-red dot, is me.

6. On my desk there is a yellowed photograph. It shows three unknown women bathers. I don't know much about the photograph, just that it was taken at the beginning of the century on the river Pakra. That is a little river that runs not far from the small town where I was born and spent my childhood.

I always carry the photograph around with me, like a little fetish object whose real meaning I do not know. Its matt yellow surface attracts my attention, hypnotically. Sometimes I stare at it for a long time, not thinking about anything. Sometimes I plunge attentively into the reflections of the three bathers mirrored in the water, into their faces which are looking straight at mine. I dive into them as though I am about to solve a mystery, discover a crack, a hidden passage through which I shall slip into a different space, a different time. Usually I prop up the photograph in the left-hand corner of the window, where the end of the lake can be seen.

7. I sometimes have coffee with Kira from Kiev, a retired literature teacher. *'Ya kamenshchitsa,'** says Kira. Kira is passionate about every kind of stone. She tells me that she spends every summer in the Crimea, in a village where the sea throws all kinds of semi-precious stones up on to the shore. She is not alone, she says, other people come there as well, they are all *kamenshchiki*. Sometimes they meet up, make a fire, cook borsch and show one another their 'treasures'. Here, Kira passes the time painting copies of various subjects. She has made a copy of the archangel Michael, although, she says, she prefers—threading. She asks whether I have a broken necklace, she could mend it, she says, re-thread the beads. 'You know,' says Kira, 'I like threading things.' She says it as though she were apologising.

8. In nearby Murnau, there is a museum commemorating Odön von Horváth. Odön von Horváth was born on 9 December 1901 in Rijeka, at

---

* 'I am a pebble-lover.'

16.45 (according to some other documents it was 16.30). When he had attained a weight of some 16 kilograms, he left Rijeka, and spent some time in Venice and some more in the Balkans. When he reached a height of 1 metre 20 he moved to Budapest and lived there until he was 1 metre 21. According to Odon von Horváth's own account, Eros awoke in him when he was 1 metre 52. Horváth's interest in art, and particularly literature, appeared at a height of 1 metre 70. When the First World War started Odön von Horváth measured 160cm, and when the war ended he was a whole 180cm. Odön von Horváth stopped growing when he reached a height of 184cm. Horváth's biography measured in centimetres and geographical points is confirmed by museum photographs.

9. There is a story told about the war criminal Ratko Mladić, who spent months shelling Sarajevo from the surrounding hills. Once he noticed an acquaintance's house in the next target. The general telephoned his acquaintance and informed him that he was giving him five minutes to collect his 'albums', because he had decided to blow the house up. When he said 'albums', the murderer meant the albums of family photographs. The general, who had been destroying the city for months, knew precisely how to annihilate memory. That is why he 'generously' bestowed on his acquaintance life with the right to remembrance. Bare life and a few family photographs.

10. 'Refugees are divided into two categories: those who have photographs and those who have none,' said a Bosnian, a refugee.

11. 'What a woman needs most is air,' says my friend Hannelore as we walk towards the nearby Andechs monastery.

'What a woman needs most is a butler,' I reply to Hannelore as I buy a cheap plastic ball with a guardian angel in it in the souvenir shop at the monastery.

Hannelore laughs inaudibly. When the ball is given a little shake, snow falls on the guardian angel. Hannelore's laughter rustles like polystyrene snow.

12. Before I came here, I spent a few days on the Adriatic, in a house beside the sea. Occasional bathers came to the little beach. They could be

seen and heard from the terrace. One day my attention was drawn to a woman's strikingly loud laughter. I looked up and saw three elderly bathers in the sea. They were swimming with naked breasts, right by the shore, in a small circle, as though they were sitting at a round table, drinking coffee. They were Bosnian (judging by their accent), probably refugees, and nurses. How do I know? They were recalling their distant schooldays and gossiping about a fourth who had confused the words 'anamnesis' and 'amnesia' at her final examination. The word 'amnesia' and the story about the exam were repeated several times and each time they provoked salvoes of laughter. At the same time, all three waved their hands as though they were brushing invisible crumbs from a non-existent table. All at once there was a shower, one of those short, sudden summer ones. The bathers stayed in the water. From the terrace I watched the large shining drops of rain and the three women: their laughter was increasingly loud, with increasingly short intervals, now they were doubled-up with laughter. In the pauses I could make out the word 'falling' which they kept repeating, meaning, presumably, the rain . . . They spread their arms, splashed the water with their hands, now their voices were like birds' cawing, as though they were competing as to whose voice would be throatiest and loudest, and the rain too, as though it had gone mad, was ever heavier and warmer. Between the terrace and the sea a misty, wet, salty curtain fell. All at once the curtain absorbed all the sound and the three pairs of wings continued flapping magnificently in the glistening silence.

I made an inner 'click' and recorded the scene, although I don't know why.

13. 'What a woman needs most is water,' says Hannelore as we rest after swimming in the luxurious atmosphere of the Müllersche Volksbads.

14. From the start, my acquaintance S.'s life didn't go well. But still, she managed to complete her nursing training and get a job in a hospital for mentally retarded children on the edge of town. 'It won't end well. I absorb other people's misfortune like blotting paper,' she said. In the hospital she found her little personal happiness, a male nurse, much younger than her, an exceptionally small man (when I met him I couldn't take my eyes off his little lacquered shoes) who even had a surname that was diminutive. At a relatively advanced age, she fell pregnant. She decided to

go ahead with the pregnancy despite the fact that they were both diabetic. She carried the pregnancy (twins!) to term, and then, the day before they were due, the unborn babies suffocated. My acquaintance fell apart like wet blotting paper. She spent some time in the psychiatric wing, recovered and moved with her little husband to a smaller town. One day she suddenly appeared in my house. Everything was 'normal', we talked about her work, about her husband, about this and that, and then my acquaintance took a little plastic bag out of her handbag and spread her 'treasures' before me. These were two or three insignificant little shiny objects, so insignificant that I don't remember what they were. She fiddled with her trinkets for a long time. Then, catching sight of a miniature spray of dried flowers on my shelf, she said that she really liked the spray, that it was wonderful, simply wonderful, and asked me to give it to her. She shoved the little spray into the plastic bag, and then departed with her pathetic magpie's treasure.

15. Over coffee, Kira tells me something about the other inhabitants of the villa. 'You know, we're all alike in a way, we are all looking for something . . . As though we had lost something . . .' she says.

16. An exile feels that the state of exile is a constant, special sensitivity to sound. So I sometimes feel that exile is nothing but a state of searching for and recollecting sound.

In Munich where I had gone to meet Igor, I stopped for a moment near Marienplatz, drawn to the sound of music. An elderly Gypsy was playing Hungarian Gypsy songs on a violin. He caught my passing glance, gave me a smile that was both deferential and brazen at the same time, recognising me as 'one of his'. Something caught in my throat, for a moment I couldn't breathe, and then I lowered my eyes and hurried on, realising a second later that I had set off in the wrong direction. A couple of paces further on I caught sight of a life-saving telephone box and joined the queue, pretending that I had to make a phone call, what else?

There was a young man standing in front of me. Tight black leather jacket, tight jeans, high-heeled boots, a kind of insecurity and impudence on his face at the same time, like colours running into each other. A second later I knew that he was 'one of us', 'my countryman'. The way he slowly and persistently dialled the number—looking neither to right nor left, like a waiter in a cheap restaurant—filled me with a mixture of anger and pity and put me on the side of the people in the queue. And then the young man finally got through (yes, 'one of us', of course!). My country-men's habit of talking for a long time, about nothing, as though coddling, pampering, mutually patting each other's backs and jollying each other along, that habit filled me again with a sudden mixture of anger and pity. The violin was still whining sorrowfully, the young man was talking to a certain Milica, and in my head, as at an editing table, I was mixing the whine with the young man's babbling. The black-eyed violinist was staring persistently in my direction. For a moment I wanted to leave the queue, but I didn't, that would have given me away, I thought. That is why, when the young man finished his conversation and smoothed his hair with his hand (a gesture which filled me with the same mixed feelings as before, because of its unexpectedness), I telephoned Hannelore, who was the only person I could have telephoned, thinking up some urgent, practical question.

I was late for my meeting with Igor. We went to a Chinese restaurant and, as we chatted brightly waiting to be served, I observed that I was restless, absent, that my eyes were wandering, I felt as though I was covered with a fine film, like spectacles on a winter's day. And then I became aware of a sound I had not at first registered. There was Chinese or Korean pop-music playing, or at any rate pop-music from that part of the world. It was a soft, elegiac, sweet crooning, a love song presumably, which could have been from my home, or from Igor's Russian home. Just then there was a sudden downpour of rain which streamed down the restaurant window behind Igor, and finally I broke, let myself go, reacted properly, precisely, following an ancient, well-practised reflex, of which I had not been conscious until that moment. In a word, I salivated at the sound of the bell, that universal, sweet whine, the same whine no matter where it came from . . . I struggled inwardly, resisted, grumbled, almost glad that I was in its power, almost physically satisfied, weakened, softened, I splashed about in the warm invisible puddle of tears . . .

'What's happening, Igor . . .?' I asked him, as though apologising.

'The glint of the button on your blouse is making your eyes shine,' said my friend, a Russian Jew from Chernovitsa, an exile.

I looked dully down at the button. It was an opaque, plastic-goldish colour.

17. 'I have no desire to be witty. I have no desire to construct a plot. I am going to write about things and thoughts. To compile quotations,' wrote a temporary exile a long time ago. His name was Viktor Shklovsky.

18. *'Ich bin müde,'* I say to Fred. His pale sorrowful face stretches into a grin. *Ich bin müde* is the only German sentence I know at the moment. And right now I don't want to learn any more. Learning more means opening up. And I want to stay closed for a while longer.

In the silence of my room, with the romantic stage set in the windows, I arrange my bits and pieces, some I have brought with me, without really knowing why, some I found here, all random and meaningless. A little feather I picked up while walking in the park gleams in front of me, a sentence I read somewhere rings in my head, an old yellowing photograph looks at me, the outline of a gesture I saw somewhere accompanies me, and I don't know what it means or who made it, the ball containing the guardian angel shines before me with its plastic glow. When I shake it, snow falls on the angel. I don't understand the meaning of all of this, I am dislocated, I am a weary human specimen, a pebble, I have been cast by chance on to a different, safer shore.

19. 'What a woman needs most are air and water,' says Hannelore instructively as we sit in a bar, blowing the froth from the beer in our mugs.

20. The exile feels that the state of exile has the structure of a dream. All at once, as in a dream, faces appear which he had forgotten, or perhaps had never met, places which he is undoubtedly seeing for the first time, but that he feels he knows from somewhere. The dream is a magnetic field which attracts images from the past, present and future. The exile suddenly sees in reality faces, events and images, drawn by the magnetic field of the dream; suddenly it seems as though his biography was written long before it was to be fulfilled, that his exile is therefore not the result of external circumstances nor his choice, but a jumble of coordinates which fate had long ago sketched out for him. Caught up in this seductive and terrifying thought, the exile begins to decipher the signs, crosses and knots and all at once it seems as though he were beginning to read in it all a secret harmony, a round logic of symbols.

21. *'Nanizivat', ya lyublyu nanizivat','** says Kira as though apologising for something, and smiles the pale smile of a convalescent.

'Threading, I like threading things.'

22. In the glass studio at the end of our park, the Romanian couple are preparing an exhibition. The young woman uses an axe to shape pieces of wood she has been collecting around the park for days. Meanwhile, the man pins little pieces of thin, almost transparent, paper to a huge white board. On each one a bird's head is painted in soft, bright, grey water-colours. The young woman hits the wood rhythmically with her axe. At first the little pieces of paper are still, and then an invisible current slowly stirs them. The birds' heads quiver as though they were going to fall.

*Threading, I like threading things.

10

PART TWO

Family Museum

I

The poetics of the album

It is a nostalgic time right now, and photographs actively promote nostalgia. Photography is an elegiac art, a twilight art. Most subjects photographed are, just by virtue of being photographed, touched with pathos. An ugly or grotesque subject may be moving because it has been dignified by the attention of the photographer. A beautiful subject can be the object of rueful feelings, because it has aged or decayed or no longer exists. All photographs are *mementos mori*. To take a photograph is to participate in another person's (or thing's) mortality, vulnerability, mutability. Precisely by slicing out this moment and freezing it, all photographs testify to time's relentless melt.

Susan Sontag, *On Photography*

'What are Slavica and Branko doing here?' she says, taking the album from my hands and scrutinising the photograph of a young smiling couple.

'Who are Slavica and Branko?'

'You don't know them . . . You were only little . . .' she shrugs. 'If I only knew why I had put them in the album,' she murmurs to herself, emphasising 'them' and looking carefully at the photograph as though it were some rare botanical specimen.

Suddenly—with the swift movement of a hand removing a sticking plaster, she detaches the cellophane cover, takes out the photograph and tears it into small pieces. The paper sounds of the execution rip the air.

'There,' she says. 'They've been dead for ages anyway,' she adds in a conciliatory-commemorative tone, handing me back the album.

The beginning of this story is hidden in a lady's pigskin bag, which she had brought with her, along with the suitcase of modest contents in that far-off year of 1946. As soon as the first (postwar) opportunity permitted her to buy a new lady's bag, the old one settled in a corner of the wardrobe and from that moment on served as a storehouse for memories. There were new bags later, but this one, the first, stayed in the corner of the wardrobe.

Later there would be new furniture as well: new wardrobes, chests of drawers, cupboards. There would be even more suitable suitcases and bags, but that brown pigskin bag acquired a permanent place in the corner of the wardrobe, where it continued to be a treasure-trove of memories.

In my impoverished postwar childhood, deprived of things, Mother's bag was a substitute for a non-existent cellar or attic, a doll's house, a toy chest. I used to take out its modest contents, enthralled, feeling like a participant initiated into some Mystery. I couldn't know that that is exactly what I was. A participant in the simple mystery of life.

To start with, the bag concealed photographs (of my mother mainly), a few letters (of my father's), a gold coin, a silver cigarette case, a pure silk scarf and . . . a lock of hair.

Mother's photographs were exciting: in some she wore unusual hats, in others 'sailor-suits' and school caps, in others swimsuits (Mother in a boat, an unknown sea glistening behind her, a sight I had yet to see). There were also photographs of an older married couple, who must have been my grandmother and grandfather; a young woman, who must have been my aunt; and her little girl, my cousin. The pictures didn't mean much to me as I didn't know any of those people.

Apart from Mother's photographs (tied with a pretty ribbon), there were some of Father; then of me (as a newborn baby); and some of us together: Mother, Father and me in idyllic scenes of playing in the snow.

The letters had been written in 1948, in my father's handwriting, from a TB clinic ('You were still in my tummy then, you hadn't been born,' my mother used to say). As soon as I learned to read, I read those letters secretly. They were about quite incomprehensible things: about postwar coupons ('Have you got enough coupons?'); about streptomycin (someone had managed to obtain life-saving streptomycin); about bacon (someone had acquired a precious piece of bacon); and about love ('I see your face wherever I look').

The gold coin had belonged to Mother's family and she was to keep it all her life. Later on an almond-shaped gold ring (a present from my father) and a little square of gold for teeth would be added to this household treasure. These were the only valuables she possessed.

The cigarette case was made of silver and had belonged to my grand-father, Mother's father. There was a trotting horse engraved on the lid ('That's a horse trotting,' my mother used to say). I ran my fingers over the silver surface following the outline of the trotting horse, I opened the case and breathed in the tobacco smell of my unknown grandfather.

The pure silk scarf (Mother always emphasised the word 'pure') had been sent by my grandmother in a letter. That little breath of silk smuggled in an ordinary letter opened a crack in the door to the unknown. The words 'pure silk' worked like a magnet to attract other words of obscure meaning, the word 'emerald' among others. I used to enjoy rolling the unusual word 'emerald' round on my tongue, as though I were rolling a hard green menthol sweet round my mouth.

There was also a little silken tail captured like a fly in a cellophane wrapper—a lock of my hair. I used to like holding the cellophane up to the light to catch the rays of the sun.

With time the bag grew old, worn, tattered around the edges. It was no longer possible to close it, the photographs fell out, trickling from the bag, straggling round the wardrobe. We piled them up, tied them with string and put them back in the bag, in an effort to create order. Shoe boxes also appeared beside the bag. We threw the pictures into those boxes, or shoved them into books and drawers. Mother's bag remained the central store-house of memories.

My mother often grumbled that we must tidy up, that she would throw all the photographs out one day, that all decent people kept their photographs in albums, that it was disgraceful to have all this rubbish in the wardrobe, that wardrobes were meant for clothes, and not for all kinds of pictures, but despite her grumbling nothing changed: not the corner of the wardrobe, nor the bag in the corner, nor its function.

In 1973 my father died. I loved him, but I took his death rather calmly, and reproached myself for being so cold.

A month after his death a photograph of him, one of those small pass-port-sized ones, slid out of somewhere and appeared silently by my feet. A glance at that little picture, at that little, silent fact, tugged at a thread in me and I was shaken by a sudden, powerful sob which took my breath away. I shut myself in my room and wept, I thought I would never stop.

When I finally calmed down, my mother came into my room and pronounced a sentence the true sense of which I would understand only much later.

'We ought to buy some albums,' she said.

We did. The brown pigskin bag, the one she had brought with her in that far-off year of 1946, was thrown out of the wardrobe. A haphazard, disorderly heap of life burst into the light of day. I looked at the faces, smiles, bodies, those yellowish-brown, black and white scenes, those smudges of light on rectangular bits of paper—and felt uneasy, as though I'd caught sight of something embarrassing.

One day I found her surrounded by heaps of photographs, with a grimace of tragic helplessness on her face.

'Do you want me to help you?' I asked.

'No,' she said, 'they're my albums.'

The bag disappeared, the cardboard boxes too. The photographs no longer peered out of the drawers or fell out of books, they were now safe–between the canvas covers of the albums. A tidy pile of a dozen albums now lay on my mother's little bedside table, suggesting by their number and appearance a substantial dossier of life.

'And where's the bag?' I asked.

'Gone. I threw it away,' she said.

I leafed through the albums. They reminded me of the bag: the pictures were in order, admittedly, but there was no way of guessing at any kind of principle of 'organisation of the material'. Even the photographs of my mother herself, which had always been kept separate, tied with a jealous ribbon, were now mixed up with all the others.

Either there were too few albums, or there were too many pictures. She couldn't decide or didn't know how to organise them. She had given up the battle with genre at the outset.

One day she rearranged the albums, seeking to establish a chronology of events, but for some unknown reason the principle broke down there as well. As a result a photograph of me from my student days turned up beside Slavica and Branko, the unknown young couple.

Within that flimsy chronology, she tried to establish some kind of hierarchy, but if she decided to erase the unimportant Slavica and Branko from her life's dossier, the smiling faces of an equally unimportant Branka and Slavko would still be there.

The principles of a chronology of events and their significance in her life was destroyed, it seems, by her inner sense of things. So, for example, she devoted an exceptional amount of space to photographs of the weddings of some distant nephews, although she was barely in touch with them. She must just have liked wedding pictures.

Once I noticed a little triptych in one of the albums: three photographs of her, arranged next to each other. On the first she could have been about twenty, on the second thirty and on the third about forty. The most recent picture of her was off in the corner, outside the triptych.

'I've aged terribly, haven't I?'

'No,' I said, examining the photographs carefully.

Covering a distance of some ten years with each picture, her face certainly had changed. Its roundness turned into an oval, her big brown eyes grew smaller and became somehow slanted, her full lips became flatter and lost their appealing pout, two lines by her mouth began in her thirties to turn downwards, in her forties there were already barely perceptible little pouches on either side of her face. By the most recent photograph her mouth was visibly sagging sadly.

'No,' I said once more, closing the album.

When I picked up the same album again later, the triptych had been removed, the pictures rearranged and the newest, the one with the sagging mouth, had disappeared for ever.

In 1976 I went to Armenia with a group of students. We travelled through the dark-red Armenian spaces, above which the ghostly shadow of snowy Ararat hovered, vanishing and reappearing like the Cheshire Cat. In the Gerard Monastery, a wondrous building dug into the rocks, we met a monk. Handing round his pointless visiting card with equally pointless busyness, the monk led us to his cell. There was nothing in the cell apart from a bed, a table and a chest of drawers. On the bureau—equidistant from one another—stood three framed photographs.

'This is a picture of me at twenty, this is me at thirty, and this is me when I was forty,' the monk announced in the voice of a museum guide.

At the foot of each frame, there was a little bunch of dried flowers tied with a ribbon.

With time, Mother did succeed in putting her albums 'in order'. The one I liked best continued the pictures she had brought with her in that far-off year of 1946. Liberated from its ribbon, the bunch of yellowish-brown photographs now spread through the album in all the beauty of their patina. Young Grandmother and Grandfather with friends with striking features ('Family friends, Armenians,' said Mother) gathered round a gramophone with a speaker like a giant lotus; sitting on the grass, with a white cloth beside them and on the cloth baskets of grapes; there were Mother's appealing girlhood pictures on a beach, in a boat, on a walk with girl friends, in the shadow of trees, on an outing . . . Young girls in silk dresses, among them Eli, my mother, and young men in white trousers and dark jackets . . .

'Look,' she says, pointing at a smiling young man with a face like a young greyhound, 'he was my first love . . .'

I recognise the face, she used often to point at that picture, always saying the same words: 'he was my first love'.

'Who knows whether he is still alive . . .' she says, stroking the cellophane cover with her fingertips as though it were a crystal ball.

As I travelled through America I visited my Zagreb acquaintance, who had moved there some fifteen years earlier with her husband, a doctor, and was now stranded somewhere in American suburbia. They lived in a nice house, they had two children, she possessed credit cards and cheque books, she went once a week to yoga, once a week to a fitness centre, attended a course in Japanese ('Mark my words, in the twenty-first century, this will be Japan!'), she nosed around local antique shops, looking for pieces of furniture to suit the 'European' arrangement of her house, she roasted a turkey on Thanksgiving Day, drove her children to school and to tennis lessons, she stuck American flags in birthday cakes—and once a week got her friends together for a 'hen party'.

We sipped chilled Martinis beside her pool and chatted about this and that.

At a certain moment my acquaintance looked at me, her eyes shining with the Martini or momentary rapture, and said: 'Go on, tell them what Miroslav was like!'

I was bemused. I simply couldn't remember who Miroslav was.

'You know,' my acquaintance prompted me, 'I've already told them everything a thousand times, they know it all already . . .'

'Aha . . .' I said vaguely. I still hadn't a clue what it was all about. And then I hazily recalled that, before she married and came to America, she had really 'gone out' with a certain Mirek . . .

'Aha . . .' I began, but my acquaintance interrupted me.

'God, imagine, six feet tall!'

At that moment I clearly remembered Mirek, who had been barely five seven.

'God, and those heavenly blue eyes! Go on, tell them . . .'

Suddenly the picture of Mirek, whom I would never in my life have remembered, flashed into my mind, crystal-clear. Mirek had small brown eyes and a pockmarked face.

'He loved me madly . . . And when I think that I slipped away from him and married pointlessly, really pointlessly . . . He never married, did he?'

'No, he didn't. Never,' I said, compassionately.

In the verbal album arranged for her friends, Mirek's picture had been touched up on its journey from Zagreb to the American suburbs. The not quite five seven Mirek had grown into six foot Miroslav; the colour of his eyes had changed from brown to blue, and an ordinary Zagreb youth had become an unforgettable lover and the imaginary property of the participants in the hen party. Like shooting stars long since extinguished, here, on the other side of the sky, Mirek shone in his full glory.

Later, when we were washing the dishes in the kitchen, I winked conspiratorially and was about to say something along the lines of 'That's a good one, that Mirek story of yours', but my acquaintance forestalled me: 'I always loved my Miroslav, and I always will . . .' I realised that the story of Mirek was not a fabrication for the entertainment of her friends, which it might have been to start with. With time, my acquaintance had embellished Mirek's picture and come to believe in it, the touched-up version was real.

I nibbled a piece of cake, and in order to change the topic of conversation, declared: 'These cakes are good . . .' 'They're very ordinary, American. They call them brownies,' said my acquaintance in the same tone in which she had just been talking about Miroslav.

When she came out of hospital in July 1989, tormented by doubts about her survival, Mother asked me to take her photograph. Through the little eye of the Canon automatic I saw her hopelessly struggling to give her frightened face an expression which she would leave us, her children, as her last. I believe that she was sure of that. I watched that inner effort to raise her sad, drooping face and drag a smile on to it, while, no matter how she tried the effort resulted in one single unambiguous expression (which she could not see or know), a naked spasm of fear.

Suppressing a surge of emotion, hidden behind the camera, I struggled between the wish to do what she asked and the terror that, if I did, the picture really would be her last.

'That's it!' I said, pressing the shutter.

Chance ordained: there was something wrong with the camera. And Mother recovered.

Halfway through February 1988, in response to his imploring summons, I flew to Munich where he happened to be for a short time. He met me in the lobby of the Opera Hotel, sitting in a wicker armchair among clusters of white and violet orchids cascading out of gigantic vases. He stood up when he saw me in the doorway, we moved towards one another as on a stage, covering at the same time a distance far greater than those few steps.

We were to spend two days shut up in the hotel room, we would not touch, we would utter only the most essential words. He would stare dully and tenaciously at the television set, not understanding German, and I would go out from time to time on to the balcony and rub my nervous fingers on the little metal plate on the balustrade which, for some reason, had the number thirteen engraved on it (the secret set-designer of life had arranged that kitsch coincidence).

I would take frequent long showers so that he couldn't hear me crying. Under the hot water I would feel a pleasant wet languor mixed with a powerful sense of loss. I made a firm decision several times that I would get up, call a taxi, take my bag, slam the door and leave him for ever, but I stayed pinned down by an insurmountable bitter-sweet feeling of unhappiness. It seemed to me that we were caught in a kitsch glass ball, like a decrepit Adam and Eve sent back to the tree of paradise, that someone was turning the ball, that snow was falling over us, that it was absolutely immaterial whether we were alive or dead, in any case we were imprisoned for ever. At night I would be woken by his sobs, so feminine, so like my own. The same strange immobility prevented me from stretching out my arm and hugging him.

On the third day, we, actors in a silent film, got up and went outside. The sun glared like a spotlight, we walked through Marienplatz dragging with us a heavy burden of unspoken words. The air smelled of hot wine, cloves and cinnamon, it was Carnival time, the middle of February. We were like actors in a cheap operetta, again surrounded by the requisite stage set. The white sun, like a magnifying glass, revealed every little line on our faces, and we instinctively sought the protection of the icy shadows.

At the airport we sat drinking, waiting for my flight to be announced, and then walked slowly towards the exit. On the way we noticed an airport photograph booth and—goodness knows why—we went in. We sat there squeezed on to the round seat, protected by the dirty curtain, waiting for the little red light to come on. When it came on for the last, fourth time, he suddenly kissed me. The length of the kiss was dictated by the whirring of the invisible camera.

The loudspeaker announced the second call for my flight, but I was standing by the little metal opening of the booth waiting for the pictures to appear. I stared tensely at the opening as though the final answer was about to slide out. At last the Polaroid strip lazily peered out of the hole, I took it, tore it in half (two for him, two for me). Clutching his Polaroid half, he gave me a cursory kiss, and I set off towards the queue for passport control. As I walked away, I kept telling myself not to turn round, but I did. He was standing with his hands thrust into his pockets. His face, for the first time somehow lost and afraid, gleamed like a camera flash and disappeared. I crumpled the photographs in my hand, threw them away and set off. I wondered later why that secret set-designer of life had dreamed up such an unreal scenario for our parting when the pain was so real. The true end of our story, which had gone on for several years, was marked by the 'click' of the airport camera and the Polaroid kiss, which, while expressing undeniable love contained also its equally undeniable death.

Mother's albums—the way she set out 'the facts of her life'—revived before my eyes an everyday life—I had forgotten. This everyday life was arranged

21

(by the mere fact of being posed), then it was re-sorted (through the selection of photographs), but—perhaps just because of an amateur artistic impulse that the facts of life should be nicely arranged—it sprang up in the gaps, in the mistakes, in the method itself, touchingly authentic and alive.

One of the pictures would treacherously reveal my little shoes with the cut-off toes and disclose the world of postwar shortages in which toes grew more quickly than the ability to purchase new shoes, a time of workers' union outings, speeches and flags, pioneers, miniature socialist spectacles, reduced to the measure of the provincial town in which we lived, the celebrations of the First of May, children's fancy-dress processions, which were called 'the corso of flowers' (the picture shows me as a poppy!), thrilling pyramids of friendship, relay races, cross-country runs, family holidays . . . An unwritten history of everyday life emerged, which, judging by these pictures, so innocent and universal, could have taken place anywhere, but nevertheless did take place here.

In 1991, after the definitive collapse of the idea which had been for my father a realisable truth, after the disintegration of the country which had been kept together by that same idea, Mother gathered my father's old medals (for brotherhood and unity, for devoted work in the building of socialism) into a heap, put them into a plastic bag—as though they were human remains—saying sadly: 'I don't know what to do with these.'

'Why don't you leave them where they were . . .'

'What if someone finds them?'

I said nothing.

'You take them . . .' she pleaded.

But, nevertheless, that same year when the names of the streets changed, when the language and the country and the flags and the symbols all changed; when the wrong side became right, and the right side was suddenly wrong; when some people were afraid of their own names, when others, apparently, for the first time weren't afraid of theirs; when people were butchering each other, when some were butchering others; when armies with different insignia sprang up on all sides, when the strongest set out to obliterate everything from the face of their own country; when terrible heatwaves laid the land bare; when a lie became the law, and the law a lie; when people pronounced nothing but monosyllabic words: blood, war, gun, fear; when the little Balkan countries shook

Europe maintaining rightly that they were its legitimate children; when ants crawled out from somewhere to devour and tear the skin from the last descendant of the cursed tribes; when old myths fell apart and new ones were feverishly created; when the country she had accepted as hers fell apart, and she had long since lost and forgotten her first one; when she was seared by heat in her flat, as it radiated from the baking concrete and the concrete sky; when the panic-stricken light of the television flickered day and night; when she was racked by the icy fever of fear—my mother, despite everything, kept tenaciously to her dogged ritual visits to my father's grave. I believe that it was then that she looked for the first time at the moist gravestone and suddenly noticed the five-pointed star (although it had always been there, at her request) and perhaps for the first time she had the thought, feeble and exhausted as she was, that it might be possible to paint out the five-pointed star carved into the stone, and then she thrust the thought aside in shame and kept the photograph of my father in his partisan uniform in the album—as her own. It was as though it was then, suddenly confronted with the little star above my father's name, that she really accepted her own biography as well.

When she got home she sat down in her baking flat as in a train; she sat there with no defender or flag, with no homeland, virtually nameless, with no passport or identity card of her own. From time to time she would get up and look out of the window, expecting to see scenes of the war-destroyed country, for she had already observed such scenes. She sat like that in her flat as in a train, not travelling anywhere, because she had nowhere to go, holding on her lap her only possession, her albums, the humble dossier of her life.

A friend of mine was born without ever knowing his father. His mother used to say that his father had vanished in the whirlwind of war. What survived the whirlwind of war was a little, faded photograph of his father.

Later his mother died too; later he himself founded a family. One day, quite by chance, he discovered that his father had been executed after the war; he had been one of those 'on the wrong side'. He took another look at his father's little photograph and for the first time noticed that the picture was not only old but had been carefully touched-up (in all probability by his mother's hand). A little line here, a little smudge there and his father's hated uniform blurred into an indistinct suit.

Forty-five years after the war—when the 'wrong side' had experienced its historical touching-up and when the photographic light of the new times had shifted towards the 'right side'—my friend smiled at his son's question about his grandfather and replied briefly: 'He vanished in the whirlwind of war.' And he showed his son the little, faded picture.

I never liked the whole business of taking photographs. I found tourists, armed with cameras, objectionable, I found looking through other people's albums or watching their slides a torment.

During one trip abroad I bought a cheap automatic camera, and once the object was already there I shot several films. After some time I looked through the photographs and established that the scenes I had photographed were all I remembered of that journey. I tried to remember something else, but my memories stayed tenaciously fixed on the contents of the photographs.

I wondered what I would have remembered and how much if I had not taken any pictures . . .

When she went to my grandmother's funeral, my mother came back with a bundle of our family photographs which she had sent to my grandmother over the years. Among them was one of me, taken on the beach. I could have been about thirteen. On the back of the picture I discovered a text in Bulgarian written in my distant cousin's unskilled hand: 'This is me, taken on the beach, in my new swimsuit.' Under the text was her equally clumsy signature.

Now that picture is in my possession. Why my distant cousin did that, I shall never know. I am puzzled by that detail, sometimes I wonder whether it could have been me who did it, that, in fact, it's hard to prove that I didn't do it, because the picture is quite definitely of me, and then I am shaken by the nightmare thought that I might have signed my own photograph in her language, alphabet and handwriting and her name.

After the initial chaos, the initial selection, ordering and organisation according to principles of a chronology of events and their importance, after touching-up (after discarding any ugly pictures, after discarding Slavica and Branko)–the photographs in my mother's albums seemed for some time now to have settled into their permanent disposition.

Nevertheless I noticed that the currents of a new life did manage quietly to creep into the strict albums: a piece of torn-off paper with the name of a face cream, someone's telephone number, a newspaper cutting about where to buy special door locks and alarms, or an article about the noxious effects of tomatoes, someone's holiday postcard . . . As though the emptied spaces left by the discarded photographs attracted replacements through an invisible magnetism.

When the genre of the album threatened to turn into the genre of collage (in that sense the only subversive element was the lock of my hair, displayed beside my first photograph), she would tidy them, throw out the 'rubbish' which, escaping her control, had crept into her albums and disturbed the construction of her personal history.

Sometimes I would come across her leafing through her albums. Then she would close the one she was holding, take off her glasses, put them down and say: 'Sometimes I feel as though I have never lived . . .']

'Life is nothing other than a photograph album. Only what is in the album exists. What is not in the album, never happened,' says a friend of mine.

Once in Moscow I met a certain Ivan Dorogavtsev from the village of Fryazino on the outskirts of Moscow. He was a translator of Shakespeare, and the local madman. Dorogavtsev wore a threadbare, woman's wig, evidently with the intention of approximating his physical appearance to that of the one he admired, his unattainable god William. Dorogavtsev's worn suit was decorated with a large home-made badge on which was written (in Cyrillic): William Shakespeare.

Dorogavtsev produced heaps of paper materials. Kitsch postcards (mostly Czech, Bulgarian, Polish, which were easier to come by, and, of course, local, Soviet ones) on to the back of which he glued his translations. So the line *My mistress's eyes are nothing like the sun* was juxtaposed with the Chapel of Betlem, fragments from *Othello* with a birthday greeting, '*S dnem rozhdeniya*', printed on the back of the postcard. He himself made booklets, which he bound with postcards, so that Dorogavtsev's translation of Hamlet's monologues typed on a bad typewriter was bound with a picture of Muhina's famous monument *Rabotnik i kolhoznitsa*. Dorogavtsev sometimes inserted his own lines, thoughts and commentaries into his translations, and Shakespeare's renowned dark muse had its rival in the blonde Olyechka, an inhabitant of the village of Fryazino.

Dorogavtsev persistently wrote letters to President Brezhnev requesting the support of the Soviet state. In his letters he explained the greatness of his cultural mission, maintaining that he possessed the secret key to revealing the facts of life, ordinary reflections and astounding technology of Shakespeare's work. Everything that Mankind (Dorogavtsev liked to write some words with a capital letter) knew about Shakespeare could be safely and immediately (!) thrown on the rubbish heap of History, because when he, Ivan Dorogavtsev from Fryazino, published his Revelation, Russia would become the first and only Authority on the greatest genius, the Man of the Universe (he meant Shakespeare, of course).

In his booklets Dorogavtsev mercilessly denounced his predecessors, earlier translators, quoting details of the accuracy of their translations in precisely calculated percentages. So, according to Dorogavtsev's research, the most famous of them, Boris Pasternak, for the accuracy of his translation of *Hamlet* got precisely 0! And after the zero allocated to Pasternak, Dorogavtsev placed a resolute exclamation mark.

If there is in every madness, as in every lie, a glimmer of truth, then in Dorogavtsev's case that truth shone forth—from a photograph. Dorogavtsev showed me that photograph ceremonially, as though it were the greatest secret. The picture was a photo-montage, the work of an amateur photographer, which thanks to its bad technique and the virus of Dorogavtsev's madness (ah, blessed amateurism!) concealed exactly what should be concealed and disclosed exactly what should be disclosed.

In a word, on the photograph, shoulder to shoulder, their eyes gazing into eternity, like the best of friends, stood William Shakespeare and Dorogavtsev himself. They stood as though it were the most natural thing in the world, as though they had always been there, Will and Vanya. The photograph alone could confirm what madness refuted: that Ivan Dorogavtsev from Fryazino did indeed possess the 'key' to Shakespeare's secret.

In my earliest childhood I used to cover my eyes with my hands and say 'I've gone', and then, opening my hands, 'Here I am.' This would provoke the joyful, squealing approval of all present. 'There you are!'

That most elementary child's game—which fixed certain concepts in the consciousness: here I am, I exist (therefore, I see), and I've gone, I don't exist (therefore, I don't see)–had a somewhat more grown-up version. I remember that as children we used to curl our fingers into a 'telescope', put them to our eyes and with a special jokingly threatening intonation announce to our partner in the game or those around us: 'I see you!' Later we replaced our hands with paper tubes. The tubes reduced the boundless and unmanageable world to something bounded and manageable, to a little piece of world, a little circle, a frame. The little tube presupposed choice (I can examine this or that). Broken down into little circles, the world through the white paper tunnel reached the eye in sharpened beauty. That jokingly threatening exclamation—I see you!—acquired its full meaning. Through the little tube one really could see, without the tube one only looked. With the help of a simple paper tube one could achieve the desired measure of the world, the photograph.

When I visited New York for the first time (thrilled at the prospect that I was going to see it at last) I was confused by the absence of any kind of emotions connected with the fact that I was walking down its streets. I mentally pinched my cheeks, massaged my heart, but, apart from a dull indifference, I did not succeed in rousing any kind of feeling, none at all.

And then when I got into a taxi (in which a radio was playing loudly) in the windshield in front of me I recognised (!) a screen and I gasped at the tide of pictures rolling over me. Thanks, therefore, to the cinema conjured up by an ordinary drive in a taxi (movement, music, a window like a screen), I finally recognised the town and myself in it. I had a tube (I seeee you). Through the magic tunnel New York was rushing in all its beauty towards my eye.

A photograph is a reduction of the endless and unmanageable world to a little rectangle. A photograph is our measure of the world. A photograph is also a memory. Remembering means reducing the world to little rectangles. Arranging the little rectangles in an album is autobiography.

Between these two genres, the family album and autobiography, there is undoubtedly a connection: the album is a material autobiography, autobiography is a verbal album.

Organising a family album is a deeply amateur activity (amateur because it is not devoid of artistic pretensions). And writing autobiography (regardless of any artistic achievements) is also an amateur activity.

The advantage of 'amateurism' over 'professionalism' (let us call it that for want of a better word), or at least the difference between those two, is contained in the point of indistinct pain, pain which an amateur work (like extrasensory perception) can touch and thus provoke the same reaction in the observer/reader. The lavish strategies of so-called works of art rarely reach that point. The point of pain is a chance target preserved only for blessed amateurs, a target which only they can touch, without actually knowing what it's all about.

I remember a morning picture which my glance happened to snap from a tram. A young couple came out of a doorway; he was in an untidy post-man's outfit, with a postman's cap on his head; she was a small, nondescript woman. The city doorway spat this pathetic pair, illuminated by the grey morning light, out on to the street. The way she stretched up on to tiptoe (in old worn shoes with high heels), turned her neck and bent her head back; the way he put his arms tenderly round her waist, bending her slightly backwards like a doll; the way he kissed her passionately, knocking his post-man's hat to one side; the way, abandoning herself to the kiss, she raised one leg—that, I am certain, is something that even the best professional film actors would have had difficulty in acting out (the couple kissed as 'amateurs', imitating them, the film stars). That morning photograph, which I snapped with my glance, smiling to myself, and remembered, provoked in me a deep, unerring, indistinct pain, the pain of difference.

Both the album and autobiography are by their very nature amateur activities, doomed from the outset to failure and second-rateness. That is, the very act of arranging pictures in an album is dictated by our unconscious desire to show life in all its variety, and as a consequence life is reduced to a series of dead fragments. Autobiography has similar problems in the technology of remembering; it is concerned with what once was, and the trouble is that what was once is being recorded by someone who is now.

There is only one thing that both genres can count on (but they never do count on anything because calculation is not in their nature) and that is the blind chance that they will hit upon the point of pain. When that happens (and it rarely does), then the ordinary amateur creation emerges victorious, on another non-aesthetic level, turning even the most splendid artistic work to dust.

In literature such a work is an object of envy (springing from a sense of failure) only for real writers. Namely, such a work has achieved with divine ease what they, for all their efforts, will never achieve.

I once met a man who in the old communist days was employed in an important institution as a kind of 'editor', more precisely he prepared short autobiographies. These were autobiographies of people proposed by their institutions or work places for decoration. The 'editor' had a superior, an 'editor-in-chief' or passer-on of the autobiographies to those above. It was they who decided who was to be given a medal.

Although the authors of the autobiographies themselves more or less knew the genre, it was the 'editor's' duty to make them all consistent. There were not only requisite genre and linguistic clichés, but personal facts had also to be pressed into clichés.

'But this man was not born into a poor, working-class family! It's all written here in any case . . .' the 'editor' protested.

'Just write it like I say,' said his superior.

'But then all the autobiographies are the same! How then can they know who to give the medal to?'

'That's what is required. What is permitted is just two lines of difference. Just two lines!' said his superior sternly.

Both the album and autobiography respect the subject they are concerned with (the subject is so personal, how could it not be respected?). Compiling an album and autobiography are activities guided by the hand of the invisible angel of nostalgia. With its heavy, mournful wing, the angel of nostalgia brushes aside the demons of irony. That is why there are hardly any comic albums, ugly photographs, humorous autobiographies. It is in these most sincere and most personal of all genres—the album and autobiography—that the scissors of censorship are most assiduous. If the humorous (comic, ironic) permeates an autobiographical text, then the reader will shift that kind of text into the category of 'inauthentic' (professional, literary), into another order and type.

Autobiography is a serious and sad genre. It is as though somewhere deep within us there was an encoded assumption about the genre, and both the author and the reader submit to it: they harmonise the rhythm of their pulse, their heartbeat, slow down their breathing, together lower their blood pressure . . .

Autobiography and albums are the first genres we learned together, the only ones we repeated together. The album is only a variation on pre-school albums with all kinds of little pictures, a variation on later school techniques: flower presses, collages, binders. . .

Autobiography, and albums too, remind me infallibly of school and the genre of a straight 'A' essay.

In my day, in writing and literature classes there were essays on a set and a so-called free topic. These free essays presupposed the skill of good expression, while the set ones required some knowledge. The straight 'A' free essay was easier to do, it was possible to earn the desired 'A' with less effort.

Namely, the free essay entailed surprisingly rigid cliches: first-person narration and a stereotypical opening. Thus, for some unknown reason, the 'A' essays always began with rain ('I am sitting by the window against which the first drops of autumn rain are beating . . .') and ended, on the whole, with the same kind of precipitation. What is more, autumn rain was at a particular premium. The most artistically effective were the verbs 'teem' and 'trickle' ('The rain teems . . . trickles . . .') and elliptical sentences suggesting the rhythm of the heart together with the rhythm of rain drops. In these essays, like tedious toothache, the same contemplative-nostalgic tone rang persistently, generated by the precocious meditation on the leaves falling from a nearby tree and profound anxiety over the so-called transience of life.

All in all, those wet essays provided the major part of the future reading public with the foundations of its aesthetic principles. Once the first seal had been imprinted long ago by a romantic primary school teacher, children left school with developed 'literary taste', knowing exactly what was 'beautiful', and, besides, they had their written proof, their 'A's. Some of these pupils became teachers themselves and imprinted watery seals on their own pupils, some of their pupils themselves became teachers . . .

And when a well-known critic, the fiery promoter, translator and analyst of the work of Marguerite Duras, began her text about her visit to the living writer by saying that that day it was raining, that, in other words, that day, when she, the critic, stood in front of the house of Marguerite Duras pressing the doorbell excitedly, it was pouring with rain, I heard the familiar ring of the tone of the 'A' essay learned so long ago. And, from that day on, the pages of the famous writer have rung for me with a familiar, insistent, toothaching tone and the smell of rain . . .

Both albums and autobiography, as amateur activities, like a kind of home craft, endeavour to be beautiful. Albums and autobiography are like school essays that rush towards their 'A's (we'll show the album to someone, and someone will one day read our autobiography). Both the genre and its consumer have a shared assumption about what is beautiful. 'Have you read X's book?' 'Yes, it's just a series of stylistic tricks, nothing special . . .' 'And have you read Y's?' 'Yes, beautiful and authentic . . .'

Beautiful and authentic—these are two aesthetic criteria fixed for ever in the consciousness of most readers. Both the writer and the reader sweetly submit to the rhythm of the genre: they adapt the rhythm of their pulses, the beating of their hearts, they lower their blood pressure, breathe together . . .

An English friend of mine once wrote me a letter. She knew Croatian reasonably well. She had written the letter at a time when she was upset. The content of the letter sincerely touched me, but I could not suppress my laughter as I read its lines. My friend had written the letter in Croatian on an English typewriter. Before my eyes crawled little touching sentences shoving past each other to express their pain as fast as they could. All the seriousness of the message was destroyed by the absence of the necessary diacritic marks ('With those little guys on top?'as an American official had once put it when she tried to write my name and surname). And the image of pain had been transformed into its opposite.

While I was at university, another girl moved into the house where I was living. She came from a provincial town, enrolled in the English department and set about studying assiduously. We shared a kitchen and bathroom and did not talk much. She was quiet and withdrawn.

Coming home one day, I found a doctor in her room. She was lying on the bed deathly pale. She had swallowed a large number of sleeping pills. We spent the whole night trying to keep her awake.

She recovered, we did not mention the event. And then one evening she came quietly into my room, sat down, pulling her nightdress tightly over her knees and told me in English—with great difficulty, searching for words—why she had tried to kill herself. It was a banal story: an affair with a married man. When she had finished, she went quietly back to her room, and we never mentioned the episode again.

That girl shook me: she could only tell her painful, personal story in a foreign language. The foreign language helped her to cough up the little lump of pain that was stuck in her throat. An inner sense of good taste prevented her from telling the story in her own language. It was a banal tale (for the outsider, the audience), besides, by telling it she would have destroyed the reason for her pain. As it was, carrying out a complicated linguistic and psychological convolution, she told her pain in a foreign tongue and at the same time preserved it by not destroying its nucleus.

It seems that we can only easily express pain, and curses, in a language which is not our own. It was, I suppose, the same good reason as that of my quiet fellow-student, that drove the Russian poet Joseph Brodsky to write his autobiographical pages about his parents in English. The reason lies partly also in good taste: passing through the filter of a foreign language, the invincible nostalgia of the genre acquired, instead of wetness, a fine, dry quality.

Some time ago I myself bought an album. An elegant one, with a nice brown pigskin cover, which I had been trying to find for a long time.

A little while ago I picked it up. Leafing through the pages, I stopped at a photograph of myself. I examined it carefully and noticed two little lines around my mouth. They pointed downwards, making on either side of my mouth a small, barely noticeable pouch. With a swift movement, as though removing a sticking plaster, I detached the cellophane cover (the paper sounds of the execution ripped the air), took out the photograph, tore it into small pieces and abandoned it to the eternal darkness of oblivion.

In the bottom, deepest drawer of my desk there is a jumble of photographs. When I open the drawer, faces, smiles, bodies—those smudges of light on rectangles of paper—pour out. I have kept one bundle of pictures in an envelope, stuck it down, tied it with a ribbon and pushed it right to the bottom. From time to time, looking through my things, I come across it, I touch it, I feel the pain with the tips of my fingers and I know that it is not yet time to open it. But one day, when I think that the pain has gone, I shall open it, look at the pictures and arrange them in the album. I shall select them carefully, arrange them meticulously, taking care that there should be no mistake. And all the while I shall be sitting by the window where the first drops of autumn rain are beating . . .

II

The notebook with the flowery cover

1

And now he himself slices, he collects the seeds in a special piece of paper and begins to eat. Then he asks Gapka to bring him ink and, in his own hand, he writes an inscription on the paper containing the seeds: 'This melon was eaten on such and such a date.' Were there to be some guest present, then: 'So and so participated.'

> V. N. Gogol, 'How Ivan Ivanovich
> Quarrelled with Ivan Nikoforovich'

In 1986, when I walked across the boards of a dark, dusty loft and found myself in the illuminated space of a studio belonging to the Moscow painter Ilya Kabakov, I made an inner 'curtsy'. I was in the domain of the unacknowledged king of rubbish, a descendant of the line of Kurt Schwitters, a line which had developed its secret tribe, 'archaeologists of the everyday', Robert Rauschenberg, Fernandez Arman, John Chamberlain, Andy Warhol, Leonid Sejka (the great 'philosopher of the garbage heap'), and many others.

The Russian branch of this tribe runs from Gogol to the avant-garde artists (who indeed took only Gogol with them on their famous 'steamship of contemporaneity'!) and the formalists who beat their heads against the everyday, *byt'* (a word which means far more in Russian than its equivalents do in other languages). The most bizarre literary figure in this secret tribe is the forgotten avant-garde writer Konstantin Vaginov. Through his novels stroll characters who dream of founding a Museum of the Everyday, *byt'*, organisers of the society for collecting old and contemporary junk, collectors of trash, fingernails, matches and sweet wrappings, 'great systematisers' of the trivial, classifiers of cigarette butts like the incomparable Zhulonbin from the novel *Harpagoniada*: 'Classification is one of the most creative activities,' he said when all the cigarette butts lying on the table had been entered into the inventory ledger, 'essentially, classification shapes the world. Without classification there would be no memory. Without classification it would be impossible to imagine reality,' reflects Vaginov's hero.

Sensing that the Soviet epoch was coming to an end the same task was taken up some thirty years later by descendants of the Russian avant-garde, Russian alternative artists. The Moscow artist Ilya Kabakov began his project of 'making sense of reality' first of all by painting scenes from everyday life, exactly as they had been recorded long ago in newspaper photographs, in volumes of photographs about the Soviet Union, cinema posters; scenes, that is, which had already been articulated iconographi-cally in the consciousness of consumers as typical, Soviet.

In that way, in Kabakov's paintings hyperrealism and socialist real-ism are brought into a confusing, ironical connection. In these paintings Soviet everyday life appears 'realistic', but at the same time it is a metade-scription of the everyday/*byt'* as it developed in the art of socialist real-ism. The everyday in Kabakov's paintings seems to have adapted to time and merged with its previously 'formulated' socialist realist face. Thus in one painting Kabakov copies a socialist realist reproduction from an album dedicated to a 1937 exhibition of socialist realist painting. Kabakov the 'archaeologist' used (factual) material from everyday life: the Soviet album is a legitimate part of that material.

In Kabakov's paintings, the textual sometimes completely eliminates the pictorial. On enormous canvases Kabakov will carefully copy and magnify documents of the Soviet everyday: train timetables, house rules, announcements on bulletin boards, various Soviet documents and forms. At the same time, Kabakov's artistic intervention is minimal, it quite sim-ply takes everything from Soviet everyday life: both the form of commu-nication (boards, hoardings) and the contents of the message (house rules). Magnified like that, the message is read in several ways: as bureau-cratic discourse devoid of meaning which acquires a decorative function; as a text which invites renewed reading; as a conceptual provocation to official art (a list of house rules may also be a work of art). Kabakov him-self, however, does not suggest any one of the proposed readings. The material of bureaucratised everyday life transposed on to magnified boards obliges the observer/reader to read into it his own meaning.

Kabakov transposes on to his canvases themes which had previously been the exclusive right of literature. In his 'kitchen series', Kabakov actualises the everyday life of the kitchen in a 'communal flat' (this residential-social phenomenon of Soviet daily life has now disappeared). These 'kitchen' canvases usually had a (real!) kitchen utensil attached to them (a knife, a grater, a sieve), and a fragment of dialogue ('Whose is this grater? Anna Mikhailovna's. Look, someone has left a knife! It's Petrovich's knife!').

In the project entitled *You've got something boiling, Ol'ga Georgievna!* Kabakov uses the language of the everyday to create a bizarre piece of art. The installation consists of a room-divider made of wallpaper, which opens out to a length of 45 metres. On either side are strips of paper containing text, written in a special bureaucratic script. The text is composed of remarks by the anonymous residents of a communal flat, participants in a marathon conversation. The residents gossip about one another, criticise one another, discuss moving out, but at the same time it is as though they are not communicating, as though the conversation is being conducted among deaf people. With documentary precision, Kabakov reproduces everyday conversation, which places the observer/reader in a trap of ambivalent feelings (from sympathy to anxiety) towards the brutal aesthetic of everyday life.

His involvement in Soviet everyday life logically brought Kabakov to the multimedia project *The Man Who Never Threw Anything Away.* Kabakov's whole project is a transmedia diary, a kind of total autobiography. That is, the author of Kabakov's project is an anonymous Soviet citizen who has his own outlook on the world, his own conception of beauty, his own language in which he writes this unusual (auto)biography.

Kabakov's project consists of albums with an introductory story told by the author, the anonymous Soviet citizen; then large panels on which is stuck or fixed, systematised in an orderly way, the most various real rubbish; then groups of objects tied in hanging bundles or placed in boxes, and each of these objects has its own catalogue label; and finally numerous exercise books, folders, files, *Books of Life.* The author, the owner, the subject and object of all of this is the ordinary Soviet citizen.

Some panels have small fragments of litter stuck on to them, the date and time of day are usually recorded near the top of the panel (i.e. 15 March, in the evening) and a brief description of the situation in which the rubbish was found (In the corner by the bed, when I got up, and there was

35

no broom so I borrowed one from Ol'ga Nikolaevna; In April, on the table, when I decided to tidy up; it was pouring with rain). Under each exhibit (an eggshell, string, crumbs, finger nails, hairs, a razor blade, etc.) there is a catalogue note (Eaten for supper; From Nikolai; I was picking my teeth; I don't know; Off my slipper; I was sewing something; I don't remember; I was eating an egg; I was sharpening a pencil; shaved 15 times).

In his narrative procedure, Kabakov does not reproduce only the thoughts, world view and aesthetic taste of his ordinary Soviet citizen, but he also uses an appropriate technique of expression. Or rather, he takes over what are to him, an ordinary citizen, the accessible collectors' techniques of family albums, collage, popular-educational collecting of postcards, stamps, matchboxes and the like. The panels containing somewhat larger objects have more detailed catalogue notes. So, for instance, under the wrapping for some tablets he writes: 'Volodya had a headache, he asked whether I had anything, I didn't have aspirin, only paracetamol, it helped'. Or under an empty glass jar: 'This is the jar in which Vika brought egg mayonnaise.'

Anchored in the chaos of the everyday, *byt'*, Kabakov transcribes a grandiose, transmedia (auto)biography of triviality. The albums entitled *My Life*, which are of course compiled by Kabakov's little anonymous author, reveal the kitsch of a personal life measured in postcards from summer holidays, newspaper cuttings, messages, notes, sketches, photographs, letters, certificates, personal documents. Kabakov shapes his (auto)biography measured in 'rubbish', the grotesque (or tragic) character of which is increased by the absence of the personal! The personal destiny of the anonymous citizen and author of the autobiography is simply the result and image of the System (in this case Soviet), Its taste, Its opinions, Its language. By taking the mask of an ordinary Soviet citizen, and adopting his innocent technique of collecting everyday junk, Kabakov reveals the complex permeation of the system, politics, ideology, media, culture, education, the everyday and the personal life, and radically challenges official culture by the mere act of giving priority to 'rubbish' over the so-called great themes of high art.

In 1986, when I walked across the boards of a dark, dusty loft and found myself in the illuminated space of Kabakov's studio, I made an inner 'curtsy'. I had never faced a more terrible, painful or touching scene:

the total (auto)biography of an ordinary man, clear, painful, bare, reduced to 'facts', so terribly marked by the system.

I left the memory of Kabakov, that uncrowned king of rubbish, my guide through his own museum of the extinct Soviet epoch, a guide who did not expect that anyone would ever enter that museum apart from friends or chance guests, like me, in that illuminated Moscow studio, where it belonged.

Just three years later, strolling through New York's SoHo, I came across a painting of Kabakov's in a gallery. It was a small piece: the background was an illustration torn out of a child's book and on it were stuck indecipherable, crumpled pieces of paper. The illustration was neutral in itself, the scraps of paper a kind of dead addition; the price of the picture was dizzying. A little prick of vague disappointment told me that Kabakov's dark frescoes, composed over the years in a dusty Moscow attic, would soon make it into the world. I wondered whether exposure to the air and light would destroy their nature. Would that painful beauty created from the trash of ordinary life be transformed into trash deprived of meaning and purpose?

Postscript

The nature of 'trash', (auto)biographical material, is not, it seems, all that straightforward after all. I was to see Kabakov once more, a full eight years after our meeting in his Moscow studio. This time I saw him in the Berlin Podewil, where he put on an unusual concert in February 1994. Lit by a small reading lamp, Kabakov stood on the stage reading from a little music stand sentences spoken by the anonymous participants in the marathon conversation which took place in the communal kitchen. It was a stage performance of Kabakov's old project *You've got something boiling, Ol'ga Georgievna!* A second male voice (that of the drummer Tarasov) read the rejoinders from another music stand. The two men performed a kind of two-voiced canon. From somewhere came the sound of radio music, the typical Soviet radio repertoire: sickly sweet tunes, patriotic and military songs, classical music, Swan Lake of course. The reading was at times accompanied by the banging of pots, spoons, forks, and black and white slides of authentic Moscow 'communal kitchens' projected at the back of the stage.

It was a requiem for a vanished epoch, its sad resumé, the very heart of the system. The exhausting verbal flagellation provoked physical nausea in me, it was an attack on the memory tattooed with sentences, a hallucination in sound, the painful noise of a vanished age.

I was deeply moved by Kabakov's performance on the Berlin stage. And I cannot say for certain what it was that provoked that emotion. 'Communal kitchens' were not part of my everyday reality. And yet, I wept. What is more, I felt that I had an exclusive right to those tears. Be that as it may, Kabakov's performance pulled a thread of undefined sadness in me, that of a shared 'East European trauma'. 'Traumas acquired in the formative years are never forgotten,' says my friend V. K. and adds: 'Some people call that nostalgia.'

2

All at once I felt as though an ice-cube of anxiety had been thrust into the pit of my stomach.

Milan Kundera,
The Book of Laughter and Forgetting

9 January
Mirjana came. She cooked me lunch and left, dear, good Mirjana. I managed to iron my son's washing, he ought to come and collect it. I must remind him to lay it carefully folded in the cupboard. He telephoned and said that Bubi had called to say she had arrived safely. I am worried that she hasn't called me as well.

It's almost twelve already, but I don't feel like sleeping, I don't have a temperature, but I'm coughing a lot. They say there's a kind of Asiatic flu around, why does it have to be me! I'll try to read a bit, maybe I'll fall asleep.

10 January
I'm ill myself, luckily Boža has got over her flu, and she can look after us, me and Verica. Verica asked me for a cigarette to disinfect her throat. Another of her 'pearls' of medicine. Our Verica has a talent for everything, what would we do without her. Sometimes we get fed up with her 'knowledge'.

My neighbours Boža and Zvonko have gone shopping. Zvonko has raised the interest rate, Boža likes spending money, but Zvonko won't let her. Every year in January there's a real 'home theatre'. I'm sorry I'm not a writer to describe it all. But still, if it weren't for them, I'd be far worse off than I am.

I'll have to make some tea. When will I be rid of this flu? It's a glorious day outside.

12 January
I got up at about ten o'clock, someone was knocking at the door, it must have been Boza inviting me to coffee. I went to the bank, I wanted to know how much interest I had earned. I had 50 million, enough to pay the electricity and running costs. It will be tight, but I think that my pension will be enough to keep me going through the month.

On my way back from the bank I took the mail out of my postbox. There was a letter from Dimitrina with New Year greetings and the announcement of Sokle's death. It was such a sad letter that I cried. She had poured out her heart, she described everything she had been through. To send a man with an open stomach home from hospital, that I never saw in a horror film, let alone in real life! Dimitrina had to go through all of that with Sokle, she had herself barely survived.

I was so saddened by that letter that I can't get to sleep again. I keep thinking of our whole family, all those who are no longer with us. I remember Sokle's mother, Auntie Cvetanka, my aunt. What a cheerful woman she was! All my mother's family was cheerful, all except Granddad who was a heavy drinker, that's what killed him.

When he was little, Sokle always had a runny nose and I didn't like him much, that's probably why. Later he became a good-looking man, civil and pleasant, everyone liked him, unlike his brother, who I don't much care for even now. Good people don't see well, Sokle included. He wasn't happy with his first wife, Mima, he was with Dimitrina, but only for a short time, unfortunately. That's human destiny for you!

Now in the village all that's left of that large family are Auntie Pavla and Uncle Toshko.

I liked Auntie Pavla more than all my other aunts, and I had four of them. Only two of the five sisters are still alive: Auntie Pavla and Auntie Natsa. Auntie Pavla, the youngest and prettiest, married, without love, the handsome, but stupid Slavcho, fortunately they have lovely children. I shall never forget her wedding. As she didn't love Slavcho, she invited me to sleep with her. When I went home and told Mother all about it, she put *her hands to her head; I nearly got a hiding. What a disgrace for a bride-groom! How old was I then, twelve I think . . . My eyes are smarting, I can't read, and how I'll get to sleep, I just don't know.*

15 January
I got up early, cleaned the flat, got lunch and waited for my son. He came, we had lunch, talked a bit more than usual in fact. He stayed a little longer out of politeness, but I knew he could hardly wait to go. I can read him like an open book, only I pretend not to notice, so that he doesn't feel bad.

I can't blame him. I used to long to leave home myself, but my parents were a thousand times stricter than I am. In the middle of summer I had to be home by nine o'clock, while it was still light, and I couldn't even dream of any kind of 'assignation'!

16 January
I got up early again today, took down the curtains, washed them, dried them and put them straight back on the windows. Generally, I gave the place a thorough clean. Still no letter from Bubi.

19 January
I had a temperature again last night, I don't know whether it's flu or something else. The fog and cold affect my rheumatism badly. Still no letter from Bubi.

Today for some reason I kept thinking of Petya. My dearest friend. I shared all my little secrets with her, we went to school together, we were in the same class, we both lived in flats in the old railway station. God, the things that went on in that station, my whole childhood!

It was nicest in summer, when all the trains had gone through, and we would gather on the platform. Ivan, my first love, played the guitar, we danced, sang . . . Now I no longer know whether I loved him because he played the guitar or because I really liked him. But it doesn't matter any more. We were neighbours, he was in the third year of secondary school and I in the last year of elementary school. I think I was fifteen, nowadays little girls of fifteen know all there is to know about love, for me it was enough just to look at him. He liked climbing mountains, I remember he once brought me an edelweiss. I kept it for a long time in a book as a memento.

Petya was a thin, undeveloped little girl with blonde plaits. The boys didn't take much notice of her, but in the end she went off with the handsomest. I was even a little envious. She later married him and I went abroad. I shall never forget the day I left Varna. Petya came rushing up with Gosha at the last moment, with a bouquet of flowers for me. Later, when we used to come to visit my parents, Petya would always come to the station to see us off at the last moment. Later we came by car, so there was no longer any need to run. There, I remember that well. Now we're both widows.

Tonight I feel as though I could write till morning, but my eyes hurt.

24 January
I've become so lazy lately, I've just lain around, eaten, watched television, drunk coffee with neighbours, listened to stories about their illnesses, about their hard and soft stools, about tea for opening and closing the bowel. Sometimes I don't know whether they're the ones who're mad or I am. How can they not notice that they keep saying the same thing, some things five times over, and I listen out of politeness as though I were hearing it for the first time?

I can hardly wait for Ankica or Mirjana to come. To have a bit of a laugh with Ankica. Mirjana doesn't particularly like to laugh, but she has a way of soothing me, and I like being with her. Ankica is like my Petya used to be in Varna.

I remember there were six children, each one just a head taller than the last. Their father was a drunk, their mother had a constant headache, I never saw her smile. She didn't know how to cook, she never cleaned the house, or else she couldn't with so many children, so Petya ate with us every day; my mother was an excellent cook.

My Petya liked all of that, and we weren't mean, and to my great joy she was our 'third' in the house! I think I loved her more than my sister, my sister was younger, but stronger than me, and she often fought me. I liked Petya more. But still, I envied her on two occasions. First, when she was given a wonderful georgette dress, blue with white daisies, and although I had nicer clothes, and had far more things, I envied her that dress. The other thing was Gosha. He was the only good thing she had in her life.

That was all so long ago and I wonder how I could have envied her. But I liked that dress so much that I can still see it before my eyes. Strange.

41

Still no letter from Bubi. It's already one o'clock in the morning, I'll try to read and fall asleep. I'm reading Chekhov's short stories.

28 January
Today at last there was a letter from Bubi. She's well and that's a weight off my mind.

I watch TV, the politicians tell us that the situation in the country is very bad. I'm afraid. There is less and less money, everything is terribly expensive. How we'll manage I just don't know. I'm used to taking the rough with the smooth. I never had much, and I expect I'll manage now, at my age one doesn't need much anyway.

When I remember what life was like before the Second World War, and for ten years or so afterwards, this is still good. Just let there not be a civil war, as many people are saying. Heaven forbid.

My son's coming to lunch tomorrow. I'm glad.

4 February
The fog hasn't cleared for two months now, and there's no sun. The air is poisonous. I have no energy for anything. This morning I woke up at five o'clock, put the radio on low, listened, listened, and fell asleep again. But I got up around nine nevertheless, went to the market, bought what I need-ed, spent five million, the only expensive item being a kilogram of meat, the rest was just bits and pieces. I daren't go to the market every day, but only every third day. I am afraid of what life is going to be like.

I'd really like to change at least something in the house, just so as not to look at the same things all day long, but I get nowhere, I don't think any-thing can be changed. I really like being at home, I like nice things, I like changing the furniture, I enjoy it when my house gleams, but never mind…

My neighbours Boža and Verica have the flu, I'm surprised I haven't caught it from them. Every day I hear the same stories, it's really boring, it's so boring that I'm really sick of it, but I go on listening patiently, and I go on having coffee with them. Who else is there?

10 February
Ankica was here for three days, it was nice, we went shopping, I bought a nice raincoat, cheap what's more, which is very important in this day and age, when there's not much money and everything is very expensive.

11 February
There hasn't been any rain, there'll be restrictions on electricity and water. That's all we need!

12 February
My son's away, it's Sunday. The week passes somehow, but it's terribly sad when I have to eat by myself on Sundays, I'd prefer not to eat. I feel rest-less all the time. I'd like to travel somewhere, but I don't know where, and besides I couldn't travel alone. It's enough that I'm alone all day at home.

Boza and Verica again. I'm fed up with them, but I can hardly wait for them to invite me for coffee in the morning, or I them. And it's always the same boring stories, every day. But if they weren't there, I'd be even worse off . . .

15 February
I took my blood pressure today, 170/100, it's the first time I've had such a high blood pressure, I'm worried.

I watched the film Philadelphia Nun *tonight. So-so, nothing special. I'm going to bed. I can't watch television for long.*

21 February
Flu again, more serious than the last, luckily Mirjana is here and she's looking after me. We were in town yesterday, I bought some coffee cups and sandals, quite cheap, but nice. Mirjana bought some boots, cheap, but quite nice.

She gave me a gift of a crocheted tablecloth. Good old Mirjana! What shall I give her? You can't really repay such hard work!

23 February
I'm lying in bed listening to the news. The political situation is getting worse. It's extremely tense in Kosovo. Heaven forbid that what people are whispering about should happen! The flu doesn't let up, it's a really bad dose. I can hardly wait for Mirjana to get back from town so that I'm not alone. She went off in the morning and she's still not back.

24 February
Today's my son's birthday, he's thirty-two, and he's still a big child. When

he'll grow up, I just don't know. I bought him a modest gift, there's no money for anything else. But I made a cake, he'll come on Sunday.

My son's thirty-two, my daughter forty, I must have got old. You can't be young with such old children.

25 February
I feel better today. At last it's raining, but not very hard. We need it to pour and make real rivers.

The news is bad. The miners in Kosovo haven't left the shaft, they won't take any food, they won't give up their demands. The political situation is still tense.

11 March
I feel uneasy, I don't know how to help myself. Sometimes I remember little things and think about them to try to drive away the dark thoughts. That's how I remembered that on Sundays we always used to have boiled beef, soup and tomato sauce. My husband's favourite food. On Sunday mornings we went to the market, I liked it when we went together, and when, tall as he was, he carried my basket. And I, small as I was, walked beside him.

12 March
I saw two good films. The spring weather is lasting. Bubi's well, she wrote me a letter.

13 March
Another nice, sunny day. It seems that we've missed out winter. No one sends me Martenice *ribbons any more and that saddens me. Those March ribbons remind me of my childhood, of spring, of something that only the Bulgarians wear to mark the spring, sun and love. I have a whole collection of them.*

15 March
I've got a sore throat, I ought to go to the doctor, but I don't feel like it. I've been sort of indifferent to everything lately, I'm tired all the time, I feel sleepy, I'm afraid of getting depressed again, all the symptoms seem the same as eight years ago, when I had a good reason, but now? What's

44

the reason now? Idleness, the emptiness of existence? But it's better not to 'philosophise', that will only make it worse. But what can I think about, except the past? I have no future.

20 March
At last someone thought of sending me Martenice, Sashka no less, the last person I thought would have done. It made me happy as usual. The TV news has just started, I'll carry on tomorrow.

27 March
Bubi's birthday, I sent a telegram. I can't believe it! Forty, but she'll always be twenty to me. All it means is that I'm sixty-three, but I don't feel it. I miss her. The weather has been wonderful lately, real spring, and it warms my heart.

30 March
I had just got back from the doctor when Zlata called to say that Vikica had died. That family seems cursed. They keep dying one after the other.

1 April
I haven't heard from my son, and nothing is happening about the cemetery. I don't understand how it is they can have so little sense of duty, if nothing else. I'll have to go and tidy the grave myself. They'll forget me as well, as they have their father. Sad.

I'll have to have lunch on my own again tomorrow, I can't bear eating alone on Sundays.

Bubi ought to write, I can't wait for her to be back. And I haven't filled even half the notebook! Everything is so empty and pointless. Nothing interesting happens. I just hear that someone has died, nothing bright or cheerful, my neighbours are ill, I'm not particularly well myself. So what can I write about?

The political situation is still terribly tense, we live in the constant expectation that something is going to happen, but what—we don't know ourselves.

Something funny has happened, though. I bought a hat I shall never wear. Me and a hat! Really funny.

4 April

The laboratory finds aren't especially rosy. Increased lymphocites, borderline sugar levels and all sorts. We'll see what the doctor says.

I'm irritable, I'd like a quarrel with someone, only there isn't anyone. I'd like to go somewhere, but I don't like travelling alone. Once, when I was young I used to like travelling alone, but not now, I don't know why. I wonder why it is that I always feel alone, even when I'm in a great crowd. I've always been, in a way, absent.

The only things that interested me were books and films. How Mother used to scold me because of those films! I was never beaten, my sister 'copped it' more than I ever did.

We two sisters were completely different. When Mother was angry with me, it used to make me shut myself up even more. I was an excellent pupil, an obedient child, while my sister did everything wrong. But I always felt that my father loved my sister more, he was just proud of me. He called her Marushka, Marche, Miche, while I was always Vete. But Mother often called me Eli.

Sometimes I feel that I had a happy childhood, but sometimes that I didn't. I remember my first journey from Varna to Sofia. That was an experience, I was fourteen. Free, without that constant: 'Vete, look at the way you're standing, Vete, look at the way you're sitting, cover up your knees,' and so on . . . 'Mind who you talk to, watch out for thieves, watch out for men, take care, take care.' And I did, in the end, I kept myself for a good-for-nothing, but I won't think about that now, it makes me feel ill to remember.

But then I passed my first exam. And after that it was easier to travel. Now I wouldn't even go to the shop alone.

I remember my first journey, then in '46. I was frightened, but I didn't want to let my parents see. When it came to that terrible moment—when the customs men examine your luggage—I was so nervous that I dropped my suitcase, apples and books scattered over the floor, of course, there could not have been anything there to pay duty on, especially not in '46, but I was paralysed with fear, and I can still feel that fear today. How many times have I crossed the Bulgarian frontier, and every time it's like that first trip . . .

I don't remember much about that journey. It rained all the time, out of the window of the train you could see nothing but ruins, so that at a cer-

tain moment I wanted to go back. There's just one nice detail I remember from that gloomy journey: an old man peeled an apple for me, made a rose out of the peel and made me a gift of the rose.

I remember another journey, by aeroplane to Leningrad and back. I was so frightened that I was bathed in a cold sweat the whole journey, I was so happy when we landed on the earth, I didn't enjoy the flight at all, but after that my impressions were wonderful.

I'm enjoying it all now, as I write and remember everything. I didn't have any other important journeys in my life, except those annual Zagreb-Varna ones, which were the ones I liked most, now unfortunately even if I wanted to I've no one to go to, apart from Petja. My dear Petja.

15 April
It's already 15 April and nothing significant has happened. The politicians are fighting tooth and nail, and there doesn't appear to be any way out of the whole situation.

At last it has begun to rain properly and it's a little cooler. Ankica and Mirjana have left, I enjoyed their company. Now it's my neighbours, Boža and Verica again, coffee again, bonjour, boredom.

I'm having a bit of fun with the remote control, but that gets tedious too when there's nothing sensible on television.

I worked like crazy for two days cleaning the flat and now I'm twiddling my thumbs again.

The only nice thing was when Bubi called, I felt warm round the heart all day. But that was just one day, and I need at least three hundred of them in a year.

Tomorrow I'm expecting my son for lunch, if he doesn't go away again. I've grown so used to being alone that I hardly notice if he's not here. But if he doesn't call, I begin to worry.

On television there's only repeats, nothing but repeats. I'll carry on tomorrow.

25 April
Last night I went to the cinema with Tina, we saw Rain Man *with Dustin Hoffman, an excellent film. Tina saw me to the tram, I hardly made it home, my back hurt, I felt dizzy, that all spoiled my enjoyment of the film.*

I'm having injections, but they're not much use. I'm afraid of going out into the street alone again, I don't know what to do. I've been for tests ... It's all the same, everything is within the limits of the normal, but I feel bad. Shut up and put up with it, what else can I do?

The night before last I talked to Dina, they're well, they're going to Varna for Easter. If I could fly there, I'd go too. I wouldn't have remembered that it was Easter if she hadn't reminded me. Our Easter customs were nice. Mother used to bake a special cake, we painted eggs and decorated the front door with willow branches.

When my sister and I were little, we always used to get patent leather shoes for Easter—I don't know why they had to be patent leather—and new little dresses. I remember those shoes well, because they always rubbed, Mother never bought a size or even half a size bigger. So I put up with the pain, but I always looked nice, while my sister would take them off and go home barefoot, and always got a smacking.

I liked St George's Day best of all. We always went on an outing with the school, we made swings, put garlands of flowers in our hair, while the grown-ups roasted a lamb, it was wonderful. Been and gone.

I don't know where my son is, he hasn't called all day. He hasn't mentioned where he's going for the First of May holiday. I'll be at home, as usual, with my neighbours, Boza and Verica, what would I do without them!

2 May
It's the second day of the holiday, it's been raining ceaselessly, all over the country. It's spoiled a lot of people's holiday. Not mine, I don't go anywhere anyway, but I'm sorry I couldn't get to the cemetery.

I'm expecting Mirjana tomorrow, she's coming for her pension, and I'll pick up mine as well. I like it when she comes.

I keep watching the news on television. The Albanians have started sabotaging things, they've apparently broken the main pipeline in Priština. They won't be satisfied until they've got a republic. I don't understand why they can't have one, if they want it so badly!

I've got nothing new to read, so I'm reading The Encyclopedia of the Dead by Danilo Kiš again, I like it.

It just keeps on raining, and that depresses me, and the heating's poor, so I'm cold as well. I can hardly wait for Bubi to get back. I've been thinking about her a lot lately.

20 May
At last something has happened, the worst possible thing, to me of all people.

31 May
More tests and a stay in hospital. I'm sick with fear.

2 June
They're reducing my sugar level, I'm less frightened, I'm going home for the weekend, but it'll soon be Monday, when I'm having the operation. I'd like Bubi to be with me . . .

3

What I need today is not a book and movement forwards: I need a destiny, and grief as heavy as red corals.

Viktor Shklovsky, *Third Factory*

At the beginning of 1989, before I went abroad for several months, I gave her a little notebook with a flowery cover.

'What's this for?' she asked cautiously.

'So you can keep a diary,' I said.

'I've never kept a diary. Not even when I was very young.'

'Something else, then. Anything . . . Notes . . .'

'I'm not a writer. What would I write about?'

'Samuel Pepys wrote that on 1 January 1660 he got up and put on a suit with long, wide trousers which was all he had been wearing of late, and that on 1 January 1669 Captain Beckford offered him a magnificent bed warmer . . .'

'So what? . . .'

'Pepys wrote in his diary that he had to take his wig to the wigmaker to have it cleaned of fleas . . . There, just the most ordinary things, but how interesting it is today!' I said.

'I don't see anything interesting about it,' she said. 'There's nothing to write about!' she said caustically, bringing the conversation about the notebook to an end.

When I came back, I found her in hospital. She recovered, left hospital and one day she handed me the notebook.

'Here you are,' she said simply as though she were giving me a completed piece of homework.

For a long time I did not dare touch the flowery cover. The very idea hurt me. And then one day I did open it after all and what its pages scattered on an already open wound was . . . salt.

I cleaned the sentences, removed the burrs and mud, spat into a handkerchief and washed them with my own saliva.

Now in the palm of my hand there's a heap of her misused words (she wrote 'draught' instead of 'shaft'; just as she once said in angry protest: 'you've all bitten me off', when what she meant was 'written me off'), wrongly used case endings, spelling mistakes . . .

I soothed the rhythm with full stops and commas, removed the misplaced exclamation marks (those dear little exclamation marks!), took out the Cyrillic script (she always wrote Varna in Cyrillic), took out the frequent, and unnecessary quote marks, changed the capitals into lower case (she always wrote parents with a capital letter). I left the over-used word 'nice', clichés such as: 'The political situation is becoming tense', which she had learned from television, her unexpected poetic comments such as: '*Bonjour*, boredom'; and the half-redundant sentence which I imagine refers to her commentary on the weather forecast: 'We need it to pour and make real rivers'.

I ask myself what is left? Because here, in the palm of my hand, are the shells of her language, her identity, touchingly misused accent marks, intonations which only I hear, words whose meaning only I know, her handwriting which changes depending on her mood, self-censorship which only I sense . . .

To start with I began fiddling with feeble ideas about genre, hoping in a sly corner of my mind for literary effects, but now I'm just in its painful centre, as in quicksand, and I can't get out . . .

'I sometimes think I have forgotten everything. Why does a person live at all if he forgets everything anyway?' asks my mother.

'Memory betrays everybody, especially those whom we knew best. It is an ally of oblivion, it is an ally of death. It is a fishnet with a very small catch and with the water gone. You can't use it to reconstruct anyone, even on paper. What's the matter with all those millions of cells in our brain? What's the matter with Pasternak's '"Great god of love, great god of details"? On what number of details must one be prepared to settle?' says Joseph Brodsky.

'Even what was mine, and only mine, I remember so little of it . . .' says my mother.

'A normal man doesn't remember what he had for breakfast. Things of a routine, repetitive nature are meant to be forgotten. Breakfast is one; loved ones is another,' says Joseph Brodsky.

'Then what's the sense of it all . . .? If I have no future, and can find no base in the past . . .' asks my mother.

'As failures go, attempting to recall the past is like trying to grasp the meaning of existence. Both make one feel like a baby clutching at a basketball: one's palms keep sliding off,' says Brodsky.

'In the end life is reduced to a heap of random, unconnected details. It could have been like this or like that, it's absolutely immaterial. I wonder where is that point I can still take hold of before I slip into nothingness,' asks my mother.

'What memory has in common with art is the knack for selection, the taste for detail. Complimentary though this observation may seem to art (that of prose in particular), to memory it should appear insulting. The insult, however, is well deserved. Memory contains precise details, not the whole picture; highlights, if you will, not the entire show. The conviction that we are somehow remembering the whole thing in blanket fashion, the very conviction that allows the species to go on with its life, is groundless. More than anything, memory resembles a library in alphabetical disorder, and with no collected works by anyone,' maintains Brodsky.

'I've read a lot, I've submerged myself in books . . . Everything I've read is just a confused jumble of words. I try to remember my parents. I'm ashamed that I know so little about them. Then I console myself with the thought that at least I know my children . . . I feel a chill round my heart when I realise how little I know about them . . .' says my mother.

'Sometimes I was troubled, but usually I just stared at them without understanding; I had forgotten the signals, our little rituals had lost their meaning for me. Defeated by my indifference, they put less and less conviction into their efforts to pull me back into the world of our common memories. In the end they ran out of words. What moved me the longest were their gestures: my daughter's way of tossing back her hair, the way my son takes the bows of his glasses between his teeth or my wife persists in straightening her tired back. These are gestures that cut to the heart. But then they give way to new ones, or perhaps to old ones that I never noticed. And thinking of the past, I was bewildered: how were we able to live together, when I knew so little about them?' says Georgy Konrad.

'What I do remember sometimes are the strong desires of my youth. They seem stupid now. For instance, as a child I adored horses, I dreamed of riding a horse one day . . . I didn't even do that,' says my mother.

'In my childhood I was a fervent worshipper of the tiger: not the jaguar, the spotted 'tiger' of the Amazonian jungles and the isles of vegetation that float down the Parana, but that striped, Asiatic, royal tiger that can be faced only by men of war, on a castle atop an elephant. I used to linger endlessly before one of the cages at the zoo; I judged vast encyclopedias and books of natural history by the splendour of their tigers. (I still remember those illustrations: I who cannot rightly recall the brow or the smile of a woman.) Childhood passed away, and the tigers and my passion for them grew old, but still they are in my dreams. At that submerged or chaotic level they keep prevailing. And so, as I sleep, some dream beguiles me, and suddenly I know I am dreaming. Then I think: this is a dream, a pure diversion of my will; and now that I have unlimited power, I am going to cause a tiger.

'Oh, incompetence! Never can my dreams engender the wild beast I long for. The tiger indeed appears, but stuffed or flimsy or with impure variations of shape, or of an implausible size, or all too fleeting, or with a touch of the dog or the bird,' says Borges.

'It seems that I've spent my whole life longing for something, but I never knew exactly for what. It was all so hazy . . .' says my mother.

'Longing is an intensive and enduring experience in which instinctive impulses have acquired a predominantly emotional and symbolic form, so that its contemplative character finds itself in conflict with an indistinct need which does not lead to action . . .' affirms the *Philosophical Dictionary*.

'When I really think about it, the only thing I clearly remember is fear. As a child the thing I was most afraid of was gloves turned inside out. That innocent object provoked horror in me,' says my mother.

'Actually, my moments of horror are brief, and what I feel is not so much horror as unreality . . .' says Peter Handke.

'You know, the first horror is growing old . . .' says my mother.

52

'Horror is something that obeys the laws of nature: *horror vacui* in the consciousness . . .' says Peter Handke.

'That doesn't mean anything to me. I have the feeling that everything would have been different if I had been born a man . . .' says my mother.

'For a woman to be born into such surroundings was in itself deadly. But perhaps there was one comfort: no need to worry about the future. The fortune-tellers at our church fairs took a serious interest only in the palms of the young men; a girl's future was a joke . . .' says Peter Handke.

'No one can accept the fact that his own life is a joke,' says my mother.

'Life is well ordered, like a *nécessaire*, but not all of us can find our place in it . . .' says Viktor Shklovsky.

'Perhaps the problem really is that I was born a woman . . .' says my mother.

'Human women are incomprehensible. The human routine is awful, meaningless, sluggish, inflexible . . .' says Shklovsky.

'One way or another, I always lose . . .' says my mother.

'I call on the ink and the pen and what is written with the pen to bear witness; I call on the uncertain darkness of twilight and the night and all that it brings to life to bear witness; I call on the day of judgement and the soul which reproaches itself to bear witness; I call on time, the beginning and end of everything to bear witness—that everyone, always, loses,' confirms Meša Selimović.

'Sometimes I am horrified at the banality of my life. Some people do have lives which resemble a well-thought-out story. I was always jealous of people like that . . .' says my mother.

'There is no reason why a well-thought-out story should resemble real life, life strives with all its might to resemble a well-thought-out story,' says Babel.

'It's all of no importance now, in any case . . . Now I no longer know who I am, or where I am, or whose I am . . .'

Postscript

I added the sentence 'Now I no longer know who I am, or where I am, or whose I am . . .' to the text I had already written, later, on the day when my mother uttered it: 20 September 1991. I thought that it might be the

53

last sentence I wrote. The idea of a genre that I had been swinging around to start with had now stretched into a double knot. The sentence was incorporated into the text between two air-raid warning sirens. We spent September in a blacked-out flat or in the shelter, tormented by the sounds of the sirens, television pictures of our destroyed country and fear. We took our personal documents with us into the shelter so that if there were a bomb we would not be anonymous, but properly identified corpses. The touching and naive sentence from her diary—'Heaven forbid that what people are whispering about should happen'—had become reality. What people were whispering about happened.

In 1946 she travelled through a Yugoslavia devastated by war. She came at the end, having missed the beginning. Now, at her own end, she was seeing what she had missed. As a child, what she was most afraid of was a glove turned inside out. Reality has turned inside out like a glove.

Every time she went to the shelter she would take with her . . . a cage containing her budgerigar! She directed all the love she had left over on to that budgie, which I had given her just a month earlier, despite her opposition. She did not seem too anxious about us, her children, or even about herself. The whole of her—who no longer knew who she was, or where she was, or whose she was—was wrapped with her last breath around that tiny caricature of an angel. Faced with possible death she carried into the shelter just two things: her identity card and her budgie, a little replica angel, a heart beating pit-pat, pit-pat, pit-pat . . .

III

'Kinder-egg'

Do you recall objects which you lost the following day?
They beg you meekly one last time
(in vain)
to let them stay with you.
But the angel of loss has touched them with its careless wing;
they are no longer ours, we retain them by force.

Rainer Maria Rilke

LITTLE SMOKE SIGNALS

I turn on the answerphone and listen to the tape. There is a message.
'Come on, Bubi . . . where are you? You're never there . . .'

She calls every day. The messages she leaves are virtually identical.
First there is a silence, then at the other end of the line I sense an indrawn
breath (she's inhaling cigarette smoke), then I clearly hear an exhalation
(she's breathing the smoke out). She's playing for time, courageously
overcoming her momentary defeat. The intonation is always the same:
false cheerfulness, apparent unconcern. She calls me Bubi. She pronounces Bubi languidly, with a kind of uncertain affectation, a little flirta-
tiously. Bubi is an invitation to a cuddle, almost directed to herself, like
whistling in the dark to drive away fear. 'Bubi,' she says to herself in the
deaf silence of the receiver.

The phrase 'You're never there . . .' follows after a longish pause, and
is a verbal extension without meaning. The phrase contains neither a real
reproach, nor what it is that's troubling her. The phrase serves to extend the
deafness, she's listening to her own voice, there is also the faint hope that
my voice might suddenly pierce through the silence at the other end of the
line. She breaks off suddenly, I sense her putting the receiver down rapidly, as though she had committed some kind of childish sin. And she almost
seems glad that I'm not there. Talking to me could have been painful; as it

is she's 'had a chat' and nothing hurts. She's not aware that the messages are always the same. She draws on her cigarette, inhales, exhales, her cracked voice sends out little SOS smoke signals. No one hears them but me. And I do nothing.

THE KISS

I often wonder how it is that I know so little about her. Her life seems to me like a little piece of cheap cloth, allocated to her once and for all, which cannot be stretched, or let out, or shortened. From outside, that's how she relates to it as well, as though towards a little cloth: she washes it, irons it, mends it and keeps it tidily in a cupboard.

I wonder how it is that I know so little about her and that what I know seems so unimportant. She knows far more about me. She alone, like a proprietor or a thief, knows my password, the password of my pain. I know nothing about that pain either, I don't know where it comes from, I don't know why I'm not capable of overcoming it, why it so infallibly takes my breath away.

I know all her gestures, movements, expressions, the tone of her voice. I recognise them in myself. In the mirror, for an instant, for a flash, as in a double exposure, instead of my own reflection, I catch hers. I see two lines round my mouth creeping inexorably downwards and ending their journey in (for now) barely perceptible little bags.

I wake increasingly often breathing heavily, I smack my lips the way she does. I watch her secretly during her afternoon sleep. There are tiny beads of sweat on her upper lip. I wonder whether when I'm asleep my face shows as clearly my sinking into despair.

Sometimes I catch myself swinging my legs, crumbling the air with my toes, the way she does.

Sometimes I am washed by a sudden wave of anxiety, like an unexpected blow, and I wonder then whether I have at that moment as helpless and vulnerable an expression as hers. Do I cough slightly pretending that nothing has happened, the way she does?

Sometimes I catch in my voice something of her cracked voice, sometimes her voice breaks in under mine, I speak in a duet, I keep stopping, drawing out the words as she does, waiting for it to pass.

I remember once long ago—running home from a romantic rendezvous at which the excited boy and I had practised our farewell kiss

56

over and over again—and I had come home wrapped in a mist of adrena-
lin, and absentmindedly repeated what I had been repeating until a
moment before, running the images together in my brain, I kissed her
soundly on the lips in the same way. This clumsy gesture provoked a
strange disquiet in me. To say now that what I did then was kiss some
future me, as though in a mirror, would be too simple.

When I recognise her in myself, when the images merge, that first
picture chimes in me as well, that beginning, that kiss on the lips, her
wide-open, slightly alarmed eyes in which was reflected my equally
embarrassed gaze.

NAME AND SURNAME

'Name?'
'Elisaveta . . .'
'Surname?'
'Simeonova . . .'
'Father's name?'
'Simeon . . .'
'Date of birth?'
'2 August 1926.'
'Place of birth?'
'Varna.'
'Where's that?'
'On the Black Sea . . . In Bulgaria . . .'
'And are all Bulgarian girls so pretty?'

I believe that she must have had similar conversations often in those
years. In customs and police stations, in offices, councils, with grey civil
servants, anonymous dispensers of documentation. I believe that all those
who wrote down her modest details must have first asked her inquisitive-
ly why she had come here? The sentence 'Are all Bulgarian girls so pretty?' in fact belonged to my father and was spoken somewhat later, with
sincere admiration, I believe. 'I didn't know what to reply,' she says. It is
to her bewilderment, his momentary audacity and that banal sentence,
that, in the end, I owe my own birth.

At twenty years of age, with a past not worth mentioning, with that
round number 20, glowing with health and brimming with dreams of the
future, she set off in the summer of 1946 from distant Varna to Yugoslavia.

She travelled by train. From Varna to Sofia, from Sofia to Dragoman, the border crossing and the last known point. As she crossed the Yugoslav border she was suddenly afraid, either because of the customs official's black moustache, or the finality of her decision. And as she opened her suitcase, thinking in panic that she still had time to change her mind and go back, it slipped out of her hand and scattered its modest contents over the floor. She remembers the rolling apples ('There were lots of them, lots of apples,' she says. 'I don't know myself why I had packed so many.'). Her memory was stuck on that picture of apples rolling over the floor. And it was as though the apples had made the decision and not her: she had to pick them all up, and then the train left . . .

She doesn't remember much. She juddered in the half-empty train in that distant year of 1946 across the devastated land ('Everything was destroyed, everything . . .'). She put her things tidily back into her suitcase: little summer dresses of silk georgette, elegant velour shoes, books, her sandals with cork heels made according to the latest Parisian fashion magazine. (That winter the sea had brought into the Black Sea port of Varna huge quantities of cork from some scuppered ship. That summer the girls of Varna clattered softly over the warm cobbles in light cork sandals which left a smell of the sea in their wake.) She put her apples back on the top.

She peered through the greasy window pane hoping to see something new, but everything was destroyed, so hopelessly destroyed, and then it began to rain, a sticky drizzle that fell for hours, blocking out the window, and she curled up in the empty compartment and thought about her fiance, a young Yugoslav with a wonderful smile, a sailor, whom she had met in Varna, on the promenade by the sea. She imagined their future shared home, she repeated to herself for the hundredth time the name of the station where she had to get off, she imagined his smile awaiting her at that station, and then she fell asleep from the warmth of that indistinct future. She juddered like that for hours, dozing, occasionally waking and eating her apples.

And the only thing she remembers clearly ('I don't know why I should remember that, of all things,' she says, emphasising 'of all things') was an old man ('He had a noble face') who came into her compartment at one of the stations. She offered him an apple, he took out a penknife and peeled the apple deftly making the peel into a rose.

'There, young lady,' he said.

('It was wonderful, I had never seen such a rose!')

She got off at the station whose name she had repeated so often to herself, holding her suitcase in her hand, no one was waiting for her, a sticky drizzle was falling and it was dark.

There, in that place, she covered over her past with a cloth of darkness. From time to time I shall just pull the occasional thread out of that cloth.

THE FIRST PHOTOGRAPHS

'He had a lovely smile,' she would say, having first destroyed all the photographs of him.

He was a sailor in the home guard, on a ship that was stranded and forgotten in the port of Varna which was not rocked by the storms of war. Thanks to that historical detail several young girls from Varna would be whisked away to Yugoslavia after the war.

She would find him, marry him, be raped on her wedding night (once and never again), come to hate him, leave him after a few months, quickly learn the language and typing ('It was easy, I was surrounded by illiterates'), get a job in the local sawmill, later in a local office, rent a room, move, erase it all, forget it all . . .

Meanwhile, under that cloth of darkness stir dim images of a dirty neglected house, his constant lies, oaths and pleas, a partisan girl, another fianceé, waving a pistol and threatening to kill him, swarms of flies, a mother-in-law with an enormous goitre, a toothy father-in-law dandling his goitrous wife on his knees, kneading her bosom with his huge hand, grunting pigs, filth, sweat, sweaty, greasy windows without curtains, night, the forest at night where she had been sent for wood, 'the little lady', 'the foreigner', her tears in the forest because she could not remember in the darkness on which side of the world her Varna was, as though things would have been easier if she had been able to remember, her tears over that, the distrustful gaze of those around her, her own despair, damp walls, the sharp smell of boiled beet, looks as sticky as flies . . . All those images merged and solidified into a dull sense of humiliation, into a hurt as heavy as a goitre. Because of that hurt, that invisible goitre, she decided at a certain moment that she would not go back, that she would stay, she would stay . . .

'Are all Bulgarian girls so pretty?'

'That's where the first photographs begin, her modest dossier, her true, bright story, with a hero as young as she was, a man of the new age, who emerged from the war fighting on the right side. There was the first snapshot. Her wedding in a little silk georgette dress and cork sandals. And for the wedding lunch chicken, real chicken!

WORDS

Those were lean years. People shopped with coupons. The only material you could buy was homespun. There was nothing. No-thing! They were hungry . . . They cooked paupers' food . . .

'What's paupers' food?'

'Caraway soup.'

'Just soup?'

'Cabbage, potatoes, beans, turnip stew, tripe with cabbage, dumplings, bread and dripping, egg beaten with sugar, that was for the children . . .'

'We conceived you in hunger as well,' she says. She was pregnant. Father was in hospital. He was coughing blood. It was hard to get streptomycin. Hard to get food. She remembers that she somehow managed to come by a jar of honey. In the morning she found a dead mouse in the jar. She wept, she didn't know whether it was for herself or the mouse . . . They ate what they had. Everyone was poor. 'We had to skimp and tighten our belts.'

Every day she washed the wooden floor of the rented room with lye. She turned the mattress because of bed-bugs, she washed their clothes, boiling the washing, dried it in the sun, ironed it, cleaned the room until it gleamed, cleanliness is half-way to health. Cleanliness was a substitute for abundance. The windows sparkled like diamonds, the bedclothes shone like satin, the wooden floor gleamed like old gold, even the mouse's corpse was the colour of amber. The smell of cleanliness drove out all other smells. Those were years without smell.

Words whose meaning I don't actually know: 'lye' (used for washing), 'coupons' (a substitute for money), 'bed-bugs' (insects that existed at the time).

Words whose meaning I dimly remember: 'homespun', 'bread-and-sugar' (a substitute for cake).

Words from Mother's vocabulary of that time: 'tripe', 'dripping', 'turnip stew', 'bread-and-sugar', 'coupons', 'bed-bugs'.

1949

In the year I was born the dictionary of the world contained . . . a world.

That was when Harry Truman became the thirty-third President of the United States, which was celebrated in Washington with a parade seven miles long; an earthquake in Seattle was proclaimed 'a catastrophe ten million dollars bad'; in Paris the Council of Europe was founded, a community of ten European states, the embryo of the future united Europe; in Great Britain rationing ended, restrictions on sweets were lifted, after ten years of darkness London shone with neon lights; in China the civil war was still going on and then ended with the proclamation of the People's Republic of China; in the American city of Miami a new architectonic wonder was opened, a 'futuristic university'; Israel was accepted into the United Nations, which moved in the same year into a new building, 'the most important building in the world', as President Truman called it on the occasion of its opening; in Great Britain the rate of exchange between the pound and the dollar altered drastically in favour of the pound; the little state of Monaco crowned its new ruler, Prince Rainier; in London the damaged St Paul's was restored; the summer of that year was tropically hot; Prince Charles was a baby with a charming curl; the Marshall Plan of economic aid for Europe was in place; Berlin was divided, the Soviet zone became East Berlin, the capital city of the German Democratic Republic, while the three other zones became West Berlin; a new double-decker aeroplane flew from London to New York in under nine hours; the USA and the USSR entered the period of the 'cold war'; Erroll Flynn, Gregory Peck, Douglas Fairbanks and Rosalind Russell were invited to a royal party given by the British Queen; a new anaesthetic was discovered which allowed women pain-free delivery . . .

In the dictionary of the world there was a world. In the dictionary of the world there is no sign of us. In our dictionary there is no sign of the world. On the day I was born, 27 March, physical education was developing successfully in the Belje agricultural estate, the progress of the Velimirovac commune was noteworthy, the country was preparing for the full completion of the spring sowing plan, and 10,000 women from Split joined the Front Brigades. On that day there was a distribution of tinned milk for D-1 consumers, two tins per coupon of the consumer's ration. That day the Balkan cinema in Zagreb was showing the Soviet film *The Young Guard*, the Zagreb cinema was showing the Soviet film *A Train Goes East*, the Jadran cinema was showing the Soviet film *The Adventures of Nasredin Hodža* and the Romanija cinema, *The Cruiser Varyag*. Also a Soviet film.

In my mother's dictionary there is no world. In her dictionary there is me, a husband who will not die and caraway soup.

CARAWAY SOUP

3 tablespoons of fat or butter
4 tablespoons of flour
1 teaspoon of caraway seeds
1.5 litres of water
salt to taste
bread cut into little squares and fried in fat

Heat the fat, add flour and cook until light brown in colour. Add the caraway seeds, cook a moment and add the water, stirring constantly. Add salt and continue to cook for 15 minutes. At the table place a little fried bread in each bowl and pour the soup over it.

THE DOLL'S HOUSE

When we moved into the new little house (I must have been three or four) with two rooms, a large kitchen, bathroom, pantry, verandah and garden, I began to explore the world (it was round like an egg) and Mother got what she had always wanted, a large doll's house. Our move marked the beginning of that joyful time in which everything was a first!

My parents' first bedroom suite, bought on hire purchase, of real walnut, with a large double bed, bedside cupboards, a spacious round-bellied wardrobe that gleamed like a mirror and a low chest of drawers with a large upright mirror on it, a piece of furniture oddly named a dressing-table. The suite would soon be joined by kitchen fixtures including a dresser, their first gas cooker, the bathroom boasted the first wood-heated boiler ever seen, which looked like the rockets seen much later, while the crowning glory was the first radio called a 'Nikola Tesla'. When we moved into the house I experienced for the first time the enchanting taste of the southern fruit called an orange, I was given my first doll made of India-rubber, dressed in a little dirndl, which vaguely suggested the existence of some other country in which differently dressed little girls lived.

Later all these things would change. We moved into a new flat, but the joyful age of new things did not end, some other first things came along: the first mass-produced Gavrilović pâté, the first television set, the first gramophone, the first washing-machine, the first Volkswagen 1300 car. Mother would light her first cigarette and start smoking. Another new age would begin. The collective life of the street where our first little house was (we called the street the colony) and that street-syndicate collectivity would be replaced (with the appearance of the first television) by another, media collectivity. The idea of the world being round and whole as an egg would be supported by the same popular songs *(Marina* and *Mustapha)*, but the idea would very soon shatter. Out of the splinters would spring up the contours of other worlds: first, for some reason, there was only Mexico, Mexicans and their *Mamajuanita*, then for a short time Indians. The existence of these others would be confirmed by the collective tears of some twenty million Yugoslavs provoked by watching melancholy Indian films. Then some other countries would shove their way in, mostly African ones. Their existence was confirmed by their representatives. We would wave little flags and stutter their mysteriously unpronounceable names: *Nkrumah, Sirimavobanderanaike, Nasser, Haileselassie* . . . Mother would maintain that before I was born there was a country called Russia, but at first I didn't find any traces that would confirm any such thing.

SOOT

'Soot' was one of the first words I learned, as natural as the words 'mummy', 'daddy', 'bread', 'water'. We lived in a small industrial town in which there was a soot factory. My father worked in that factory. 'Oil' was a natural word as well. Not far from our town there were oil boreholes, soot was something obtained from oil.

The street where we lived was called the colony (short for workers' colony) and the little houses in that colony (including our own) were at that time models of future 'modern' workers' settlements.

Mother often took me to the factory baths (which was much simpler than lighting the 'modern' boiler in our bathroom). The workers' eyelashes were thickly matted with soot, they looked as though they were wearing make-up, they fluttered their eyelashes like dolls. In the cold, stone cabins with hot showers, I remember the little streams of black water trickling in all directions, seeping through the grey heaps of soap suds.

Mother waged a daily battle against soot. In the morning she would wipe the window sills with a damp rag.

'There's been another fall of soot . . .' she used to say, running her index finger, that precise measuring instrument, over the window pane. She would move her finger importantly and say, in the tone of Marie Curie just after she discovered radium: 'See?'

'Yes,' I replied, staring at mother's finger smeared with greasy black pollen.

Every day she would open the windows, peer outside, look up at the sky, curl her lip in annoyance, and close the windows.

'There's soot in the air again!'

Soot was the fifth element.

On grey days, grains of soot would fall steadily from the sky like slow drizzle. On sunny days the air trembled with tiny golden spiders. Breathlessly, I watched their quiet, irresistible invasion. When one of these little spiders fell on to my hand, I would squash it, and the gold would be transformed into a black, greasy mark.

In winter, when snow fell, the soot would spread at night over the snow cover. In the morning we would break off the grey frozen crust, stare excitedly at the white snow underneath and 'make angels', leaving the traces of our children's bodies in the snow.

The chain of my memory always links the word 'oil' with the same phrase: Tito in the flesh. One year the opening of an oil bore-hole was attended by the President himself, Tito in the flesh. The bore-hole suddenly spurted towards the sky in a terrible jet and the guests were spattered with oil rain. My father's new suit, made for the occasion, could never be worn again.

'It can't even be turned inside out . . .' said my mother sorrowfully.

THE GLASS BALL

The first useless object in the house, in that age of first things was a glass ball. In the ball there was a little town, above the town stretched a dark-blue sky. When the ball was turned upside down, snow fell on the town.

The ball was a magical object, I examined it from every angle, twisting and turning it to see whether I could shake anything else out of the scenery apart from the reliable snow.

Some time later many magic balls were thrown out of homes (for some reason they had been declared kitsch).

I imagine its smooth coldness under my fingers now, I stare intently into the scenery of the little town, it seems to me as tiny and distant as another planet. Entranced by the magic I turn the ball over. From the earth to the sky waft snowflakes, small as particles of soot . . .

THE SINGERDUCHESS

'Excuse me, have you got any scraps . . .?' A huge woman sat watching us with brilliant, piercing eyes. We arranged ourselves side by side like apples, we just reached the window sill, we peered inside. With a broad sweep of her hand the woman took a handful of rags out of a sack, scooping them up like withered leaves, and gave each of us a handful through the window.

We withdrew with our treasure and, pink with excitement, examined the contents impatiently. The treasure glittered before our eyes: rags with stripes, rags with spots, rags with checks and squares, patterns and flowers, all one colour, multi-coloured . . .

The Duchess was the most important person in our little street. Her surname was Duke and, with the greatest respect, everyone called her the Duchess. We needed the rags for our dolls. The dolls were cobbled together from white canvas, their head and body stuffed with straw (or rags), hand-sewn. We used a 'tintenblei' (a wonderful pencil with a thick soft violet centre) to draw their eyes, nose and mouth (a dot, a dimple and a curl—and there's a pretty little girl). We dressed those bald rag dolls in dresses sewn from the Duchess's scraps.

We made clothes for our dolls from her scraps, while the Duchess sewed clothes for our mothers and for us, little girls. The Duchess was a dressmaker and in that pre-ready-made-clothes era she was a very important person, almost as important as the doctor, if not more so.

'Let's go to the Duchess!' Mother would say and I eagerly stretched out my hand to take hers.

I never saw that huge woman outside. As though she had grown completely into her little room, that jungle in which the most varied and dangerous fauna lurked at every step. It seemed that in that room everything was just temporarily in the Duchess's power, it seemed that all that was needed was a second's inattention for the dangerous beasts to come to life. A tape-measure snake wound itself tamely round her fingers, but it would often slip out of her hands and dart away into a corner. There were innocent, fleet-footed, toothless spools that jostled and shoved one another and dangerous pillow-like hedgehogs always bristling; untameable rags the colour of parrots twisted around in the sack and kept leaping out and wriggling over the floor; ribbons and lace like luxurious lianas created shadows in which bugs dozed: snap-fasteners, hooks, metal buttons; pins spawned in plastic boxes; metal thimbles yawned with a threatening grey yawn; studs like cockroaches lured by light kept scuttling over the floor; unfinished dresses hung on hat-racks besieged by an army of white ants, 'tacking'; and everywhere, from every corner, from the floor and the ceiling, threads of every possible colour invaded inexorably.

That immense woman seemed to have grown into her Singer sewing machine. The two of them together were: Singer-duchess. The Singerduchess's huge body used one foot to move itself (the other was placed calmly behind it at the time), one hand to turn the black wheel, the other to tame the living cloth and prick it with pins. Like an enormous beast the Singerduchess buzzed, spat, drew threads around itself, stuck pins . . . The Singerduchess was ruler of the jungle and her powerful humming overcame all other sounds: tinkling, clanging and rustling, the sound of the dull, soft fall of insects and snakes on to the floor.

In the corner of the jungle stood a fetish in the shape of an armless, headless torso, divinely blind, deaf and indifferent to the life of the jungle—a wooden tailor's dummy.

In that distant pre-ready-made era the Singerduchess sewed everything: panties, bras, swimming costumes, dresses, blouses, skirts, trousers, coats and wraps. The Singerduchess took father's worn suit, turned the material inside out and made an elegant suit for my mother, and sometimes there was enough left over for a skirt for me. The Singerduchess could make a blouse like the one Katharine Hepburn (whom my mother resembled) wore in the film *The African Queen* and a dress like the one Ava Gardner (whom my mother would have liked to resemble) wore in the film *The Snows of Kilimanjaro*.

Only sometimes, for some unknown reason, the Singerduchess would become wilful.

'We'll have a jabot here, Duchess . . .'

'Just an ordinary plastron,' the Singerduchess would say shortly. And the women would submit.

She stitched straight or gathered, in pleats, and tucks, she tamed linen, calico, crepe, georgette, baize, chintz and silk.

'We'll have a ruche, Duchess . . .'

'A ruff . . .' the Duchess would reply. And the women would submit.

Thanks to the Singerduchess, her former life in Varna, a real, big city compared to our little town, and her acquaintance with the art of film, in the pre-ready-made era my mother was the most elegantly dressed woman in town.

The unstoppable threads advanced from everywhere, from all the corners, from the floor and the ceiling, they hung, crept, crawled—and they stuck to the Singerduchess's customers like leeches.

Seeing her customers out, the Singerduchess would first pick the threads off them, and finally, lifting up the last little thread like a recently killed insect, she would say significantly: 'Someone dark is thinking of you.'

She would say that, if the thread was white. But if the exemplar of the dressmaker's fauna was black, the Singerduchess would say: 'Someone blond is thinking of you.'

The Singerduchess had a daughter whom people called Gina, after the Italian actress Gina Lollobrigida. Gina really did look like Lollobrigida, the very double, and she was as beautiful as an actress! She had a full white face, lively black eyes, full lips, white teeth and an unusually narrow waist.

'Gina has a waist like this . . .' said the women, joining their thumbs and forefingers in a circle.

Gina had shiny, black, short hair which she wound into curls on her cheeks and forehead. She put her thumb and forefinger to her lips, as though she were about to count a wad of money, licked them, and then used that same thumb and forefinger to moisten a lock of hair and deftly twist it into the figure 6. On each side of her face Gina had at least six of these sixes, and on her forehead two, curved like two big black snails.

Although she was as beautiful as an actress and dressed like a doll, although black and white threads stuck to her abundantly, although many dark and blond men must have thought about her as a result, Gina never married.

'She didn't have any luck with men . . .' said the women.

Who knows, perhaps the unhappy Gina was in the power of the Singerduchess's spellbinding dressmaker's fauna. In any case, I have a photograph of me with Gina, on a workers' union outing, where our parents had taken us children. In the photograph the wind is billowing Gina's white calico dress, which emphasised her narrow waist still further. Behind the parachute dissipation of Gina's dress, I can be seen, with a white ribbon in my hair. Behind us burns the eternal flame. The flame comes from the grave of the Unknown Soldier on Avala mountain, where the photograph was taken.

AUNTIE PUPA

I stand on the tips of my toes on the polished parquet warmed with golden light, I stand straight, my tummy pulled in, my neck stretched, there is a book on my head, I take a careful step, the yellow parquet throws sheafs of light towards the loft, I swallow air, hold my breath as though I were diving, I stretch out my other leg and the book slips to the floor with a crash.

'Beoffwithyou!' says Auntie Pupa and laughs raspingly, as though she were coughing.

Tante Puppe. She was tall, dry, bony, her nose curved into a thin beak, with blinking, bluish eyes which looked at the world as though they knew everything already. She had a slight limp, but she held herself unusually upright as she walked, lightly, her head held high, she would stretch her neck like a long-necked animal and carefully sniff the air with her fine nostrils.

She lived in a little detached house with a porch and a large garden. The rooms were large, sunny, with doors that opened wide leading from one room into another, like new worlds. As you entered the house you put on capacious felt slippers. People slid noiselessly through her house, like in Russian museums. For some reason all she grew in the garden were luxuriant bushes with 'clumps' of flowers: they were white balls of flowers that she called 'dumplings', large hortensias which changed their colours like chameleons and sumptuous pale-pink and white peonies. I liked clumps of flowers, as she did: I spent hours studying the life of ants on them.

Auntie Pupa was a pre-war schoolteacher ('she's a pre-war schoolteacher!'), she knew German, she played the piano and was the absolute authority in questions of elegance.

She tried unsuccessfully to teach me the art of walking well. She was firmly convinced that a pleasing walk was one of the most important, if not the most important thing in life.

'Watch animals,' she said. 'Just how elegantly they move!' I studied the available animals attentively.

'What about hens?'

'Hens are not without a certain elegance,' she would say solemnly.

I remember a sun-filled room, she was sitting upright in an armchair, tapping the floor with a stick like a ballet master. I stretch on to tiptoes ('Pull your tummy in!'), I pull my tummy in ('Hold your breath!'), I hold my breath ('And now breathe lightly . . .') . . .

I did not learn the art of walking well. I did not understand how it was possible to breathe with one's stomach pulled in, but I did all I could just so as to spend as much time as possible with her. I would die of happiness when, sometimes, with a regal gesture, she would let me stay the night.

I lie in her bed, with the covers up to my chin, I am hiding, the door which leads to the next room is wide open. Her son comes out of the bathroom, his skin is golden like King Midas himself, he has a towel round his neck. From the radio comes a popular song. He rubs himself with the towel in time to the music, shakes off golden droplets, sways in a dance step. Istanbul, Constantinople, Istanbul—left—Constantinople—right, Istanbul—up, Constantinople—down . . .

Auntie Pupa appears in the doorway, she slowly sniffs the golden air around her, steps easily, upright, then she points her fine beak and sees a pair of wondering eyes peeping out from under the bedclothes . . .

'Beoffwithyou . . .!'

Sometimes, now, I'll be sitting in an armchair, reading, then suddenly I get up, place a book on my head, stretch on to tiptoe, pull in my stomach. I feel the weight of the book on the crown of my head, I feel a vague physical pleasure . . . And then I go back to the armchair, pick up my book and think that in the art of walking well there really is some kind of secret, a kind of truth, which, like all higher truths, is not accessible to everyone. Auntie Pupa knew that truth.

AUNTS

I often pleaded with Mother to tell me about her Bulgarian family, numerous and scattered like dandelion seeds.

'First there were Grandfather Milan and Grandmother Lyuba,' she began the story from Grandma and Grandpa.

'And then?'

'And then Grandfather Milan and Grandmother Lyuba had seven children: Bogumil and Todor, Eksena, Pavlena, Anastasiya, Vasilka and Tsvetanka . . .'

She would cross out the intrinsically uninteresting Bogumil and Todor at once and start to talk about Grandma and the aunts . . .

'Eksena was always called Asenka, Pavlena Pavla, Anastasiya Natsa, Vasilka Vasilka and Tsvetanka, hmTsvetanka,' she went on, enjoying my enjoyment.

'And then?'

'Eksena married Simeon, Pavlena married Slavcho, Anastasiya Vancho, Vasilka Tsvetan and Tsvetanka Levcho . . .'

I was a little disappointed that Tsvetanka had not married Tsvetan, but there was nothing to be done about it.

'And then? What next?'

She listed the branches and sub-branches of the family tree (Pavlena and Slavcho had four children, Rumen, Dunka, Ilcho and Milanka . . .) and I listened to the simple enumeration intently as though it were the most interesting fairy-tale in the world. Vasilka was the prettiest, but she died young, Pavlena married the stupidest husband, who later became the richest, Eksena married the handsomest, Tsvetanka the cleverest, while destiny, which left no one out, bestowed on Anastasiya the biggest farter!

'He was the biggest farter in the family,' said Mother enjoying the fact that she was pronouncing a forbidden word. 'He let out "pigeons" that made the whole house shake,' she said replacing the forbidden noun with the permitted phrase.

Eksena, Pavlena, Anastasiya, Vasilka and Tsvetanka were my imaginary dolls, my charms and my chants (Eksena chops the wood, Pavlena sweeps the floor, Vasilka prepares the food, Anastasiya bolts the door—while Tsvetanka, while Tsvetanka's just—good!), magical names, children's cards, five ladies, heroines from a fairy-tale. It was enough for Mother to tell me just a few details (Anastasiya used old matches for make-up; Eksena, my grandmother, was swept away when she was not quite sixteen by a handsome young man, my grandfather, and taken to the far side of the country, to the shore of the Black Sea; Pavlena cheated on

her stupid husband and God rewarded her with fine-looking children)—
and I dressed my dolls in imaginary tales, sewed them destinies, added
children and husbands . . .

Eksena, Pavlena, Vasilka, Tsvetanka and Anastasiya—along with
Pandora and her box, King Midas, partisan tales, the Argonauts and their
search for the golden fleece, with children's stories about Tito, who once
stole a pig's head and used it to feed his hungry family, with the unhappy
Medea, with Russian folk tales, with the boy Nemecek out of *The Hero of
Pavlova Street* and Audie Murphy, the American actor, hero of Westerns—
would be preserved in the enduring fund of my childhood myths.

Nowadays I remember hardly anyone of that scattered dandelion family, although I met some of them, but the real live Aksena, Pavlena and
Anastasiya had lost their fairy-tale aura and with time had become its grey
opposite. For some reason the only vivid image to survive was that of the
completely unimportant Vancho (ah, capricious memory!), the biggest
farter in the family. Although my imagination had created his image in my
childhood, today, as one of the few left in the album, it has the full 'reality' of a photograph.

I 'remember' him, therefore, with an enormous belly raised towards the
sky, with a snub nose on a face which had been all kneaded upwards by
God's hand, in baggy white trousers, a white shirt, with a white sailor's cap
with a brim, with a blind man's round black glasses on his nose and the
inevitable cane in his hand, walking along a sunny promenade by the sea.
Behind him flutters a flock of pigeons' shadows. He turns, angrily drives the
birds away with his cane like flies, but the skittish flock carries on hovering
behind him. Then he gives up, he steps out importantly, the sun glares, the
shadows—his own, the shadow of his cane and of the flock of pigeons—are
drawn after him like a fluttering regal train. The Farter King is on his way.

BINA

'Here you are,' Mother would say, thrusting a bundle into my hands.
'Take that to Bina and ask her to pick up the runs for me.'

In my inner album, I have preserved, for a reason known only to my
capricious memory, the image of Bina the Italian ('They are Italian,' said
Mother, although I didn't understand what that meant).

Bina picked up runs on stockings. With their vanished use (torn stockings would soon simply be thrown away) the words would vanish ('I've

71

got a run in my stocking; the runs need picking up')—and with them that tiny skill would vanish as well.

Pale-faced, taciturn, with a tired smile and foxy eyes placed at a slant, Bina picked up runs. Only she possessed a magic needle with a hook, and women would bring their torn nylon stockings to her (known as *najlonke*), rarer than silk ones, at first the ones with a seam, later seamless. With her magic surgeon's hook Bina would patiently pick up thread after thread, tiny loop after tiny loop, and deftly mend the shameful whitish stripes as though they had never been there.

It was as though she found some satisfaction in that minute work. Her bandy-legged little husband beat her violently, her bandy-legged mother-in-law drank all day long and fished in a nearby stream (where one day when she was drunk she would be dragged by the leg by the Water Man down to the depths, never to return), and her snotty, constantly hungry children were not much comfort to her.

When I got nearer to their little house, I would slow down. I liked to watch her (she always sat by the window), driving flies away with a shake of her head, catching the last of the daylight with her tired eyes, putting a transparent stocking on to her hand, tracing the treacherous run with her eyes, then, taking the stocking off her hand like an expensive glove, she would put it on to a wooden 'mushroom', place the run in the centre and with her twinkling hook gather, one by one, the runaway threads. When she caught sight of me, she smiled, framed in the window like a living photograph, shaking the flies from her head and squinting her foxy eyes.

One day, having first picked up the runs on all the stockings, some-where around midnight, when everyone was soundly asleep, fastening her hooked needle on her breast, she went out into the courtyard in her slip-pers. She stood still for a moment, glanced at the starry sky, and then, as though under a spell, she went slowly into the garden and stopped beside the well. There she took off her slippers, glanced at the reflection of the moon in the water, perhaps it seemed to her that in its shiny pale-yellow silk she could see a run that needed to be picked up, and so, with her glint-ing needle in her hand . . . she jumped into the well.

In the morning they found a pair of slippers placed neatly side by side. At her funeral her little bandy-legged husband, his bandy-legged mother and four children, all in black, cried shrilly and swarmed around the coffin like flies.

I often used to see the image of slippers beside a well, floating, for some reason, above the ground at the level of the well. And when after that event anyone mentioned that someone had died, the first thing I thought of would be a pair of slippers.

THE HEAVENLY TREE

In my mother's friend Tina's garden there was just one tree, a Japanese apple tree.

'Come here,' commanded Tomica, Tina's son and the same age as me.

I trotted obediently after him. We came to the tree. A dark-pink flowery cupola stretched above us.

'Now we're going to climb it,' said Tomica. We climbed on to the short-stemmed tree and sat down among the comfortable web of branches.

'See?' said Tomica importantly, waving his hand over his territory.

We sat in the heavenly tree completely concealed by its flowery cupola. The rays of the sun penetrated through the cupola, dappling us with flickering light. We sat like that in that warm apple bowl intoxicated by the humming of insects and the scent of the dark-pink blossom. It was all sweet and thick, so unbearably fragrant and somehow close, like under a magnifying glass. For a moment the sweet headiness made me think I was going to fall. I grabbed hold of a branch, carelessly rubbing my hand against the rough bark, and grazed my finger.

A little drop of blood slipped out of the pink cut and fell silently on to a petal.

'Quick, suck the blood . . .' whispered Tomica.

'Why?'

'Cos if you don't you'll die . . .' he said in a mysterious, terrible voice.

Obediently I sucked the little drop of blood from my finger. It tasted sweet and strange. My heart thumped with unclear emotions: it seemed to me that I was on the verge of some great discovery, some great secret. I trembled, I inhaled the heavy scent of blossom, I sniffed the air around me like a blind person trying to find traces of that magnificent, unknown secret whose depths I could only guess at. The word 'die' rang and stayed hovering in the air like a golden ring. I sat swinging my legs, staring at the little golden hairs and pink flesh under the grazed skin over which a large ant was walking. I was so tiny, and the ant so huge.

'And now we'll make snow,' said Tomica and began shaking a branch.

On to the green grass beneath us fell dark-pink snow. Among the petals hovering in the air I saw mine, the one with the drop of blood on it. We sat like that, tiny, inside a glass ball, caught up in a snowstorm of blossom, quite alone in the world, Tomica and I.

BORDERS

The secure world in which a sooty pollen-like drizzle fell constantly had its sharply defined borders. And at the borders lurked the dangers of mysterious distances and terrible depths.

One of the borders was the railway line. It was beyond the railway line that the unknown distances began. At night they gleamed dark-blue, pulsating and emitting noises among which could be made out the whistles of steam engines and the croaking of frogs. By day the distances quivered lazily in a tranquil light-blue haze. There beyond the railway line, concealed by the blue silk of distance, lived Gypsies *who stole little children.* I often thought I caught sight of them on the horizon, I imagined them drawing that silk in, covering me with it as with a scarf and I would vanish for ever. The way many inquisitive children had already vanished . . .

The other border was deceptive: in spring it would appear like an alluring ribbon of snow-white lace, and in the winter like a prickly black hedge. Beyond that border lurked a danger more terrible than the Gypsies *who stole little children.* Its name was 'The Water Man', a mysterious being who lived in the stream and had dragged many inquisitive children down to its depths. Trembling with fear and sweet trepidation I pushed my way through the hedge, hid in the green river ferns, crumbled the damp clay in my excited fingers and stared into the yellow water anticipating his sign . . .

Between those two dangerous worlds which lay in wait beyond the borders I set off for a third, the first class of primary school.

THE PRIMER

By chance my first primer happened to slide out of a box of old papers. The first page and the first four pictures moved me deeply. I remembered, when I started school, staring long and fervently into those fresh clear colours (mostly bright blue and bright green), I remember adding depth to the simple, flat lines through the energy of my entranced gaze. It was not that I was thinking up stories, I was just meticulously examining every detail, every smallest detail. I examined the pictures with my gaze as a fish does the limpid river bottom.

Even now I recall the pleasure with which the pencil in my hand multiplied the apples, pears, plums, the joyful little spheres (clusters of grapes); the pleasure with which it drew symmetrical little tails on tree trunks, green pines (I filled my notebooks with orderly forests of them). I remember those endless rows of orderly carrots, onions and potatoes. I recall the touching optimism of multiplication. And I can almost hear those pears and apples of mine now soundlessly rolling out of the notebook and filling another, imaginary space. All those lines and streaks, thick ones and thin ones, all those little circles and snails, all those little hooks and snakes, all those loops and dots—they all rustle, crinkle, mingle in that imaginary space, they have not disappeared, one day someone will let them out to become a real window, a real pear, a real word, a sentence . . .

I scrutinise the pictures. I can't read yet. I notice the brightly coloured, pleasing harmony of the most varied objects and concepts: here are a horse and a harp, a man and a mouse, fingers and a flower . . . Each of them contentedly making its own sound: a boyah; a girloh; a sheepbaa; a cowmoo.

I notice the objects: an antiquated radio, archaic pens and erasers. I notice the passionate faith in progress: in one picture children are waving at an aeroplane, in another a happy family is gathered round a table. And on the table—a radio! An antique steam engine is racing into a cloudless future, bridges span rivers, chimneys puff cheerful smoke, tractors plough the soil, and ships the sea. People (men, I see only now) work cheerfully: pilots and tractor-drivers, doctors and miners. Women are only mothers. Or little girls.

The sky is blue, the sun is shining, there are no clouds or rain anywhere, not even at the letter C, nor at the letter R.

I learn the letters. A—for apple; E—for elephant; O—for orange; U—for umbrella. *Sara, see the sea! The smooth, silky sea! Bit, sit, hit, bat, sat, mat, how, now, cow . . .*

I learn sentences. *Jemal and Jafer are good friends. They come from Bosnia. Jafer has no family. He lives with Jemal. Jemal's mother loves him like her own son. Jemal and Jafer go to a distant town to learn a trade. Jemal's mother puts an apple in each of their pockets. As they leave she says: 'Work hard, children, light of my life. Gladden your mother's heart with good reports!'*

The sentences make soft imprints, outline some common coordinates in the empty fields of our future personal biographies. Some letters stand out: F – for family; H – for homeland. (*Like a mother, with its Plan, the state takes care of every man.*) B – for brother. All people are brothers, especially Africans.

A very long way away, in Africa, live peoples with dark skins. They greet our sailors joyfully. They point to the red star on our flag. They shake our sailors firmly by the hand and shout in their own language: Yugoslav sailors are our brothers!, reads a passage from my primer.

There are Serbs and Croats. They are brothers too. And *When brotherly hearts unite—nothing can oppose their might!* So my primer proclaims.

The coordinates of the primer's system are not built on opposites. In the world of the primer there is no evil. There is only good, without its opposing side. It's good to learn, to be clean (*Every day/come what may/wash the dirt/and grime away*) and diligent (*All young and strong who never shirk/Come along, and join in our work!*) Only the Fascists are evil. They usually come with the adjective 'black'!

In my primer the Homeland seems to have no borders. There is Pula (*Let's send a postcard to our pal Pero the pioneer in Pula . . .*), there is Filip from Slavonia and Frane from Dalmatia, there is our sea. But it's not called the Adriatic anywhere.

The names in my primer are Croatian and Serbian, Slovene and Macedonian, fairly distributed. As many Petars as Mitars, Djordjes as Ivans . . .

The world of my primer is realistic. The picture of a mother in a clean apron seeing her little boy off to school is overlaid for me now with a picture of my own mother. I remember Mother's snow-white aprons, the clean bed linen, curtains and cushions, the aesthetics of poverty. In the general postwar deprivation we all shared, a vase of wild flowers, a little curtain and a cushion successfully concealed the lack of things.

C for car—and the drawing of a car opens the pages of an unwritten story of Yugo-everyday life. I remember that passionate faith that each new day would bring a better future (this year we're buying a car, and next year we'll go to the sea).

'Sara, see the sea! The smooth, silky sea!' was not an alliterative sen-

tence to practise writing the letter 's', but what we really said each time we caught sight of the sea. The picture of the family at the train window (you can clearly see the initials of the Yugoslav State Railways, in Latin and Cyrillic scripts) matches the exciting reality of travelling by train to Zagreb, the capital of Croatia, to Belgrade, the capital of Yugoslavia.

In the drawing of the radio I clearly recognise the first 'Nikola Tesla' Yugoslav radio (I remember staring intently in the dark at the magic flickering green eye), and the family gathered round the table will certainly be listening to the *Sailors' Requests* programme . . .

The Tito of my primer was the real Tito too, the one to whom we sent letters on his birthday. I remember rolling the letters into tubes and pushing them into a wooden, handmade baton . . .

The primer has given us new faithful friends is written in capital letters in my primer. *Those friends are letters. Woe betide anyone who does not have these friends!*, threatens my primer.

I started school in 1957. That year I got my passport to the Gutenberg galaxy, and another, inner one. The primer is a kind of passport for several generations. Several generations are a whole nation. I recognise that 'nation' of mine today. It hatched out of the primer like those multiple pears and apples from my beginner's notebooks. I always do recognise my people, even in international airports, where, mixed up with others, they are harder to discern. I recognise them by a kind of twitch, by the way they glance shyly around them, and the way they try not to, by the way they check in their luggage, I recognise them even when they're travelling in the opposite direction . . . After all, we're out of the same primer.*

THE GREY ZONE OF OBLIVION

'You write about me—for yourself; I write about myself—for you' says Alya, to whom Viktor Shklovsky's love letters were addressed.

*The primer, which was initially synchronised with my life, soon became a dusty document of passing time. Life went off to conquer lovelier, richer images.

In 1991, when the last bloodiest phase of dismantling the Yugoslav Utopia began, time rolled up into a circle and everything went back to the beginning. Tired of the hysterical strategies of the media war with all its sound and fury, the dismantling returned to the bare, clear little sketches from my primer. Jovans are attacking Ivans, the Cyrillic alphabet is quarrelling with the Latin script, Serbs with Croats, Djordje and Jafer are fighting. The green aeroplanes with the red star from my primer took to the air . . . *Our, Yugoslav* sailors shelled our ports and *our lovely blue sea* from their ships. The homeland without borders began to carve new borders. Books, our *best friends*, burned, splinters of centuries-old churches flew through the air together with splinters of Tito's plaster heads. Letters, figures, symbols from my primer rushed to annihilate themselves. Like Eristochtones, the Utopia was devouring itself before our eyes, and in the empty spaces, like harmless eggs, there began to appear the outlines of new primers!

Writing about her, my mother, I am hunting for pictures of myself in the darkness of oblivion, but all our pictures are shared, even if she is not in the picture for a moment, she is present.

When I look through photographs in albums I notice a symmetry between photographs and remembrance. Where *our* shared photographs stop (and *my* photographs from school, *my* photographs from school outings, *my* photographs with my friends . . .) is where the zone of possible remembrance stops as well. After that I don't seem to remember much. As though only shared photographs were a guarantee of remembering. Where our shared photographs separate (into increasingly numerous ones of *me* and increasingly few of *her*) is where the grey zone of oblivion begins. Perhaps I do remember facts (that year we travelled to this place or that, that year we changed this or that in the house), but they produce few images.

THE BLACK SEA

Memory, it seems, is not simply *capricious*, it winds along secret paths of its own, following subtle laws of symmetry.

I was to see her Black Sea (as she showed me photographs she would say, 'there, that's *my* Varna, that's *my* Black Sea') once from the other side, in Odessa, dimly recalling that I had seen a similar town and similar sea somewhere before. A momentary daze (or a quite legitimate curve of memory) would not allow me to remember. The simple notion that Varna, where I had been so often, was on the other side of this sea did not so much as cross my mind. I listened to the sound of the sea in the arms of my lover, weak with a powerful sense of hopelessness. I was to remember an intense smell of half-dried apples on a metal plate (which the invisible hand of the kind owner of the house had left on the bedside table). The scent of those apples merged with a sense of hopelessness and they remained for ever linked.

Many years later in New York, in an apartment on Washington Heights, I was to smell the same scent. I discovered that the tenant of the New York apartment was an *émigrée* from Odessa, and that it was she whose 'invisible hand' had once, long ago, placed a metal plate with half-dried apples on a bedside table for a man and a woman . . . Ah, the fathomable paths of destiny!

I was to remember the Black Sea quite clearly on another occasion

78

and in a third place. One summer, on the long wooden pier in Brighton, I bought candy floss, sat down on the beach wrapped in a wind—cheater (fluffed up like a bird, like the English people there), breathed in the strong, cold wind, melted the little threads of sugar wool with my tongue and for a moment felt quite clearly that I was eighteen, that I was sometimes called Eli and that there, on the other side of the sea, on another shore, was a town in which I had once been as someone else—the town of Varna!

'Memory, I think, is a substitute for the tail that we lost for good in the happy process of evolution. It directs our movements, including migration. Apart from that there is something clearly atavistic in the very process of recollection, if only because such a process never is linear. Also, the more one remembers, the closer perhaps one is to dying.

'If this is so, it is a good thing when your memory stumbles. More often, however, it coils, recoils, digresses to all sides, just as a tail does; so should one's narrative, even at the risk of sounding inconsequential and boring. Boredom, after all, is the most frequent feature of existence, and one wonders why it fared so poorly in the nineteenth-century prose that strived so much for realism.

'But even if a writer is fully equipped to imitate on paper the subtlest fluctuations of the mind, the effort to reproduce the tail in all its spiral splendor is still doomed, for evolution wasn't for nothing. The perspective of years straightens things to the point of complete obliteration. Nothing brings them back, not even handwritten words with their coiled letters.'
(Joseph Brodsky, *Less Than One*)

MOTHER'S TREASURE

Mother's greatest treasure was books, the ones which she brought with her in the suitcase full of apples, and the ones she began to buy when she arrived.

My birth was marked by a book too, Maxim Gorky's novel, *Mother*. Without reading it, but beguiled by the fitting title, my father bought the book and took it to my mother in hospital on the day of my birth.

In the general postwar poverty, one of the most pervasive ideological slogans (on a par with *Cleanliness is halfway to health*) was *Books are our greatest treasure.* The propaganda messages, that *Knowledge is power*, that *Books are our best friends*, were reinforced not only by folklore in which *The mind governs, while strength shifts logs*, but also by little apocryphal tales about great socialists, self-made men, who seem to have done nothing but *read, read and read*, like Lenin; they did it even at night, by the light of the moon, like Maxim Gorky; men who transformed themselves, through education, from insignificant peasants into scholars who spoke several foreign languages, and virtuoso piano players, like Tito. (This cliche connected with great socialists would be repeated some forty years later, when the new Croatian president was building his media image, having himself photographed in the pose of an engrossed reader of a novel, which was nothing more or less than one by the American writer John Irving! As I looked at that nauseating photographic set-piece, I remembered another Irving, the writer Irving Stone who had a place of honour in my mother's postwar library.)

My mother's authentic passion, not engineered by anything, infected me too in my early childhood so that her modest library became ours. Because of a lack of books intended for my age, such as *The Hero of Pavlova Street* and *The Apprentice Hlapić*, I very quickly chose instead *Lucretia Borgia (The Pope's Daughter)* and Upton Sinclair and his *Petroleum*, one of the first books in our library. I think that my father bought the book in 1946, because of the title again, since he worked in the oil industry. Upton Sinclair, together with Irving Stone and Theodore Dreiser, was Mother's favourite American writer. Somewhat later a series of 'books of the film' appeared, with a picture, a scene from the film, stuck on to the first page, and Stone's *The First Lady of America* took up a permanent position in Mother's library.

The titles of my mother's library are today a valuable source of information about the first postwar publications and translations, because my mother conscientiously bought every new book that appeared on the poor literary market after the war.

So the two of us forged our taste together, we could not make up our minds which was better: Trygve Gulbranssen's *The Wind From The Mountain* and *No Way Round* or Robert Penn Warren's *All the King's Men*, Lajos Zilahy's *Deadly Spring* or Pierre la Mure's *Moulin Rouge*, Daphne du Maurier's *Rebecca* or Balzac's *The Troublemaker*, Stendhal's *Armance* or *The Egoist* by George Meredith, Cronin's *Hatter's Castle* or *Marianne's*

80

Life by Marivaux, Zola's *Truth* or *The Leviathan* by Julien Green, Fielding's *Joseph Andrews* or Dickens's *Pickwick Papers* . . .

In 1951, Mother bought Gertrude Stein's novel *Melancthe*, but I don't think she ever read it. She bought that book because she liked women's names in the titles: *Anna Karenina, Emma Bovary, Carrie, Armance, Rebecca, Lucy Crown* . . . Women's names in the title promised in advance a destiny with which she would be able to identify, comparing her life with that of the heroine of the novel. Sometimes she liked the titles themselves, as for instance Guy de Maupassant's novel *Strong As Death*.

Nevertheless, we really did share one novel: Hardy's *Tess of the d'Urbervilles*, purchased in 1954.

The Book of Knowledge, a popular lexicon with pictures, was my favourite book for a long time. In a childhood without picture books, television, cartoons, videos and computers, where all today's distractions were concentrated into one: the book. My hungry, muddled, book-filled and puzzled child's head would think in just the same way about pictures of fish, flowers, butterflies, boats, Latin names, people's names from *The Book of Knowledge* and assumptions about life acquired by reading mother's novels.

We joined the library and I made friends with Margita, the librarian, a quiet and passionate consumer of books. Margita lent me books without any criteria, or rather, according to some criteria of her own. So, for instance, while other children were raving over Karl May, she lent me Kafka's *Metamorphosis*. If it was a book about someone who became an insect (thought Margita), it would surely interest a child!

Parallel with this sweet commune of readers founded by Mother, Margita and me, there began a quiet, unconscious betrayal on my part for which, who knows why, the French were to blame.

One of the magical words in my childhood was a word of indistinct content: 'Sorbonne'. Mother had once said of someone, 'He studied at the Sorbonne!' in a tone which expressed a fact worthy of wonder and the unassailable credibility of the person to whom the fact referred. I pronounced the magical word wrong, 'Sobronne.'

The other magical word was 'mansarde'. It sounded as enchanting as 'Sobronne'. The meaning of both words was not quite clear, but my conviction that mansardes existed only in Paris was cast-iron. I could not be quite so sure about Sobronnes.

Little by little, the French language became attached to the words 'mansarde', 'Paris' and 'Sorbonne'. I turned the dial on our first radio until French would start to gurgle and seep into my grateful ear. Through the green eye of the 'Nikola Tesla', skimming along the gurgling French language as over water, I floated out of the sooty little provincial town into the great, unknown world. I secretly decided that I would become as famous as Minou Drouet, the star French children's writer. Later I changed my mind and decided that I would become Francoise Sagan. As a first step, I cut my hair short like Jean Seberg in the film *Bonjour, Tristesse*.

Later I decided that I would find someone like Jean-Paul Sartre and live with him in a 'mansarde'. There was no room for my mother in that 'mansarde'. Later still I would give up the idea of the 'mansarde' and Jean-Paul Sartre, but the French fascination had done its work: the first few books of what was just 'my' library began to appear.

CHEWING-GUM STORIES

She adored the cinema. In our little provincial town to start with there was just a projector, set up in an improvised hall in the local hotel. Mother would take me to the cinema every day, she would watch the same film several times over.

She subscribed to the magazine *Film World*, full of wonderful pictures and delectable material about the lives of film stars, scandals, marriages, divorces, affairs, drunkenness, unhappiness. She devoured these stories until she knew them all by heart.

Somewhat later came chewing-gum packets with little pictures of film stars in them. Once I inherited (from an older child, who had decided to grow up) a real treasure: an album with pictures of actors from chewing-gum packets. I examined the album, and Mother knew a story to go with each of the pictures: about Ava Gardner, the poor farmer's daughter, the 'bare-foot countess', the most beautiful woman in the world, who could not be saved from an unhappy fate even by her beauty; about the lovely Susan Hayward (Mother cried as she watched the film *I'll Cry Tomorrow*); about *Gilda*, Rita Hayworth, the 'goddess of love', who married Aly Khan, the richest man in the world; about the capricious Vivien Leigh, the beautiful Scarlett O'Hara from *Gone With The Wind* and the unforgettable 'old maid' from *A Streetcar Named Desire*, about her marriage to Laurence Olivier; about the honourable Jean Gabin, a builder who became an actor and the husband of Marlene Dietrich; about the romantic dreamer Gerard Philippe, the unforgettable hero of *Le Diable Au Corps*, destined to die young from cancer; about the handsome Rhett Butler, Clark Gable, the adventurer with the irresistible moustache; about Martine Carol, about Leslie Caron, about the mysterious Michele Morgan, about the equally mysterious Greta Garbo, about the stern and spiteful Joan Crawford and the strange Bette Davis; about the charming and cheerful Carole Lombard, Clark Gable's wife, who was tragically killed in an aeroplane accident; and the melancholic cynic Humphrey Bogart, Bogey, and his wife Lauren Bacall; about the enduring love of Spencer Tracy and Katharine Hepburn . . .

Later came other stars, just mine, the first of which was the American actor Audie Murphy, the bearer of twenty-four medals for bravery, the hero of Westerns; but the splendour of the first film stars combined with their lives, which my mother related so well, will never fade.

And when once later, far later than I should have done, I saw Ford's film *How Green Was My Valley*, a momentary glint of vague remembrance, a brief mental collage returned me to the album with the chewing-gum pictures. Only instead of Maureen O'Hara's picture there was . . . my mother's!

MR PINE TREE

The cinema operator, a Czech, was a small, brown dwarf of a man with an eternal cigarette stuck to his lower lip. He always answered the question 'How are you?' in Czech: 'Like a pine tree!' At the same time he would hastily straighten up, beat his breast vigorously with his fist, as though testing the firmness of the material, and stretch a smile over his face. His figure, always followed by a faithful little cloud of cigarette smoke, had absolutely nothing evergreen about it.

He let us children into the cinema without tickets, to sit on proper seats, or, if the cinema was full, on folding ones. At the Sunday matinees, the only audience was us kids and the wife of the local teacher, who had given birth to a crowd of children and then refused to be anyone's mother or wife any more and returned to her childhood. She went to the cinema every day. Empty-headed, noticing no one around her, with a large protruding stomach, the local teacher's wife entered the auditorium with an ice-cream in one hand and a bag of sweets in the other. In the darkness she crunched the sweets loudly with her teeth and rustled the papers.

The cinema operator would close the door after us and then, accompanied by his little cloud of smoke, he would climb into the small projection box. For a long time Mr Pine Tree carried out all the duties in the provincial cinema himself: he sold the tickets, ordered the films, tore the tickets at the entrance, closed the door behind the audience, and projected the films.

Nowadays, in the darkness of cinemas, I sometimes expect to see the shot I had seen repeated innumerable times: in the narrow, vertical ribbon of light his face and the little cloud of smoke above his head, and then the heady anticipation in the dark, the duration of which is measured by steps (as many as it took the projectionist to reach his little box).

After many years I happened to meet him, and was delighted to see him. To my question—'How are you?'—he answered by drawing himself up, stretching a smile like a little flag over his face and beating on his breast with a feeble hand. 'Like a pine tree,' he said. A few days later he died. As he had tapped his breast for the last time, testing the firmness of the material, so he died, always evergreen, Mr Pine Tree.

MOTHER IN THE BALL

I walk my finger over the glass surface of the ball. I take it on my palm like an apple, I warm the cold glass, cool my warm palm. Snow falls from the dark sky on to the little town. In the ball sits my mother, licking the snowflakes from her finger.

I watch her through the glass, I think about her, I try to feel her core. I turn the ball round and over her face pass the shadows of Emma Bovary, Maureen O'Hara, Tess, Carrie . . . The shadows wind round one another according to some secret intimacy, they intertwine, connected by secret threads. I recognise the same sparkling eye, a starched white detail, a hair-grip in the hair, a stance of the body, a gesture, expression, movement, a way of speaking . . . They were held together by the same glue, the secret energy produced by women's destinies, recognising themselves in others, seeking each other's reflection as in a mirror.

I watch her in the ball and it seems to me that they are all her true core and that with them, with Tess, Maureen, Carrie, Ava, Anna, Emma, Bette, she is both real and unreal at the same time. I see those two lines which are heading inexorably downwards, ending in sorrowful little bags, I see that grimace of enduring dissatisfaction because of her destiny which had begun like a novel, which had not ended like a novel, which had stopped halfway, destined to ageing without true, strong emotions, to languishing, to a vague longing, to a glass ball. I read in her face the silt of the novels she had read, the films she had seen, the silt of women's destinies, strong, romantic, passionate, which end the way the writer and director dictate, while hers continues in vague, enduring bitterness, as great as her assumptions about her future life had been passionate and bright.

I turn the ball and suddenly I feel sorry for my mother, so small and confined, she must be terribly alone, she must be cold . . . I take the ball in my palm like an apple, hold it to my lips and warm it with my own breath. Mother disappears in the mist.

THE FIRST SNAPSHOT OF AGE

I remember her attacks of laughter when I was a child. I would watch her in amazement, a little afraid, I thought she was going to choke on her own laughter. My father would simply wave his hand and take himself off. And that would provoke another fit of laughter. It seemed as though that laughter let her for a moment break through an invisible, firm, inner membrane, in which she had always been captive. Now it seems to me that that skein of laughter which unwound swiftly and inexorably, meant claiming a kind of freedom (she knew of no other), a deep inhalation before she returned to her former, usual shape.

When she had stopped, which happened equally abruptly, she would wipe her eyes, sigh deeply and contentedly, chuckle a couple more times, anticipating a new attack, relax her clenched jaws, and then, certain that she had calmed down completely, hug me: 'it's all right, don't worry, the storm of laughter is over . . .'

Shortly after my father's death we found ourselves with some family friends on an outing. She was in black, in a tight skirt, in clothes unsuited to a walk in the woods. As we walked quietly she suddenly inhaled deeply and without any reason, lifted her skirt a little and began to run. She ran swiftly, lightly, holding the skirt like a little girl, she ran amazingly fast, stretching her body forwards as though in just a moment, in just another step, she was going to break through that invisible inner membrane. When she stopped, out of breath, she made a vague gesture of her hand, as though drying her eyes (after laughing) and apologising at the same time.

I think that that was the moment she began to age.

'I liked dancing, Daddy and I used to go to parties once, but he didn't know how to dance and he was bored, so little by little we stopped going,' she said.

'I liked laughing, but Daddy was always so serious, and little by little I stopped,' she said, without a trace of accusation in her voice.

I believe that at a certain moment she looked round: her former homeland was no more, her mother and father and sister had died, there was no reason to go there any more. Little by little, on some inner map, Varna had been gnawed away by the damp of oblivion and become a blot of indistinct loss. She directed her gaze forwards: her husband was no more, her children had left home, her friends had grown old and little by little disappeared, ahead of her was only the postman who brought her pension on the first day of every month. That simple calculation took her breath away, she felt dizzy, she thought she was going to fall . . .

I believe that from that moment she began to refuse to go out. Outside she would be overcome by sudden fatigue, a painful sense that she was going to fall, a strong attack of palpitations which took her breath away, she would be bathed in sweat, turn pale and her face showed fear. 'What are you afraid of?' 'I'm afraid I'm going to fall,' she replied persistently. 'No, you won't, I'm with you'. 'I shall, I shall fall . . .'

She was afraid of shops, restaurants, walks, people, noise, cars, dogs, children, nature, squares, markets, everything provoked a painful anxiety, everything bothered her, she would calm down only in her own flat, trembling like a frightened wild animal.

It was as though she had begun to like her own captivity. She felt secure only in her slippers, although for years she had secretly dreamed of one day exchanging them for little shoes with wings . . .

After some time she did peer outside. Little by little, she began to go to the market, to her friends, but the world had definitively shrunk and her fear did not disappear, it was only concealed.

Fear of the unknown, fear of people, fear of illness, fear of death, fear of open space, fear of closed space, fear of unpleasant news, fear of travelling, fear of new places, fear of accidents that could happen, fear of war, fear of hunger, fear of the street, fear of rudeness, fear of aeroplanes, fear of the telephone . . .

She channelled some of her fear into rituals, but she managed to invent only two of them: Sunday lunch and regular visits to the cemetery, to her husband's grave. With iron persistence, she expected us, my brother and me, to participate in her ritual. Sometimes she would drive that quite new and unknown iron will on to some innocent task: she had to have some kind of plug, a part for the cooker, a bulb, a rivet . . .

Instead of slightly increased sugar levels, she imagined a seriously increased level and worried about it like her own child. Sometimes she broke the rules and didn't fail to tell me. 'You know, I had a bit of chocolate yesterday!' She would be disappointed when I said: 'That's fine, you didn't do anything terrible . . .'

She read books she had already read again, she didn't embroider, she didn't knit, she didn't sew, she didn't prepare food for the winter ('Who for, you know my sugar level is high!'), she didn't want a dog or a cat or a bird, she had never liked animals ('What would I do with them if I went away somewhere?' she would ask although she never went anywhere), she didn't have a hobby, she no longer went to visit old family friends ('What should I do there without Dad?'), she refused to travel ('I'm not going on my own for the world!'), she liked only her two old friends, both widows like her: with Ankica she thought about the past and laughed, while Mirjana soothed her.

It was as though everything she did went wrong. Only delicate African violets in pots on the window-sill bloomed under her hand with large, pink and white flowers.

It was only when she was taken seriously ill for the first time that I was astounded by the extent of her solitude. She experienced the hospital and the daily visits of her friends and old acquaintances as a kind of birthday. It was as though those bouquets of flowers and daily chatting had made her forget where she was. After a long time she was not alone, everyone, from the doctors to her visitors, sincerely wished to know how she was . . .

'KINDER-EGGS'

That change came about quietly, almost imperceptibly. She had always liked pyjamas, she liked them to be new, fresh colours, she used the hospital as an excuse to buy new ones. 'I'll keep them here, I'll need them, what if I suddenly have to go to hospital . . .'

And then she began to insist that she needed a new housecoat. She

87

had several, quite new housecoats, but for some reason she had conceived a desire for a kimono.

'A silk kimono, like the one you want, is a cheap item of clothing, it costs a couple of dollars,' I observed.

'Then why didn't you buy me one?'

'Because they look so cheap.'

'Not to me,' she insisted stubbornly.

On one occasion she bought some cheap violet and green silk and had it made into a housecoat that looked like a kimono. She never wore it. And then on another occasion she bought one like the one she wanted, imported, cheap, made of artificial silk, with a huge dragon on the back. That kimono aroused a mixture of anger and pity in me. She never wore it.

She discovered a pale-pink silk housecoat in my wardrobe which I had bought somewhere abroad and she began to plead like a little girl for me to give it to her. A momentary cruelty towards her childish weakness, so inappropriate for her age, prevented me from simply giving it to her.

One day, when I was abroad, she took the housecoat herself. 'It's too small for you anyway,' she said, and that was true. She put the pink, glistening piece of material into her wardrobe. She never wore it.

More and more frequently she would proudly show off some new pullover, skirt, blouse, she chose increasingly ugly clothes, she who had always been known for her good taste.

She began to take pleasure in shopping at the improvised flea-markets where Polish, Romanian, Russian and local small-scale retailers would sell goods. She would bring back some unnecessary bedspread, superfluous pliers, a worthless clock, she brought ever more useless and ever uglier objects into her tidy doll's house.

She had never had and never wanted jewellery. Suddenly she began buying cheap ornaments, chains, she insisted on buying me a gold ring, she wanted to buy her son a gold signet ring as a memento.

She began to go more and more frequently on shopping trips organised for pensioners to Graz, where she bought rice, kilos of raisins, coffee. The others would buy the same things: rice, raisins and coffee. Her larder was full of unnecessary supplies.

Her neighbour Verica found a little gift in some Italian washing-powder: an idiot-camera. For some time she insisted that I buy her Italian washing-powder, and when I refused (with the same mixture of anger and pity), she confided her wish to my friend. She did it with a certain flirtatiousness, slight self-irony ('I know, it's silly, but . . .'), as though she were telling him a little sweet secret ('I've always wanted to take photographs, you know').

That detail hurt me like a sharp needle. Her naïveté (she expected to find a little camera in every packet of Italian soap-powder!), the innocence of her wish, that childish iron persistence to come by the desired object opened up a little gap, cast her in a new light. Perhaps that was all she wanted. Someone who would make a rose out of an apple! A small miracle. A 'kinder-egg'—in which she would find some sweet surprise. Nothing more. A little trifle that would make her life more bearable. A silk handkerchief from a hat, a dove, a magic wand, moving pictures. A snowstorm in a glass ball. An apple rose. Nothing more. Heavens, was that such a lot? Heavens, was that all?

AN APPLE ROSE

In that distant year of 1946, in the empty train which was moving slowly across the war-ravaged country, she was travelling into her future. A little old man with a noble face (the only detail she remembered clearly), the one who came into her compartment with the windows curtained by sticky drizzle, took out a penknife and, with a surgeon's accurate cut, separated the peel from the apple she offered him and made a rose. Perhaps at that moment the stranger was cutting the cloth of her destiny. A simple, poor one, making an apple into a rose.

As a child she had been most afraid of gloves turned inside out. In every reading cards mean one thing but at the same time the opposite, one side of a coin and its reverse. Perhaps the peel, which separated itself soundlessly from the flesh of the apple and wrapped itself round the stranger's fingers like a snake before being transformed into a rose, contained her whole life, all its details, perhaps even a little hint of the surgeon's cut of her breast that she was to have a full 43 years later.

LITTLE SMOKE SIGNALS

I turn on the answerphone, and listen to the tape. There is a message. 'Come on, . . . Bubi . . . where are you? You're never there . . .' In the half-dark, the little machine grinds, squeaks, clicks decisively, produces angry plastic sounds. And then emits its last beeeep!and that's it, there's nothing more.

I sit, stretched out in an armchair, wrapped in silence and the lemon-coloured light dripping from the bedside lamp. I pick up the receiver, prop it between my shoulder and cheek, rub my cheek on the cold plastic. Maybe I should call her, have a chat before she goes to bed, rock her to sleep with words that mean nothing, complain of my low blood pressure, she'll wake up then, I've got low blood pressure as well today, she'll ask whether I've been to the doctor, I should tell her everything in detail, ask her whether she's been to the market, tell her I've been myself, tell her how expensive everything is, it's terrible, it's terrible, she'll say, ask about her neighbours, tell her I've bought a new tap, it doesn't drip any more, then she'll say no, it's a good thing you've had it fixed, how much did you pay, tell her how much, goodness, that's terrible, ask her what she's going to cook tomorrow, and what the doctor said about her sugar level, a little bit up, she'll say, be surprised, how come, I really don't know, she'll say, and then say something cheerful and wish her goodnight.

Instead of her number I dial the speaking clock, eleven fifty-five and three seconds, says the voice. I sit silently holding the receiver against my face, caressing it, rubbing my cheek against the cold plastic, eleven fifty-five and five seconds, says the monotonous voice, I open my mouth as though I'm going to say something, I form it into a little circle for some little round words, eleven fifty-five and seven seconds, says the voice, soundlessly I pronounce 'Hello, here I am, it's . . . Bubi . . .' the little balloon words rise into the air, eleven fifty-five and ten seconds, says the voice, the little balloons hover, swarm around me like moths . . . Time pours indifferently out of the receiver, cooling my weary temples . . .

I imagine her in bed, she's reading something. Her eyes sting, she slowly takes off her glasses, shuts the book and places her glasses on it. She sits up, sits for a moment on the edge of the bed, swinging her legs, crumbling the darkness with her toes. Then she looks at her swollen hand, puts it under the bedside lamp and examines it carefully. She picks up the remote control, turns on the television, changes channels—there's an empty screen on all of them. The emptiness hums monotonously, snow seeps from the screen into the room. She turns off the television, goes lazily to the bathroom. There she sits on the toilet for a long time, crumbling the air with her toes, urinating. In the half-darkness she listens to her own sound. From the bathroom she goes to the kitchen. She doesn't turn on the light. She opens the fridge, stares at the illuminated display, looking for something. On the white wire shelves are a yoghurt, a carton of milk, a little piece of cheese—a mouse's supper. She closes the fridge, without taking anything.

She goes over to the window, touches the velvety leaves of the African violets in the dark. She leans against the window sill, smoking, gazing into the darkness. Beneath her, large green leaves rustle and glint. Illuminated by the moonlight, they look like silver trays. In a year or two the green trays with a metallic sheen will reach right up to her window. Large-leaved trees grow so quickly . . .

She hears her heart beating in the darkness. Pit-pat, pit-pat, pit-pat . . . she feels touched, as though there were a lost mouse inside it, beating in fright against the walls. She strokes the velvety leaves of the violets, soothing her heart.

Here and there a pale light glows in the windows of neighbouring buildings. In one she sees the dark, motionless figure of someone smoking. In another a motionless woman is leaning on the sill smoking. She watches the woman like her reflection in a mirror. Three pins of light, three sparks, glimmering in the darkness, the luxuriant leaves absorb the thin mist of smoke. She feels a sudden desire to wave to them. She rejects the idea, but smiles, concealed in the darkness. And she imagines her hand moving. Her little, discreet signal with her finger. And she imagines the two smokers in the dark sending her the same signal.

PART THREE

Guten Tag

23. '*Guten Tag*,' I say to Herr Schroeder when I meet him. '*Tag*,' he nods his head and smiles vaguely. Herr Schroeder is our postman. Although I don't often speak to him, he is the only person I see every day.

Herr Schroeder collects postage stamps. 'Keep me any interesting ones, especially those new, Croatian, ones,' he says. 'Just leave them for me on top of your postbox.'

And I do, almost lovingly.

Herr Schroeder comes every day at exactly 10.30. I monitor his punctuality from my first-floor balcony. If I feel there's a chance that he might see me—all he has to do is look up—I slip behind the curtain. And I feel a vague excitement as I do so.

The minute he leaves, I hurry down to the ground floor to see whether there is any post. From the top of the stairs I already note with inexplicable satisfaction that he has taken the stamps I left for him the previous day.

That sequence—the movement of my hand taking hold of the thin curtain as I slip behind it to hide, bowing my head, and somewhat later the grey nape of Herr Schroeder's head as he walks away along the path to the right (always to the right!)—that sequence often comes to my mind, as though it were taking revenge. It is the full measure of my Berlin solitude.

24. In many places the streets of Berlin are arched with pipes. The pipes—pink, yellow, mauve—wrap round the city like gigantic metal lianas.

In Berlin people sleep more than in other cities in the world. I don't know myself how to cope with this excessive sleep. I wake up, have a coffee, smoke a cigarette and fall asleep. I wake up again, make another coffee, and before I have finished drinking it I am already drifting irresistibly into sleep. Sometimes I worry that one day I shall simply not wake again. I told an acquaintance, a Berliner, about it, I ought to go to a doctor, I said, I sleep all the time.

'Didn't you know?' she said. 'Everyone knows that people sleep a lot in Berlin!'

'It's because of the damp coming through the pipes from the sea,' said an acquaintance, an American.

'I wouldn't know . . .' said Zoran. 'People used to say that Berlin was an island. But that was because of the Wall.'

'We're actually a seaside town,' confirmed a chance taxi driver.

25. Vladimir Nabokov, who spent some time in Berlin as an exile, wrote a short story, 'Guide to Berlin', in 1925. In it he describes the 'iron arteries of the streets', the pipes unloaded in front of the building where he lived. It was snowing, someone had written 'Otto' on the snowy covering with his finger, and it occurred to the writer 'how beautifully that name, with its two soft o's flanking the pair of gentle consonants, suited the silent layer of snow upon that pipe with its two orifices and its tacit tunnel'.

26. 'I have walked a long time on the bridges over the tracks that intersect here, just as the threads of a shawl drawn through a ring intersect. That ring is Berlin,' wrote Viktor Shklovsky.

27. The house where I am temporarily living often sways. There is a large main road not far from the house where roads intersect like the threads of a shawl. I don't hear the noise of the traffic, my windows face the quiet side of the street. But Brigitte often complains.

'The din and smog will do for me,' she says every time we meet on the stairs.

Brigitte is my neighbour. When Brigitte says that the din and smog will do for her, it sounds very convincing. Brigitte has dark rings under her eyes, a dark expression in them, dark hair framing her greyish face. Actually, I have no idea what Brigitte's name is. She signs her poems and sketches, which she now and then kindly leaves in my postbox, with a different, artistic name. Brigitte is very concerned about: a) the possibility of one of the numerous nuclear power stations in Europe, especially Eastern Europe, blowing up; b) the oil pollution of the environment in Siberia; c) encroaching fascism; d) the rule of the global mafia; e) the bloody war in Bosnia.

'The world is slowly sliding towards global catastrophe, we are all dying, if we are not already dead, the apocalypse is unfolding before our eyes, while people sink into an ever more profound indifference,' she tells me agitatedly.

At the same time, she brings her face right up to mine. The dark rings under her eyes, the way she pronounces the words 'catastrophe' (with the hard German 'r') and 'apocalypse' (which bores into the ear like a drill) eliminate any possible doubt about the truth of what she says.

28. Rebecca Horn is a well-known German artist. Her installations—things through which mechanical life breathes—in fact copy the cold humour of Berlin shop windows (or the other way round?). The window of the Cafe Kant on Savignyplatz displays a large Easter rabbit. If a passer-by stops in front of the window, he will notice with discomfort that the rabbit, a mechanical toy, is breathing barely perceptibly.

In Joachimstalerstrasse there is a shoe shop with a woman's shoe moving in the window. One has to stop and look hard to notice that the tip of one shoe moves, up and down, as though it were greeting the passers-by.

Many Berlin shop windows display a toy, a large boar. From time to time the boar moves its head, and its glass eyes are suffused with red light.

In winter, when the Berlin streets grow bare, grey and deserted, the illuminated shop windows and their objects giving signs of (mechanical) life fill me with horror. In Berlin the sense of isolation is very acute and unambiguous.

29. 'I'm lonely,' I tell Zoran.
'It's not surprising, everyone in Berlin is lonely,' says Zoran. 'And, for some reason, no one ever has any time,' he adds.

30. Naima Mazroup, a Moroccan woman from Agadir, came to Berlin and signed up for a beginner's course of German. Lesson 3A, entitled 'Das Picknick', describes the German Wolter family having a picnic. As homework, we had to write a short essay about it, using the vocabulary we had learned.

Naima Mazroup wrote: *'Heute ist Sonntag. Familie Mazroup machen Picknick. Der Tag ist schön und warm, die Sonne scheint. Frau Mazroup macht das Essen: Sie hat Wurst und Käse, Butter, Milch, Eier, Brot und Bier. Herr Mazroup arbeitet, er schreibt einen Brief. Hasan schläft. Husein spielt Fussball. Seine Schwester Fatima hört Radio. Aber Naima ist nich da. Sie ist krank. Frau Mazroup ruft: 'Kommt bitte! Das Essen ist fertig."*

After that essay, Naima never appeared again. I was the only one in the class who knew that she would not be coming any more.

31. It sometimes happens that there is no one on the platforms of the Berlin underground, on the lines leading to the remoter parts of the city. The empty station seems to devour the space around it and if the waiting passenger takes a look around him, at the neighbouring buildings, he will notice that their windows show no signs of life. As though the whole surrounding area had suddenly been occupied by the same absence. The waiting passenger will examine the traces of former life: posters for concerts, plays, exhibitions. A pigeon will walk along the platform, the clock will show the time, the high computer display will announce the coming trains, but the sense of the absence of life will be so strong that the waiting passenger will wonder for a moment whether he has wandered on to a station where trains never come. He will see his reflection in the glass of the station waiting room. This encounter with his own reflection on the empty platform fills him with horror. In the glass he sees the reflection of the sky, the glint of the window panes of the neighbouring buildings and the deformed clock.

And then the first human figure surfaces from somewhere, followed by another, then another, and then the train arrives. The waiting passenger glances at the clock to see whether time has stood still, and whether he has, in fact, fallen into a hole in time.

32. 'Do you have some time?'

'No. Why do you ask?' says Sissel.

Sissel is an artist obsessed with maps, measures, compasses, the countries of the world and its seas. Sissel buys maps of the world, cuts the seas out of the maps, cuts those seas up into little pieces, then sticks the pieces together again to form one surface. As she does so, Sissel follows her own inner sense of geography. When she is not occupied with seas, Sissel makes holes in pieces of paper and threads the pieces on a line, like washing. Light passes through the holes and Sissel spends hours gazing enchanted at that little starry sky. When she is not making holes, Sissel makes prints on a piece of paper with a warm iron. The prints remind one of geographical maps of course.

Obsessed with her own sense of space and her place in that space, Sissel has sent a quotation from *Winnie the Pooh* (where Winnie, having found the North Pole, asks Christopher Robin whether there are any other poles in the world) to many embassies all over the world, asking them to translate the quotation into the language of their country. Sissel now possesses a collection of translations of the same quotation in many of the world's languages. In the original the fragment goes: 'There's the South Pole,' said Christopher Robin, 'and I expect there's an East Pole and a West Pole, though people don't like talking about them.'

33. Richard gave me a present of a tourist map of Yugoslavia which he had found in one of the Berlin flea-markets. Richard's present touched me, why yes, I don't even have a map, I thought . . . I gaze fixedly at the map, I trace the contours of mountains and rivers with my finger, I count the places where I have been . . . I sink into it inwardly to the point of exhaustion, the map, like good blotting-paper, absorbs a strong sense of loss.

'I'm shipwrecked, I come from Atlantis,' I say.

'Ah well, some countries last as long as people . . .' says Richard.

I run the tips of my fingers over hills and valleys, I trace the blue meanderings of rivers. It is all small, the country looks like a child's picture book. Look, the Lake of Bohinj, a sketch of a little skier on Kranjska Gora, look there's the Postojna cave . . .! Near Sežana a tiny Lipizzaner is rearing up. There's Zagreb Cathedral, there's a miniature bear walking beside Josipdol. Look, Jajce and the Yugoslav coat of arms . . . Goodness, there's Sarajevo and a mosque . . . Mostar and the old bridge . . . There's Sinj and the Ring of Sinj, Nikšić and a little sketch of a *gusle* player, there's the monastery of Studenica. Beside the monastery of Mileševo there's an indistinct sketch of the famous fresco, the White Angel . . . Skopje . . . A poppy grows beside Strumica, beside Prilep three leaves of tobacco and a small pipe, beside Vranje there are three little women in baggy trousers, by the Romanian border Gypsies with violins . . . I move south, to Dubrovnik, to the island of Mljet, to Hvar, and then up the sea to the north . . . Two little women in national costume stand in the sea by the island of Susak. A boat sails near them. I turn abruptly inland, run my finger over the cupolas of the mosque in Počitelj, the size of a child's finger nail . . . Then north, to the little Slovenes climbing up Triglav mountain. Then east, to the inhabitants of Vojvodina harvesting their wheat . . . It is all so small and so unreal, as though it never existed . . . My tears drop into the Adriatic sea. Mare Adriatico, Adriatisches Meer, Adriatic Sea, Mer Adriatique, Adriaticheskoe More . . . The Adriatic Sea is one of the saltiest. That is all I can remember at this moment.

34. Recently I had a visit from a countryman, a Croatian writer, passing through Berlin.

'I am a dead writer,' he repeated several times in the course of our conversation. He held his finger on his pulse as he did so.

35. In 1925 when, having escaped from Russia, the Russian writer Vladimir Nabokov was living in Berlin, the Croatian writer Miroslav Krleža travelled from Berlin to Russia.

'Night silence. The black water of the Spree gleams ominously in the canals, trails of light glisten in the turbid watery mirror, while tram signals and whining motor horns echo from the city centre. There the asphalt glistens, while the dense mass of slush melts in the torrent of rubber; red-green and gold advertisements flow by, half-naked women shiver in the rainy February wind, wrapped in the fluffy feathers of fantastic tropical birds. There the night bars, lacquered Chinese boxes of debauchery, with balustrades and tempera-nakedness (monkeys on blossoming cherry branches touch naked women in clumps of yellow mimosa), a swirling on the ballroom parquet to the wail of saxophones and bassoons. A plump northern woman in a Scottish tartan skirt is dancing with an Englishwoman in a white lace dress, lined with red velvet. Drunken, corpulent Hungarian women howl, Negroes howl, saxophones howl, drums thunder, and all this violet plush, this scarlet deathly motley of starch-fronted idiots, is all pushing and shoving dementedly to the cannibal sensuous screech of bagpipes, bleating under the arm of a consumptive young man with yellowish-green skin. The massif of the city centre is deserted, while across the Spree from Altberlin comes the lyrical ticking of an ancient clock on some solitary tower . . .'

That was how my countryman described Berlin seventy years ago.

36. In Joachimstalerstrasse, right next to the Zoo station, there is a small shop, 'Internationale Press', where I buy newspapers. In the narrow space beside it there are porn shops with disco music coming from them day and

night, stalls run by Turks selling cheap food, exchange bureaux, jewellers and newspaper stands. The Döner Kebab and Imbiss stalls give off a strong smell of mutton fat. Every day I drag myself through this warm tunnel greased with its various exhalations. I buy newspapers, which I could have bought elsewhere. But this is where I buy them. When I get home I wash the print stains off my hands. From here my former homeland smells of printer's ink.

37. 'Bitter is the anguish of being in Berlin, as bitter as carbide dust,' an exile once wrote. His name was Viktor Shklovsky.

38. 'Do you have some time?' I ask Jane.

'No. Why do you ask?' says Jane.

Jane is an American who likes Berlin and knows everything about Europeans.

'The Italians are certainly the most unimaginative of all Europeans. Their jokes about my hair are all to do with spaghetti.'

Jane doesn't have any time because she spends the whole day thinking, producing artistic ideas. Jane always 'thinks big', so that the ideas she produces are always 'extra large' in size. Jane offers her ideas (leaps with artificial gold wings from Siegessäule, painting Tempelhof black, the artistic mining of the uglier public sculptures in Berlin, a mass seeing-in of the year 2000 on the Zoo station, and the like) to anyone who might be able to buy them.

Jane once visited me. She was wearing a splendid suit covered with tiny, shining circles.

'I don't know what to say . . .' she said.

After she left I kept finding little shiny circles, very like fish scales, all over the flat.

39. In the Berlin zoo, there are 13,521 animals and 2,400 birds. On wet and windy days the visitors are less frequent and more visible. It's a place where lonely people can meet, mostly women, oddballs, drunks, and couples with shopping bags, looking for some reason like East Europeans.

The zoo, situated in the very heart of West Berlin, offers the visitor's eye an unusual montage of live shots. Ostriches, Saharan gazelles, antelope, zebras move against the background of the Inter-Continental Berlin

101

hotel, lions direct their roars towards the Grundkredit bank, trains and cars pass alongside rhinoceros, a flock of pink flamingos nests against the background of powerful railway viaducts.

Those 13,521 animals and 2,400 birds are the living heart of Berlin. Here, in the Berlin zoo, a harmony is achieved between people and rhinos, drunks and monkeys, drug-sellers and wild goats, smugglers and lions, courting couples and seals, prostitutes and crocodiles . . .

As the visitor walks through the park, at one moment a view opens up of Siegessaule, a winged, golden goddess. If the more attentive visitor turns his head, he will observe that the gaze of the golden girl, Gold-Else, is at the same level as the three-pointed Mercedes star, a great metal disc which revolves slowly on top of the Europa-Center. The two glinting gods, on opposite sides of the city, monitor its heart, its pulse.

40. Lyova is a Russian writer, a minimalist. And he is very small and thin, he hardly weighs as much as forty kilos. Lyova writes his sentences on file cards.

'Do you have some time?' I ask him over the telephone.

'No,' he says. 'I'm just working on something . . .'

'Are you writing a novel?'

'Not on your life!' says Lyova the minimalist, in a horrified tone.

Lyova presented me with his book, if it could be called that. It consists of about a hundred file cards. I framed card no. 68 and hung it on the wall. I often stop in front of Lyova's sentence no. 68. It goes: '*Odnazhdy ya uvidel takuyu ogromnuyu gusenitsu, chto ne mogu zabyt' ee do sih por.*'*

41. West and East Berlin are in constant conflict. If the sun is blazing in the West, it will surely be raining in the East, if it gets warm in the East, in the West the temperature is bound immediately to fall a few degrees. It is only the wind that is equally disagreeable in both.

42. My neighbour, an exile from China, has no time either. Ever since he found himself outside China, every new place rubs him like an uncomfortable shoe.

---

*Once I saw such an enormous caterpillar, that I still cannot forget it.

'Oooo,' he says when we meet on the stairs. 'How are you?' he asks, looking at me sadly.

'Busy. I'm reading adverts,' I say.

'Are you looking for something?'

'A job,' I say. 'There's a university in Alaska looking for a lecturer in Russian literature. I'm wondering whether to apply . . .'

'Hm . . .' my Chinese neighbour sighs sadly. 'Don't,' he says.

'Why?'

'Alaska is shit,' he says briefly.

'You've been there?'

'Yes. There's nothing there but snow.'

We converse in English. My Chinese neighbour is looking for a suitable country. He has already been in many countries.

'Don't tell me you've been in Greenland too?'

'Yes, I have.'

'And?'

'Shit!'

'What about Berlin?'

My Chinese neighbour looks at me pityingly.

'What about Europe?' I say apologetically.

'Europe . . . hm . . . Europe is, I'm afraid, also shit!' sighs my Chinese neighbour.

'Why don't you go back to China?' I ask.

'China's not the same any more . . .' my Chinese neighbour waves his hand sadly. 'China has also become shit!' He brings the conversation about China to a decisive end.

'Listen . . .' I say, suddenly thinking of something. 'What about New Guinea?'

'Ooooo! New Guinea?' My Chinese neighbour raises his eyebrows sceptically.

'A place there, an island, Biak, has been confirmed as heaven on earth . . .'

And, as though I had been there myself, I excitedly relate everything I heard from a friend who recently returned from New Guinea.

'What did you say it was called?'

'Biak.'

'Hm . . .' says my Chinese neighbour, taking out a little notebook. 'Write it down . . .'

And I write it down. My Chinese neighbour reads out the name letter by letter.

'Oooo!' he says, and goes away.

43. Simone Mangos, a Berlin artist, took a photograph of the water of the river Spree, placed the photograph in a glass case full of water and locked the case. A photograph can live in water, explained the gallery manager, for about six months, perhaps longer i. ˙ ˙ water is changed. After that the photograph disappears.

44. Miroslav Krleža, the Croatian writer, stopped in Berlin briefly in February 1925, on his way to Russia. That month a popular attraction for the Berliners was the corpse of a whale.

'So, Berlin is not only a city of Rogervanderweyden brocade and Geertgen's marzipan love, it is not only a city of snobs, Egyptian bronzes and Dürer engravings, but also of a whale, twenty-four metres long, which is displayed, as a miracle for the sans-culottes and plebeians, on a wooden raft on the Spree, in front of the Imperial Palace.'

45. Berlin is a mutant-city. Berlin has its Western and its Eastern face: sometimes the Western one appears in East Berlin, and the Eastern one in West Berlin. The face of Berlin is criss-crossed by the hologram reflections of some other cities. If I go to Kreuzberg I shall arrive in a corner of Istanbul, if I travel by S-Bahn to the edges of Berlin, I can be sure I shall reach the outskirts of Moscow.

That is why the hundreds of transvestites, who pour out on to the Berlin streets on one day in June each year, are real and at the same time the metaphorical face of its mutation.

Miss Pastrana, a crazy Mexican woman with a huge black moustache, was the first transvestite star in Berlin in 1850. Somewhat later, the Hungarian lady Adrienne, with her generous feminine bust and the head of a masculine bearded male, was proclaimed queen, *Konigin der Abnormitaten.*

The history of all sorts of transvestism is the alternative history of Berlin.

46. In Kantstrasse, where Russian is spoken in many places, there is a

Café Paris. On Savignyplatz there is the Café Kant, right next to the Café Hegel. Hegel is written in Latin script on one side of the sign, and on the other in Cyrillic. The Cyrillic side faces the neighbouring brothel. In East Berlin there is a Café Pasternak. The windows of the Pasternak look on to an imposing round structure made of red brick, a water tower. This tower served as one of the 'handy' prisons for Berlin Jews. In Kreuzberg there is the Café Exile. On the other side of the street, separated from it by a canal, is the Café Konsulat.

At dusk rose-sellers swarm through the city, dark Tamils with round childish faces and moist eyes. In the half-lit streets and cafes of Scheunenviertel young people perform the post-apocalypse. White Jamaicans with their hair woven into innumerable tiny plaits pass through the streets thick with the shadows of vanished lives like angels. In smoke-filled taverns on Oraninenstrasse Turks listen to Turkish music and play cards. On Kottbusser Tor a spiteful wind licks posters where the profiles of Marx, Lenin and Mao Tse Tung hang side by side. In front of the dazzlingly lit BMW shop on Ku-damm bare-chested young Germans take each other's photographs as mementos. In Kurfürstenstrasse, not far from the Café Einstein, a prostitute, a Polish woman, walks nervously up and down. An American Jew, a writer and homosexual, looks through the bars for male prostitutes and settles on a young Croat from Zagreb, who had turned up in Berlin escaping the draft. Alaga, a toothless Gypsy from the Dubrava district of Zagreb, tinkles awkwardly on a child's synthesizer in front of the Europa-Center. At the Berlin Zoo station a young man with a sunken face sits on the asphalt baring the stump of his leg and begging. The coins thrown by passers-by thud dully on to a piece of dirty cardboard with *Ich bin aus Bosnien* written on it.

47. In the bird house, the *Vogelhaus,* in the parrot section, there are no visitors. Illuminated by the artificial light of the glasshouse, a middle-aged woman sits on a bench, looking at the largest parrot in the world, *Anodorhychus hyazinthicus.* The woman and the splendid bird the colour of bluebells look at each other silently. The woman's relaxed body and the way she sits express an awareness of a perfect point in time and space. The woman is calmly chewing bread: with her fingers bent into pincers she breaks off quite small pieces and puts them in her mouth. The blue ara watches the woman with charming attention.

48. Herr Schroeder, our postman, is the only person I see every day. Herr Schroeder collects stamps. For some time now some of my letters have been appearing with a large, decisive arrow, with long sides, drawn on them diagonally, pointing towards the top corner. This arrow indicates that Herr Schroeder would like the stamp. For some time I have been waiting with a vague sense of excitement to see whether there would be an arrow on the envelope. Berlin loneliness is as acute and unambiguous as Herr Schroeder's arrow.

49. In Berlin it often happens that I do not see the notices in the U-Bahn and I get into a train going in the wrong direction. Some people invite me to their homes and I can't find the address. The street numbers are tiny and misleading. Some people promise that they will come or telephone me and then they never do. 'Oh, are you still here then, we thought that you had left,' they say, apologising. Then I remember that I had myself promised some other people that I would call them and didn't, that I would visit them and hadn't.

Berliners are inclined to be late. Altogether, there's something wrong with time here. In Berlin buses one can see the oldest old ladies in the world. It's as though they had forgotten to die. Perhaps that is why there are so many street clocks in Berlin. Some street clocks revolve, like the one in Wittenbergplatz. When a clock revolves, it is hard to know what time it is.

And there's even something not quite right with the weather. There can suddenly be a warm, tropical rain storm in December. Then Berlin is a city under the sea. Ladybirds swarm over my desk, and disappear, just as suddenly as they came.

'On the other hand Berliners keep flowers in their windows like nowhere in the world,' says Bojana, now my former compatriot.

50. I often call my compatriots, Zoran from Belgrade who now lives in Berlin, and Goran from Skopje who now lives in London.

'I'm forgetting things,' I tell them, 'for some time I've been mixing everything up, I no longer know what came first and what was next, whether something happened here or somewhere else. It's as though I can't remember anything *properly* any more.'

'I remember . . .' says Zoran.

'What?' I ask.

'Hungarian *Palma* inflatable lilos and their smell,' he replies.

I probe further. Strangely, two things they both remember from our former shared homeland are regions into which they once wandered by mistake and roads which led nowhere. Zoran describes the horror of a place in which he ended up while he was looking for some circus.

'There was nothing there. In panic I came out on to a railway line and there was no-thing,' says Zoran, emphasising the *nothing*.

Goran recalls a railway line that led nowhere.

'It just stopped, right there! Fuck the country where railways just stop!' said Goran. 'Oh, forget it . . .' he added, driving the inner image away like a tedious fly.

'So how do we measure biographies?'

'Presumably by birth and death . . .' says Zoran.

'Start with the unimportant, perhaps that way you'll get to what matters,' says Goran.

'I've just made a list of the names of all the Zagreb streets I can remember,' says Zoran.

'The only problem is how to decide what is important and what is not,' says Goran.

'The problem is that there is no hierarchy: there is no "important" and "unimportant". Nor is movement linear: there is no "start with" or "get to",' says Zoran.

'There must be some principle . . .' says Goran.

51. Ever since war broke out in our once shared country, the architect Miloš B. has been living in exile in Amsterdam. For some years now Miloš B. has been unconsciously keeping an unusual diary. On the back of matchboxes Miloš B. draws miniature sketches of faces, objects, things, houses, dreams, encounters, people, scenes from Amsterdam streets, fragments, tiny jottings, names, telephone numbers, designs, ideas, mementos.

'Rilke once said that the story of a shattered life can only be told in bits and pieces . . .' I say to Miloš .

'Look, this is our acquaintance, Djidja . . .' he says, ignoring my remark. And he shows me a matchbox with a vague smudge wearing spectacles.

And then, throwing the little box into a sack with thousands of others, he adds: 'That's my autobiography. A time when I smoked too much . . .'

52. The Armenian artist Sarkis made an installation, an unusual short autobiography. He exhibited twelve street signs, taken from the streets where he had once lived. Beside each sign he had hung a little piece of paper with a discreet motif of an angel departing from the scene.

PART FOUR

Archive: Six stories with the
discreet motif of a departing angel

'Don't dangle there! Fly! You're an angel!'
'For heaven's sake, I can't fly with these things!'
'Yes you can, it's easier with wings than without!'
'Not with these chicken feathers!'
'What did she say?'
'The chicken feathers bother her . . .'
'Imagine you're a dove, Marion . . .'

Handke/Wenders, *Wings of Desire*

The over-emotional Lucy Skrzydelko

Although there is no difference in English between the formal and familiar forms of 'you', it seemed to me that the voice at the other end of the
line was making that distinction. It seemed to be addressing me in the
familiar form.

'An interview, you say . . .'

'I've already arranged it with the editor . . .'

I had come to Boston for just a few days. The next day I waited for
her at the agreed place. She had chosen the restaurant of the Hyatt Hotel
in Cambridge. She came late. She was a fragile, almost anorexic woman,
of indeterminate age, probably between thirty and forty, pale, with a dry
complexion, large light-green eyes, and mousey hair streaked with lighter
strands carelessly caught in a bun. She was wearing a light-grey suit and
silk blouse, elegant high-heeled shoes, the businesswoman-look, like the
heroines of the television serial *LA Law*, or something like that. I had often
come across this type of disguise in America: it suggested either a false or
a real class allegiance.

She apologised for being late and for the place she had chosen for our
meeting.

'It's the only place left in the city where you can smoke, and no one
bothers you,' she said, lighting a cigarette. She had a thin, nasal voice, as

111

though she suffered from chronic sinusitis. She blew out a few puffs of smoke as she gazed attentively at my face.

'You don't remember me, do you?'

'Well . . .'

'I can see that you don't.'

'I'm really sorry . . .'

'You don't have to apologise. Everyone forgets me . . .'

'I do a lot of travelling, you see . . . Remind me, please . . .'

'It doesn't matter! I sometimes think myself that I'm invisible . . .'

'I'm really sorry . . .'

'It doesn't matter. I did hope that at least you'd remember me . . .'

I cringed. I was embarrassed. I didn't have the nerve to ask her her name.

'Lucy. Lucy Skrzydelko . . .' she said.

The name meant nothing to me.

'I'm sorry, Lucy . . .' I said, ashamed.

'Never mind . . . What shall we have? This is on me,' said Lucy, decisively changing the subject.

We ordered a salad and a glass of white wine each.

'To our meeting!' she said, taking a small sip.

Lucy finally explained where it was that we had met. It was some four years before, she said, at an international literary conference organised by an American university. She had been in the organising team, one of the people handing out folders with the programme information and greeting guests in the hotel.

'Ah, now I remember you . . .' I said, although I wasn't sure.

'Bullshit! I already told you, everyone forgets me!' Lucy cut me off in her thin, nasal voice.

I remembered the literary conference, although my notion of time had altered over the last few years. It had been about the changes in Eastern Europe, one of the first of those meetings, an intellectual travelling circus, with 'After the fall of the Wall' as the main item. So, I remembered. It was about that time that my life radically changed. I was living in exile, or whatever it's called. I was changing countries like shoes. I was performing that fall-of-the-Wall item in my own life, in other words. With time I acquired an enviable elasticity.

112

'If nothing else, it's comforting to think that every exile is input into one's own biography,' said Lucy in her child's voice, taking a little sip of wine.

I too took a sip and passed over the observation. What could I have replied? That exile, or at least the form of it I was living with increasing weariness, is an immeasurable state. That exile is a state which can admittedly be described in measurable facts—stamps in one's passport, geographical points, distances, temporary addresses, the experience of various bureaucratic procedures for obtaining visas, money spent who knows how often on buying a new suitcase—but such a description hardly means anything. That exile is the history of the things we leave behind, of buying and abandoning hair-driers, cheap little radios, coffee pots . . . That exile is changing voltages and kilohertz, life with an adaptor, so we don't burn ourselves. That exile is the history of our temporary rented apartments, the first lonely mornings as we spread out the map of the town in silence, find on the map the name of our street and mark it with a cross in pencil. (We repeat the history of the great conquerors, with little crosses instead of flags.) Those little, firm facts, stamps in our passport, accumulate and at a certain moment they become illegible lines. Then they suddenly begin to trace an inner map, the map of the unreal, the imaginary. And it is only then that they express precisely the immeasurable experience of exile. Yes, exile is like a nightmare. Suddenly in reality, just as in a dream, faces appear which we had forgotten, which we may never have met, but it seems to us that we have always known them, places which we are definitely seeing for the first time, but it seems to us that we have already been there . . .

'Exile is a neurosis, an art of paranoia . . .' I said. 'That's why we always have to be sure that we have an adaptor with us. So that we don't burn ourselves,' I added, as a joke. I suppose that metaphorical adaptor was hovering in my head because on my way to the hotel I had called into two or three computer shops to see whether I could find European plugs for my computer.

Lucy gripped the half-empty glass of wine in her thin, pale fingers. Her salad lay untouched in front of her.

'I have the feeling that I live the whole of my life in a kind of exile, but I've never moved further than the East Coast.'

'I notice you have a Slav surname. Have you been in Eastern Europe?'

'It's Polish. My father is Polish,' said Lucy darkly. 'No, I've never been, nor do I need to go . . .' She cut me off. And then she suddenly stretched out her thin, pale hand, touched my cheek and said tenderly: 'Why should I go? I've got you now . . . You are my East European sister . . .'

I flinched. The touch of her hand filled me with acute discomfort.

'Did I scare you? I scared you too. Everyone's afraid of me. Because I'm too emotional, simply too emotional. People can't stand that amount of feeling . . .'

She had once had a lover. She had happened to burst into tears in his presence, she no longer remembered why, and she had drawn his hand towards her, and a tear had fallen on to his hand. He had jumped as though scalded. 'You fool, you fool, why did you do that . . .' As though she had infected him . . . with that tear. He hit her. She never saw him again. Then she had learned that the capacity of the human heart is limited. While she, she was suffering from an excess, an excess of emotion. That was why she seemed to find a deficit in others. And that was why she had so liked my book. As though she had written it herself. As though I had taken down her thoughts. That was why she had wanted to do an interview with me. She had never interviewed anyone before . . . Yes, she lived alone, it was better that way, she had never been married, she had no children, nor did she want any, why was I asking that stupid question when I myself had no children, she had only ever been unhappy with men, they had all left her . . . Why? Because she was emotional, too emotional, not one of them could take such a quantity of emotion. She didn't have friends, she couldn't stand those petty conversations and tepid feelings, that was why she preferred to spend the whole day at work, she was an editor in a small publishing firm, they hardly published a dozen books a year, yes, she was the assistant editor, which simply meant that she did practically everything, it was she who corrected manuscripts . . . Others signed them and gave themselves airs. At present she was working on the translation of a novel by our mutual acquaintance, an East European writer, an exile who lived in New York (you know him, don't you?). A terrible translation, by the way . . . No, she had no family. Her family had brought her nothing but unhappiness. The only legacy she had from them was fucked-up genes. The genes of a lunatic and alcoholic. Her father lived completely alone and was neglected on a farm in New Hampshire. He had never even taught her Polish, the fucking madman . . . Her par-

114

ents had parted years ago after producing six miserable offspring. Her mother, a tough bitch, had found a Texan and married again. Her grandfather had seen her through school. She wasn't in touch with her brothers. They were all scattered. Where? She couldn't say . . . She really didn't care. And they didn't care about her either. They were ashamed of her. She earned about twenty thousand a year before tax, that hardly covered her rent and cigarettes. She would die homeless, she was sure of it, she couldn't see any way out . . . Yes, she was on pills, she saw a therapist regularly . . . Why was I surprised, 'therapist' is a holy American word. And she drank, sometimes she drank too much, it's true, but she didn't take drugs, and she could barely get by. Everyone was on something in this fucking country. The most powerful country in the world had the most fragile population, they were all falling apart, they were all in a state of permanent nervous breakdown. An infantile country, that's what it was, and they all needed a coach. A coach or a therapist, it didn't matter which . . . Those were those adaptors I'd been talking about . . . Actually, if she thought about it, she didn't do anything in her whole life apart from read. Her whole fucking life, she'd done nothing but read, especially contemporary writers, she knew their books, she followed them closely, she knew the fatigue of literary material very well. C. hadn't written a decent book in years, B. spent more time spreading the myth about his own greatness than writing, D. had definitely lost it, by the way, at that literary meeting where we met, that same D. had once pressed up against her in the hotel lift and said: 'I'm going to fuck you, Lucy, in the lift . . .' Yes, that's really what he said. I surely didn't have any illusions about them? Literature had changed its values. Bad had become a literary value, bad had become good. She could see it all. Even if no one noticed her, so much so that she herself sometimes felt she was invisible, that didn't mean that she could not see. She had been reading books all her life, and if she knew anything then it was about books . . . She could feel books and she divided them into warm and cold. She liked warm books. Warm books were a rarity today. She didn't care much about terminology. I must know what she meant when she said warm . . .

Lucy was falling apart. It was as though before we met she had gathered herself into a bundle, tying the knots securely, and now all the knots were coming undone. Lucy was overflowing, I no longer knew what she was talking about, she jumped from topic to topic, she appeared drunk, she lit cigarette after cigarette with her thin fingers, her pale face was tense, she looked like the heroine of a nineteenth-century novel, all diminutives, all sighs. Her half-drunk glass still stood in front of her.

I was speechless. What's this, what kind of story have I got involved in? I grumbled to myself. Who was interviewing whom here? And why should I put up with this? I could hardly keep my own knots under control. No, you're not going to do this to me, Lucy Whatsyourname, I know hunters like that very well. They secrete the mucus of their own unhappiness and wait for the naive to land on the glue . . .

'I'm sorry, but I'll have to go,' I said, as coldly as I could manage.

She looked at me with eyes full of despair.

'I understand. I'll see you back . . .'

'No, there's no need. I'll take a cab.'

Lucy lit another cigarette and called the waitress. She gazed into my face and said tenderly, in her slightly nasal voice: 'You had your hair cut . . . It suited you better long.'

'I never had long hair.'

'It was longer . . .'

'Yes, it was longer . . .' I said appeasingly.

Intending to settle the bill, Lucy spent a long time rummaging in her handbag. Then she shook the contents of her bag out on to the table. I offered to pay. She refused. The waitress was waiting patiently. Finally Lucy found her credit card. As she stood up, she swayed as though she were going to fall.

'Do you need help?'

'No, no I don't . . . Everything's OK. I'll go with you,' she said and straightened herself with touching pride.

There was a taxi waiting outside the hotel. I tried to persuade her to get in first, I'd get the next one. She refused. She insisted on paying for my taxi. I refused. I was panicking. For a moment I thought that she would never let me go.

'Goodbye,' I said, holding out my hand.

She took my hand in both of hers.

'You're my East European sister. Tell me you're my sister . . .' she murmured pleadingly, not letting go of my hand.

'Yes, I'm your sister . . .'

116

'You won't forget me, will you? Everyone forgets me. Promise me that you won't forget me. And that you'll write to me . . .'

'I shan't forget you. I'll write . . .'

'You'll forget me and you won't write. I frightened you, everyone's frightened of me . . .'

The taxi driver watched this protracted parting sardonically. I was bathed in sweat. If she touches me with her cold, thin hand, I thought, I won't be able to take it, I'll hit her . . .

I got into the taxi. She stretched out her thin, cold hand and brushed my cheek. I closed the door and waved. The taxi set off. From the taxi I saw her staggering back into the hotel. Her head pulled into her shoulders, tiny as she was, hardly keeping her balance on her high heels, Lucy resembled a little fly. It was as though her slight body was fighting her weighty soul, striving to take off. I felt a pang in my heart although at that moment I didn't think I had one. I felt sorry for her, for myself. After all, she was my sister.

I didn't contact her. But I did not forget her.

Lucy Skrzydelko. Lucy Little-Wing. A few days later I called an acquaintance, an East European writer, an exile who lives in New York.

'I hear that you met Lucy Skrzydelko,' he said.

'How do you know?'

'She called me a couple of days ago . . .'

'And?'

'She told me a lot about you.'

'What did she tell you?'

'She said you were too emotional, simply too emotional . . .'

117

Uma's feather

I see this strong young animal every morning. As soon as I get up, I go to the window, raise the white plastic blind, which leaps up with a sharp, grating sound to reveal always the same scene. On the empty training ground, he, my gleaming jogger, circles who knows how many times. One—two, one—two, runs the young perspiring creature. Between the window panes is stretched a thin wire net. Through the brownish mesh I observe the runner with his red hair drawn into a pony tail. I imagine his golden thighs bedewed with sweat. One—two, one—two, I adapt the rhythm of my breathing. I rub my knee against the ribs of the radiator, pass my thigh over its ribs, settle into my nest, squint. It's warm inside. Hoar frost glistens on the surrounding trees. My morning runner emits little clouds of steam. One—two, one—two . . .

As every morning, I hear sounds coming from the bathroom. There, the other side of the wall, behind my desk, is Uma. For days now I have been wondering how that little, fragile girl can produce such a great quantity of sounds. Every morning she first listens, then is the first to dash into the bathroom where she stays for an hour or two. From the bathroom on the other side of the wall reverberate the sound of water, the sound of gurgling, gargling, splashing, coughing, the sound of a plastic bowl bumping against the sides of the bath, the sound of water pouring out of the bowl, then silence for a time, then again the same sounds, in the same order.

My room is off the kitchen, you reach the bathroom from the kitchen. I live on the ground floor, surrounded by the kitchen and bathroom; above me, on the first floor, are three small rooms. In them live Uma, Suganthi and Vijayashree, Vijay for short. I have never been up there, on to the first floor.

The sounds hypnotise me, I feel as though I had turned to stone. But still I get up, I go into the kitchen and knock energetically on the bathroom door. I listen. Uma is hiding on the other side of the door. I go back to my room, leaving my door open. Soon I hear the sound of a door opening, she walks past my room, drained and somehow strangely soothed. She lowers her eyes, stops, bows her head as though expecting a blow.

'Are you really intending to spend your whole life in that bathroom!' I say gruffly, choked by my own anger.

She lowers her gaze, looks at me out of the corner of her eye, resembling a beaten animal. She does not answer, but passes quickly by and silently climbs up to her room.

Every morning with iron precision Uma carries out her bathroom ritual.

'Why don't you get up earlier? Or later? Why are you in there so long? We all need the bathroom! I have to go to my lectures! You stay there for two hours! That noise is just not bearable any longer! Can't you understand what I'm saying?'

She lowers her gaze and says nothing. At the kitchen table in night-dresses of floral flannel sit Suganthi and Vijay.

'Can't you explain, for God's sake! You need the bathroom too! It's as though there were a seal in the bathroom and not a woman!'

And I go angrily into the bathroom, I turn on all the taps, I turn on the one in the kitchen over the dishwasher, and I invite Suganthi and Vijay to go into my room. I close the door. The room throbs as though it were under a waterfall.

'Now you can hear for yourselves . . .'

They look at me with their shining, dark eyes and go silently out of the room.

I close the door, I'm on the verge of tears, I sit wearily on the bed. To start with it's quiet in the kitchen, then an unintelligible soft chattering begins. They are joined by a third voice, Uma's, and the three of them, my Indian girls, are already talking quite loudly in their English, which I don't understand. I turn on the radio. Their voices grow louder, it's as though dozens of parrots were competing in the kitchen.

I open the door suddenly, they all three fall silent, they look at me with their shining dark eyes. I pass through the kitchen into the bathroom, closing the door behind me. In the bath there is a plastic bowl with several little plastic dishes (that's what she uses to pour water over herself!), long black hairs crawl over the white enamel. I turn the taps on hard, the one in the bath and the one over the washbasin, and stand by the bathroom window. The window looks on to a little empty courtyard. Hidden in that dense curtain of water noises, I stand and think about nothing. The water noises wash everything away, sweeping off in little streams the thought of the past and the future, I stand wrapped in the sound curtain of oblivion. I can't remember where I come from, who I am or exactly what I'm doing here.

I leave our house in Pine Street three times a week for the High Street, where I give my lectures. For my lectures I wear a brown or grey suit and silk blouses. I take care that my blouses are always perfectly ironed. I put a silk handkerchief the colour of the blouse in the top pocket of my suit. I pull my hair into a little bun. I keep my lectures, tidily arranged, in an elegant grey folder. I take my handbag, put the folder under my arm, arrange my face into rapid readiness for a smile.

I could spend my time in the office allocated to me. I could prepare my lectures there, read, the library is nearby, there's a large desk, a comfortable leather armchair with a standard lamp. I often wonder why I don't do it, why I always hurry back to my humiliatingly uncomfortable little room, squeezed between the bathroom and the kitchen, and prefer to prepare my lectures 'at home'.

I could take a stronger line with the faculty employee in charge of accommodating the teaching staff. I already went there, I told them, I expressed my dissatisfaction with my status, I'm a teacher after all, I said, and they're students, perhaps I bother them, I said more gently, they are vegetarians, Brahmin, Indian, there are great cultural differences, you can understand that yourselves, can't you? Yes, we're sorry, it's really awkward, we'll see, we'll do whatever we can, but the semester has started, it's hard right now, we don't have any empty flats at our disposal right now, put up with it for a little longer, we'll see . . .

I nod my head, I understand, of course, and hurry back feeling relieved. I shut myself in my ugly little room with its sparse furniture: a desk, one chair and a table. I look out of the window. The sports ground is eerily empty. The radiator is warm, I rub my knee against its warm ribs.

Through the thin mesh I look at the cold moon. I pull down the white plastic blind. I pick up a book and read. It is ghostly quiet in the house.

And here they are. The door opening, their chirruping in their English of which I can barely catch a word, they talk rapidly. I hear them moving about in the small space of the kitchen, opening the fridge, clattering dishes, pots, pans, turning on the tap, pouring water into dishes and bowls, clinking cutlery . . . I listen to their shrieking, delighted voices, I'd left them several empty instant coffee jars, *it's so sweet, it's so cute*, they like those jars and little bottles, they can use them for spices, grains, flour, rice, sugar, salt and put them all on the shelves in the larder. Each of us has her own shelves and drawers, her own part of the fridge, her own little kitchen cupboard to keep her pots, pans, dishes, plates and cutlery.

They clink and clang, they've tidied and put everything away. The kitchen and the bathroom gleam, there are little pieces of paper everywhere with neatly written messages; that smoking is forbidden (that refers to me), and how to turn on the cooker, and the ventilation, and where to throw the rubbish, and where to leave the soap . . .

They have entirely taken over the space in the kitchen and bathroom. In the evening they spend a long time preparing dinner, they arrange it in numerous little dishes and bowls, lay the table, squeeze rice in their fingers, curve their hands into little spades and use them to toss the food deftly into their mouths. They sit at the table for a long time. If I come out of my room and join them, they fall silent. I ask them something about India, about Indian cooking, customs . . . They reply briefly, I can see from their faces that they can hardly wait for me to leave.

Sometimes I take my revenge. I buy large steaks, spend a long time moving them around on a plate, transfer them to the meat board, beat them, put them in a pan and fry them. They snort, cough, and go to their rooms, driven away by the smell of the meat.

So I sit alone in the kitchen, I eat my steak wrapped in an eerie silence. I look up to the ceiling. I listen to the soft tapping, banging and rustling. It's as though the ceiling were being drilled by tenacious woodworm.

And then I withdraw to my own room, but I leave the door ajar. Every few minutes I see a dark wedge of leg, or slipper, or a fluttering hem of floral flannel . . .

Sometimes I find them with ritual little dots of colour on their forehead. Uma and Suganthi wear red, Vijay black. Sometimes they put on saris or just part of them. They tame their abundant hair with coconut oil. All three have a thick, black, gleaming plait. Suganthi, the youngest, often tosses her plait back and holds her head straight as though she were carrying an invisible jug on it.

I often wonder where my painful, wearisome preoccupation with the Indian girls comes from. Because they are completely indifferent to me. I could go for a walk, go out somewhere, invite old acquaintances in, but I just stay in the room I hate so much, even when I have nothing to do, even when I don't know what to do with myself.

Sometimes I do go out for a walk. I pass houses with gardens in which plastic deer and gnomes stand guard, sometimes there are plastic flowers growing, or a flag fluttering. I go down to the little dusty park with one single tree and a notice expressly forbidding camping. I cross the main street, which is called just that, Main Street, I walk round the shopping centre and come out through the abandoned underpass at the river. I go into the Harbor Park, a little bar on the shore, and order the same as all the other customers: whisky and prawns with tomato sauce. I sit on a bar stool, sip my drink, dip the cold prawns into the tomato sauce and listen. A woman's foot in a shoe with a high heel and a little twinkling chain round her ankle is floundering on the stool next to mine. She is talking about the importance of a strong will, about the fact that thanks to her firm will she has given up smoking, and orders a third or fourth round.

I am soon overcome by unease and I hurry back home.

I look at our house. The ground floor is lit up, the light is on in the porch. The kitchen can be seen through the wire mesh. Uma, Vijay and Suganthi are sitting at the table swinging their legs. The floral flannel is all mixed up under the table. They toss back their plaits, wave their hands, laugh, then stop, squeeze rice in their fingers, arrange it in little piles on their plate, and toss the little lumps of rice into their mouths. I stop in the porch, they hear me, stop talking, become more serious, incline their heads a little in my direction. Suganthi watches me with her shining black eyes, Uma lowers her gaze, Vijay keeps on stirring her rice with indifferent fingers. I mumble 'good evening', and quickly go into my room.

I sit on my bed, stare at the calendar above my bed, it's already April. I get up, put a cross by tomorrow's date and write in the title of tomorrow's lecture. I pull up the white blind which rises with a grating sound to reveal the empty sports field lit by moonlight. The trees are sprinkled with silver buds, the grass gleams in the darkness. God, I think, how quickly the time passes, it was only yesterday that the sports field was covered in snow.

Twittering sounds come from the kitchen. It's as though they collected words in their crops during the day, and then in the evening they scatter them over the table like grain. I can make out every fifth or sixth word. Wash! They clatter the dishes, washing their numerous containers, their little pots and plates, digidi-digidi-wash, water gushes from the tap, dagada-dagada-wash, they soak, rinse, splash, degede-degede-wash, I don't know what time it is, wash, I can't remember where I come from, wash, a sweet numbness is overwhelming me, dugudu-dugudu-wash . . .

Suddenly, like a shooting star from the far side of the sky, like a message from a dream of long ago, the parish church of Maria of the Snows in the Croatian village of Belac appears before my eyes, the image of a chipped Baroque altar with a hundred carved wooden angels whose little heads hang from the altar like bunches of grapes, their little chipped faces leering. The biggest problem is the constant battle against woodworm, sighs the local priest. I nod my head and I think I can hear them. They tap, hidden in the wood, hundreds of woodworm, the angels stir, breathe, pulsate, creak, the wood works all the time, says the priest, they flap their little wooden wings, multiply, roll their shining dark eyes, spread around them the smell of protective preparations, they spread the scent of coconut oil, they clatter, wash, clink, wash, move their hands, wash, toss food with little wooden spades into their eternally open angel mouths, crumble the food with their fingers, lick them, smack their lips . . .

With a sudden movement I open the door of my room and find them at the kitchen table, motionless in a shaft of light. They exchange frightened glances. I stand like that, holding my breath, the kitchen is filled with a silence as sharp as a knife.

And then, as though in a slowed-down film, Uma gets up, lifts her nightdress of floral flannel, reveals thin, almost boyish thighs and genitals covered in thick black feathers with an oily sheen, exactly like a bird's. With her fingers bent into pincers, Uma slowly plucks a feather and hands it to me with a conciliatory gesture.

'Thanks,' I mutter stupidly. I'm blushing, I take the feather and don't know what to do with it.

She looks at me with the expression of a beaten animal, lowers her eyes, bends her head a little as though expecting a blow and drops her nightdress.

I return to my room nonplussed, as though after a heavy, nightmarish sleep. I quietly close the door behind me. Uma's feather shines with a bluish gleam, I place it on the table, slump on to the bed. From the bed I stare at the window. On the sports field two yellow fluorescent dots are chasing each other, two huge sparks. I observe my young, beautiful animal, my night runner. The little yellow spots on his trainers rhythmically roll up the yarn of the moonlight. I make out the sweating muscles, the red hair plaited into a pony tail, the golden thighs sprinkled with sweat. I feel a strong desire to rush up to him, to my unicorn in the darkness, to my lonely runner, but I can't, I'm imprisoned, there's a mesh over the window, and they are in the kitchen, the dark angels of oblivion. I am in their power.

I don't lower the blind, I lie down fully dressed, the moonlight illuminates the room. I lie curled up, staring dully at the floor. And suddenly I see a ball of fluff like a little cat, a downy lump of dust. In the darkness I look at that bristling downy creature and I don't stir. I don't have the energy to get up and pick it up, to wipe the wooden floor with a damp cloth. There's another one under the chair, there's one in the corner . . . I look at them and sense that soon there'll be another and another . . . I don't have any energy. In any case, the rhythm of the invasion is being dictated by Uma's feather. The 'cats' chase the rays of moonlight, shine with a fluorescent sheen. People say that's because there are specks of stardust glimmering in them. That fact leaves me cold . . .

My grandmother in heaven

I saw my grandmother for the first time when I was not quite seven. Later I saw her every year, in the summer holidays, several years running. My memories of her wind themselves up as on to a modest spool, I remember only a few details.

She was not tall. She had large, heavy breasts on a small round body with narrow shoulders and a protruding belly. Her greying curly hair framed her broad face with its prominent Asiatic cheekbones. She had greenish eyes, slightly slanting, a vaguely absent look like that of the seriously ill or the very old. On her face her smile seemed to take the place of an expression: she smiled broadly, obligingly and for no reason.

I didn't like her. Perhaps it was that smile without reason I didn't like, that ever ready cordiality, that nodding of her head which made her grey curls quiver like springs. I felt that she wore that smile on her face as a kind of apology for existing at all: she humoured people with that smile, as though why she existed was precisely what everyone was wondering.

My round, Black Sea granny . . . When I saw her for the first time, she hugged me so tightly that I sank into the hollow between her large breasts. For a moment I thought I would suffocate, I breathed in her dry smell. She always hugged me the same way, too tightly. At the same time she would pat me with her plump hand and I could hardly wait to wriggle out of her embrace.

Then, for the first time, she took me to a Turkish bath. I remember her old, wrinkled, and, it seemed to me then, very large and white body. She poured water over me from a little bucket and rubbed my skin with a rough glove. It hurt, but I kept quiet and for some reason I was terribly ashamed. I didn't want her to touch me ('This is your granny,' said my mother, 'go on, give her a kiss, give her your hand, hug her . . .'). It was hard for me to restrain a vague but powerful sense of physical revulsion.

The first time I saw her, her face had merged with a huge tray of dry, brittle little cakes. She had made a mountain of cakes for our arrival, when

125

she was going to see her daughter after a whole ten years, now the citizen of a foreign country, and her granddaughter for the very first time. Now, in my memory, the little cakes blend with the colour, dryness and flakiness of her skin.

I remember the way she sat. She used to sit on a wooden stool, her legs slightly apart. She would place her hands on her stomach, hug it like her own child and move her thumbs on her belly as though she were knitting . . .

She knitted pullovers out of thick wool, usually with no sleeves. She moved her hands at a terrible speed, raising her elbows like little wings. Then, for the first time, I was given a present of a huge doll. When Mother and I left (neither Granny nor Mother knew when or whether they would meet again), she ran behind us to the railway station, knitting! She raised her elbows like little wings, the needles glinting in her hands, now in my memory I see her as a clumsy, heavy bird which cannot take off. Today my imagination adds to that image rays of sun reflecting off the knitting needles, decorating her curls, turning her hair into a halo. She runs, knits, nods her head to left and right as though talking to someone and smiles broadly . . .

Just before the train left, at the last moment, she stretched up on her toes and thrust into my hands a pair of woollen slippers for my doll. It was as though on the way she had knitted into those slippers all her fears, all those important questions she wanted (and hadn't managed or didn't know how) to ask her daughter after her ten-year absence.

In the course of her lifetime, Granny knitted many small thick sleeveless pullovers, the ones that 'warm your back'. 'She could knit a pullover like that in under an hour,' Mother said. 'Her pullovers were eternal,' she added as though she were pronouncing an incontrovertible truth. There's one in my wardrobe today. 'Keep it,' said Mother, 'it's all we have of Granny's.' That's true. That little sleeveless pullover and a few photographs are the only material proof of her existence.

When she wasn't knitting, she was cleaning the house. I remember her strong, plump arm beating numerous cushions, driving the enemy dust out of them. I remember her in clouds of pure white sun-dried sheets with which she conversed as though they were alive, smelled them, folded them, sprinkled them with water, ironed them . . .

When she wasn't cleaning, she was cooking. 'In her lifetime Granny fed many people, especially during the war,' said Mother. I observe that she herself doesn't know much about her any more, that her memories have faded and that she pronounces the words as though she were fixing little seals to them, each time her tone firms up her fragile memory. All that remains of Granny's cooking are words, my tongue delights in shifting them about, but it no longer remembers the taste.

Banici, mekici, djidjipapa (this last was an unusual, family word for a food which I recognised many years later as ordinary French toast), dozens of kinds of jam: made from roses, from watermelon with walnuts, from cherries, from grapes, from plums (with a peeled almond in each one!), jam made from little pears . . . The glass jars covered with a soft breath of dust glinted in the half-darkness of Granny's larder with a magical fluorescent glow.

The apex of Granny's talent (and a child's theatre for me) was the preparation of pastry for *banici*. For that occasion the large round table was pulled out, and I watched in astonishment as the little lump of indifferent dough was transformed by Granny's skilful hands into an enormous, silken parachute.

I remember that she took me to a nearby bakery (with a bread oven!). She carried wide tin trays of food ready for baking. Small as she was, with her large stomach, she would carry the tin tray over her head like a kind of parasol. The tray would go first, it seemed as though it was floating above her, and she was running to catch up with it, and I would trip along after her. Then the two of us, the little two-man army, would stand in a long queue. The queue consisted of people with trays just like ours. Granny would chat with them and show me off proudly, people would nod and smile. I listened to the noises, remembered their gestures (learning immediately that 'no' meant 'yes', and the other way round), sniffed unknown scents (the smell of trains and the sea), explored unknown tastes (*boza, halva*) . . . 'We live in the Turkish quarter,' she said. I didn't know what that meant.

At home the other little girls would often tease me, calling after me Bulgar (Bulgie! Bulgie!) with the same intonation that they would tease Gypsies (Gypsy! Gypsy!) when they went down our street. The words were pronounced in the same way and meant the same thing: someone else, someone who wasn't the same as them.

Before I was quite seven I met my first Bulgie, a little girl of my own age. It seemed to me that she had fallen from some other planet. With an immense ribbon in her hair (*pandelka* was, indeed, the first Bulgarian word I learned), she reminded me more of an unusual bumble-bee than a little girl. Then, without knowing it, I firmly decided that I was not like her, that I was not a Bulgie, and equally firmly that nor was I a little girl from our street.

Before I was quite seven I would acquire my first notions of geography, without knowing that's what it was called ('See, down there is Turkey, opposite is Russia, and up there is Romania'). I would confuse the words Romans ('Look, those are Romanian ruins') and Romanians ('This was the rock from which a beautiful Roman princess threw herself into the sea!').

Before I was quite seven I would also acquire my first notions of 'true' and 'false' and decided that the false was far nicer than the true. On Granny's bed I would see what was for me the most beautiful sight I had yet seen in the whole world: an embroidered cushion from which hung bunches of red strawberries, here and there hidden in dark-green luxuriant leaves. I would lie on my stomach on Granny's bed and spend a long time gazing at that miraculous creation of thread.

Before I was quite seven I would hear the word 'stalin', see large statues which were also called 'stalin'. I would receive a gift of a picture book with a wonderful young man carrying his own burning heart in his hand and illuminating a path through a dark forest for other people. The young man was called Danko, and the man who invented the young man was Maxim Gorky.

Before I was quite seven I would learn, like a blind person, the Braille of Eastern Europe, without knowing that I had learned it, and later would recognise it infallibly. I would recognise its east and its west, its north and its south, I would know whether I was in Budapest, Sofia, Moscow, Warsaw, I would know them with closed eyes, by touch, once I had learned those sad letters.

Granny died young. 'Her heart gave out,' said my mother. Other people die of strokes, but in the case of my grandmother's death, my mother always repeated that old-fashioned phrase, without noticing that for some reason she had retained it exclusively for my grandmother.

I don't know how she died. I imagine her small as she was, round, sitting on her stool, with her belly which she hugged as though it were all she had. She died terribly alone, I'm sure of that. As alone, it seems, as she had been all her life. With her eternal nourishing, knitting, cleaning and smiling—the only things she knew—she warmed the coldness that had collected around her like hoar frost. One daughter had died young, the other was far away. My grandfather, always silent and serious, died a few years after her, completely forgotten, like her helpless, abandoned child. Like the train of a gown, he dragged after him his secret, which, it seems, bore the simple name: indifference.

One year, the city authorities in Varna had the cemetery dug up, having decided to build a hotel just there. 'And now there's no longer even a grave,' said my mother.

I didn't like my grandmother. The way children dislike (or like), for no reason. I didn't succeed in loving her even later. And as though I had remembered that childish dislike, I maintained it, with childish persistence, even as an adult.

Now, as I write these lines, I feel the weight of my bust, I smile broadly, obligingly and without reason. I notice that I am sometimes overcome by a vague unease. Then as though obsessed I rush to a nearby shop, buy flour, sugar, eggs, milk, walnuts, chocolate . . . I make cakes in a hypnotic trance, smiling the whole time. When the cakes are baked, I am usually astounded by the quantity. Then I sit in my car and take little baskets and trays of cakes to my friends. 'I don't know myself what's come over me, but I just thought you might like something sweet,' I say, smiling. My friends are already familiar with my crazy whim, the only thing that disturbs them, I think, is the regularity of my 'cake-bearing visits'.

What I think is happening is that, in ever more regular stages, the spirit of my grandmother, whom I never liked, who 'nourished many people', is settling in me and obliging me once a month to follow her pattern.

I am not in contact with the heavens, but for some reason I imagine her as an angel with a large bust and hair full of white curls. Up there, in heaven, she carries out heavenly cushions, beats them with her plump, strong hand, expelling heavenly dust. In the kitchen, breathing heavily, she stretches out a dough of clouds and makes *gurabiji, banici,* to feed the heavenly beings. And when they are all nourished and replete, she sits on a cloud as on a stool, her knees a little apart, takes up her knitting needles and knits everyone sleeveless white pullovers of mist. All the while she nods her head as though she were talking to someone and smiles broadly. Sometimes she shakes her curls. I like to imagine that's when hoar frost falls from the sky.

White mouse, bless your house . . .

I'm sorry I can't use their real names: they are beautiful and harmonious, they slot into one another like combs. So I'll choose other, random, names. Vida and Janet . . .

Vida met Janet as a mature woman; a professor of linguistics at an American university, divorced, with a grown-up son, American citizenship and a decent income. Janet met Vida as a mature woman, a psychologist, an expert on suicide and suicidal behaviour, divorced, with a grown-up daughter, an American all her life.

When they met, Janet looked at Vida with her washed-out blue eyes and quickly lowered them. It seemed that with this glance lowered to her hands in her lap she was crumpling the edge of an invisible handkerchief. A little handkerchief that she would need if she began to cry. Vida looked at Janet with a glance as unambiguous and sharp as a compass whose needle promises a clear direction in life. From that moment, from that first glance, Vida would take over the role of the 'man', while Janet would remain what she had been all her life, 'a woman'.

I met them briefly when they would both have been about sixty years old. Vida was strong, large, with short hair, a deep, almost masculine, voice. She spoke English with a strong accent which betrayed her Slav origin. Her severe, grey appearance was shattered by just one detail, a strikingly large plastic Mickey Mouse brooch. The benevolent observer would be more likely to interpret that detail as a clumsy fashion error than the intentional fashion choice of an ageing professor of linguistics.

Janet was strikingly tall, taller than Vida, huge, with a bright, soft complexion and silky brown hair drawn into a little bun. Crumpling her invisible handkerchief (which she would need if she started to cry), Janet, with her large, soft, heavy body, emanated a kind of tranquil, plush dullness.

After that brief, first and last, meeting I discovered something about them, from their friends and acquaintances. Janet deceived Vida (I use that

130

old-fashioned, but in this case accurate phrase deliberately), frequently, and always with men. When I met them they both already had grandchildren. Vida's son had long since married, Janet's daughter had not so long since married, Janet had a grandson, Vida a granddaughter.

So, they were both already grandmothers, but Janet continued, with the same dull, persistent passion, to deceive Vida. Everyone knew and in their way participated. That is, Janet often needed the help of accomplices for her imaginative escapades. Or she pretended she did.

She deceived Vida all over the place: at symposia, lectures, scholarly exchanges, meetings, trips . . . everywhere. Janet deceived Vida, but she would always leave some trace, she would make some little mistake, because Vida had an eye and a nose for just such little mistakes. Janet would come home persistently, like a well-trained sheepdog, and then they would spend tormented nights accusing one another, weeping, making up and swearing to be true.

Just what professor David Beers, a famous expert on autism from Edinburgh, Tony Bonacci, manager of a pizza shop in Brooklyn, Dr Janos Szabo, author of a study on phobias from Budapest, Hans Berberich, a waiter from Munich, Professor Erik van Ostaijen, an expert on Parkinson's disease from Amsterdam, Paul Lamiche, owner of a car-wash business in Marseilles, Armando Pereda, a masseur from San Diego what they all found in the huge, soft Janet I leave to them.

I would have forgotten Vida of the deep voice and unfaithful Janet had an acquaintance not told me recently that she had paid them a visit when she was in America, and that the house where they lived was 'incredible'. The house was arranged, she said, like a grotesque shrine to the innocent god Mickey Mouse. The bed covers, pillows, sheets, curtains, towels, kitchen cloths, mats, glasses, lavatory bowls, armchairs, lamps, coat hangers, heaps of plush and plastic toys, hooks for keys, badges—all these objects perpetuated the same harmless symbol. Even their slippers, they both had the same warm, fur slippers with Mickey Mouse heads and ears! Even the telephone and Vida's wristwatch which used to show Mickey Mouse on every hour, and the postcards Vida bought and sent to her friends . . . they all had the same seal, the same sign, the same coat of arms. After all, it wasn't difficult. The American happiness industry offered Vida a rich selection.

I guess that Vida set off for America some forty years ago in search of her angel and found him in Mickey Mouse! Janet, who resembled an immense child's soft toy and emanated the same soft indifference, naturally became Vida's Mickey Mouse. Vida's angel. Everything else, that 'incredible' house, was just the kitsch setting for a deeper dream of happiness.

I don't intend (as I finger Vida's visiting card with the figure of Disney's hero in the left-hand corner) to step roughly on the motif and say, for instance, that Mickey is just . . . a mouse. And a mouse, everyone knows . . . The fact that a mouse is a common metaphorical substitute for a penis, still doesn't mean much.

It is enough to say that Janet and Vida slot into one another like combs. Slav Vida found happiness in an innocent American myth (a mouse!) which she recognised in the huge Janet. The American became gradually and enduringly infected by the Slav virus: with her blue gaze she crumples an invisible handkerchief, folds its edges, and zealously deceives.

Vida and Janet are now growing old together. For some reason I believe that large Janet will die before Vida. Perhaps because of the glance she readily lowers to her hands folded calmly in her lap. Vida's is unambiguous and sharp, like the needle of a compass. Janet will die struck down by a heart attack, unambiguous and sharp as the needle of a compass.

Vida, not knowing when they would be needed, ordered two marble urns: on each of them, like an unusual coat-of-arms, there is a discreetly engraved Mickey Mouse with soft, little wings. The observer will be unsure whether the little marble ornament is a bat or an angel.

Vida will transform Janet, her one true love, into ash, and then she will herself turn into ash. That is, Vida had wheedled out of Janet—the expert on suicide and suicidal behaviour—just one piece of professional advice: what was the least painful and most certain way of committing suicide. With a precise and reliable dose of pills in her system, she will fall asleep one day, hugging one of dozens of plush Mickey Mouses to her bosom.

But before she falls asleep for ever, she will recall an image from her Slav childhood, of a village fair and a Gypsy at the fair shouting: 'White mouse, bless your house . . .' She will sink into sleep, into the last clear shot of a mouse's paws holding a piece of paper containing her future destiny, the one which is now, here, fulfilled, and therefore no longer makes sense . . . and therefore makes . . . sense.

I shall just add to this tale the fact that, according to J. Chevalier and A. Gheerbrant's *Dictionary of Symbols*, mice are used for prophecy in many West African tribes. Among the Bambar they are doubly connected with the ritual of circumcision. The clitorises of circumcised girls are given to them, and it is believed that the sex of the girl's first-born child will be determined by the sex of the mouse which ate her clitoris. It is also said that mice carry off that part of the soul of the circumcised girls (the male part of the female sex) which must be given back to god in the expectation of reincarnation.

Gute Nacht, Christa

I met Christa in an American provincial town in the course of a stay of several months in America.

Destiny in the form of a newly baked American landlady Sally (a political-asylum-seeker from Uganda) allotted us a shared flat, or more exactly a shared kitchen. Sally—who had compressed Berlin and Zagreb into one geographical point in her imagined map of the world—allocated for our use pots and pans, plates, cutlery and glasses, ceremonially sealing Christa's and my temporary community with these items.

Over those few months the kitchen was to become our shared place, our temporary homeland, the ship on which we would sail over the past, present and future, joined by nothing other than Sally's general grasp of geography.

In the kitchen we would move, confined by the small space, open the fridge, sit squashed each on to her bench and leaning our elbows on the table, chat, eat, drink or stare out of the window through window frames richly encumbered with garlic, onions, half-dried aubergines, red peppers, tomatoes, glass jars and—across that half-alive *nature morte*—observe an American landscape devoid of features.

When I moved in, I hadn't had a chance to unpack my luggage when Christa appeared at the door of my room and invited me into the kitchen for lunch. She swayed vaguely, holding a cigarette the way Marlene Dietrich held her cigarette holder, and explained with a strong German accent: 'I cooked for thirty fishermans!'*

In the course of those two and a half months, Christa cooked, for the two of us and for crowds, drank and wept, once she jumped into the dirty

---

*Christa could not learn foreign languages. Her English, which we spoke together, was poor, but in all the languages she did not know, and she knew none other than her mother tongue, German, she made herself astonishingly clearly understood.

134

local river and was saved, twice she nearly caused a fire (by falling asleep with a lit cigarette), and she fell 'desperately' in love three times.*

In those two and a half kitchen-months I discovered that Christa was tormented by two nightmares. They were both connected in a double knot, but one was insoluble and the other, at least from my perspective, soluble. The name of the first, insoluble, one was the Berlin Wall,† and the name of the other, soluble, one was old-fashioned but none the less painful: home. Around them, like large spools, Christa wound the taut threads of her life.

It is not proper to relate other people's stories, it isn't right to compose the humiliating genre of 'the short biography' out of kitchen conversations (incidentally, Christa did as much talking about her life as cooking‡). However, while the majority of people live as in a dream—as though they were writing assiduously, and someone was following them rubbing it all out—others, a minority, employ every least and most banal happening to write their own biography. Christa was a walking biography.

Born in East Berlin, Christa lost her parents when she was a little girl (her father committed suicide) and ended up in a children's home. She was

* She fell in love with an Irishman, a Bulgarian and a Taiwanese. The Irishman declined to continue the relationship, because sleeping with Christa had in any case simply been the consequence of a joint drinking bout. The Bulgarian left Christa for an American woman whom we remembered well, because at Halloween she had slipped into the Bulgarian's room dressed as an orangutan ('Ze swine, me for an orangutan he dropped!'). She fell in love with the Taiwanese platonically, because of his beauty, and she was obsessed with him until a little porcelain goddess appeared, the Taiwanese man's lawful wife. 'China bitch!' commented Christa briefly.

† I saw the Berlin Wall from both sides. My chance and unyieldingly kind guides, Croats, a married couple of *gastarbeiter*, dragged me from West to East Berlin against my will. I remember walking painfully, for hours, along the broad streets of half-empty, grey Ost-Berlin on a Sunday. The unyieldingly kind Croat wanted to impress me with a luxurious meal (the only one he could pay for and thereby feel like 'a man') in the Moscow restaurant, where with an effort we mastered the abundant menu, from the starter to the dessert of flambéed bananas. As we did so, my chance guide recorded our every step with his newly acquired video-camera, including the final flame of the flambéed bananas. Just two hours later we watched ourselves on the television set in their modest West Berlin flat. Like a magpie's nest, the flat was decorated with sad symbols, which, just a few years later, would sprout triumphantly in their full glory in their rightful homeland and serve at the time of the destruction of one wall to erect another, this time between Serbs and Croats. Incidentally, it was just then that Christa's last, 'Polish' letter arrived.

‡ Christa cooked with pleasure and often. And as she cooked she always drank. She would slice an onion and drink a glass, chop parsley and drink a glass, cut meat and drink a glass . . . She beat out some kind of inner rhythm with the glasses she drank. She would interrupt her cooking halfway through, because she would always get drunk.

There was invariably enough food for about thirty people. She had learned her proportions on a fishing boat and never learned to adapt them later. Cooking and synchronised drinking evidently fulfilled some ritual of which only she knew (or did not know) the inner sense.

taken from there and adopted by a decent couple, but Christa soon ran away from her newly acquired home and ended up in another children's home. Later she registered at university, met a wandering Icelander who fell in love with her, married, travelled to Iceland, cooked on a fishing boat for thirty fishermen, gutted fish in a fish factory, then had two children and soon ran away from her newly acquired home again, to Italy this time, with the first of what were to become numerous lovers. After two years of passionate wandering through Italy, the lover returned to Iceland and Christa to Germany, this time to West Berlin (having been permanently expelled from the East) where she wrote poems, unsuccessfully tried several times to kill herself, drank, suffered, returned to Iceland full of hope, just as though she were returning to East Berlin, and then gave up, developing an enduring Medea complex (her Icelandic children lived in Iceland with their father). She travelled to the north, the south, the west, the east, crazily and vainly seeking a substitute for her lost homeland, she travelled everywhere, to China, Brazil, America, Romania, several times (taking clothes and tinned food to Romanian Germans).

In Berlin she went every day to the Berlin Wall, climbed up to the observation posts and spent hours staring at the other side, crouching like a bird. She protested, took in escapees, fed East German *emigres,* hated the Russians, worried about Easterners, Romanians, Poles, Hungarians, Bulgarians, Czechs, drank again, protested, hated, shook her sinewy fist (toughened in the Icelandic fish factory) from the watchtower towards East Berlin, landed from her travels at East Berlin airport, wept, and swore terribly at the East German customs officers with their stony faces, accusing them of having occupied her homeland.

She rented flats ever closer to the Wall. In Kreuzberg, among Turks, Greeks and Yugoslavs, she felt closest to her true homeland. Which was without doubt, she repeated, weeping, for the thousandth time—East Germany.

From America she wrote letters to Janek, a Pole, a builder, an escapee, a lover with whom she lived, twenty years younger than her. She wrote letters, drank vodka straight from the bottle, wept and often telephoned, listening rapturously to the gurgling of the Polish language which she did not understand, answering rapturously in German, which Janek could not understand.

In the kitchen, our boat from which there was a view of an American

136

landscape distinguished by nothing, wrapped convulsively in her two nightmares, Christa began to unravel herself in the direction of the soluble and to dream of 'making herself a home' somewhere on the Adriatic.

It was also in the kitchen that we parted, getting off our American boat which was in any case going nowhere, and sailed off each in our own direction, certain that we would never meet again.

I heard from Christa two years later, from an island on the Adriatic, where she had after all 'made herself a home'. She chose herself an island (from one island, West Berlin, to another) in a country which was neither East nor West (from a Western city wrapped in the East, to the East wound up in the West).

I visited her one summer and was astounded by the place which did not resemble Dalmatian towns in any way. It was a remote, ugly village, without a single tree, with shabby grey rocks, with hideous houses which looked like nothing on earth and belonged nowhere. Nevertheless, that was where she had 'made her home', taken her books, arranged the kitchen like a ship's store, planted pots with small blue flowers that she had brought with her from Germany.

Christa left me there for my summer holiday and, maintaining that she could not bear the summer heat, she went to Gdansk, to her new lover, a Pole again, a new Janek, a worker in the Gdansk shipyard (all of which she told me in the kitchen, of course). I spent a few days in that village in no man's land,* and when one day the sky turned black, the wind got up and it began to pour with rain, I was sure that this Dalmatian island village resembled Iceland, although I had never been there.

When I left the island, I was somehow certain that we would never meet again. I thought about her at the time the Berlin Wall fell. And then I forgot her.

A long time later, I received a letter from a village in Poland. She had built a house, a small, wooden one, with a garden. I imagine that the house had been built by no more or fewer than thirty Polish builders. Christa

---

*I learned from the locals that they loved her the way Mediterranean people love *originali*, ('oddballs'). But still they did not bother her the way they usually did such people. With her appearance she made a protective magic circle around herself, and, against their nature, the locals withdrew. They were accustomed to the fact that she went out of her house in the heaviest rain and wind, when they stayed inside, and that she would be indoors when everyone else was outside. During her stay, there was only one scandal. Christa was attacked by a local woman who accused her of stealing her husband. 'Absurd,' said Christa, 'viz zat fool! I was only drinking . . .'

cooked for the thirty builders, as she had once for thirty fishermen. I imagine that the house sways slightly. Christa sleeps peacefully in the house, like someone who has earned an eternal right of entry to heaven. Over the Polish village, over Christa's wooden house, shines a clear moon. In her sleep Christa cooks. In her sleep she cleans fish. In her sleep she builds. In her sleep things sway.

Gute Nacht, Christa. Schuöne gute Nacht . . . That's what it says in a German primer she once gave me. The primer belonged to Janek, that first Janek who—underlining the name Christa and inserting a little heart instead of an exclamation mark—got no further than the first lesson. He slipped away to Canada. He has a job as a carpenter there, as he once wrote to Christa, much later, in a postcard with an indifferent Canadian landscape.

'Imagine,' wrote Christa in the letter, 'I didn't even know that the Berlin Wall had fallen! I was completely enslaved to the building of the house, and besides it's terribly isolated here, there are no newspapers, I don't see anyone . . .'*

Over the isolated Polish village, over Christa's wooden house, a clear moon is shining. For some time, Christa has been pronouncing in her sleep words in languages that she assiduously refused to learn: in Icelandic, Polish, Croatian . . . Christa pronounces those words ever since the day the Berlin Wall came down. *Gute Nacht, Christa. Schöne gute Nacht. Schlaf mit den Engelchen ein . . .*

Postscript

Maybe the story of Christa best explains the essence of capricious memory and the unconscious process of archivisation of the 'chance' biographies, 'chance' photographs and little 'chance' objects which we keep assiduously around us without really knowing why. In the secret topography of our lives it is revealed that they—those chance objects—are with us because they may, although they need not, later disclose their deeper logic. Chance things are, it seems, drawn by our personal magnetic field: we suddenly discover a nail and a cord among our possessions, without

---

*I am convinced that Christa moved into her house on precisely the day that the Berlin Wall came down. It couldn't be otherwise.

A young German director made a documentary film about a young East German girl who was involved in a traffic accident and was in a coma for a time. When she recovered it turned out that one year was completely wiped out of her memory: 1989, the year the Berlin Wall came down.

being able to explain how they came to be here or why. In the final, always banal analysis, it turns out that the nail is there in order that we might one day hammer it in, that the cord is there for us one day to hang ourselves.

Christa's biography entered my magnetic field drawn by something which I did not know then, nor could have known. I wrote the story of Christa and several years later—just as I was writing this postscript—I happened to find myself in its centre. I am in Berlin, I am pursued by two nightmares around which like large spools I am winding the taut threads of my life. The name of one is home, the one I no longer have, and the name of the other is wall, the one which has sprung up in my lost homeland. In Berlin I often stretch up to invisible observation posts and vaguely shake my fist in the direction of the south. In nightmare dreams, I build a home which is always destroyed anew. I have brought with me Christa's Janek's German primer. My German isn't going well. In my temporary Berlin dwelling-place, I often rock myself to sleep, with the sentence *Gute Nacht* . . . I whisper the last bit about the angels too. For the moment, that's all I know.

A night in Lisbon

The first thing that occurred to me in connection with Lisbon, a city in which I was to be for the first time, was the title of an old novel by Remarque, *A Night in Lisbon*. Remarque's novel is concerned with the already forgotten time when 'a man meant nothing' and 'a valid passport everything'. I came across that quotation as I waited several hours in a West Berlin office to have my German visa extended, and then some two hours in the small East Berlin office of the Portuguese consulate, with Remarque in my hand. In my passport, well decorated with visas, the handsome Portuguese visa looked promising.

I travelled to Lisbon with a huge amount of luggage, or entirely without luggage, depending on how you looked at it. I had lost my homeland. I had not yet got used to the loss, nor to the fact that my homeland was the same, but different. In just one year I had lost my home, my friends, my job, the possibility of returning soon, but also the desire to return. All in all, too long a story to be told here. At forty-five years old I found myself in the world with a bag containing the most essential items, as though the world were a bomb shelter. My memories of the shelter, where I used to go with my fellow-countrymen during the air-raid warnings, were still fresh. My luggage seemed to me at times too heavy, at times shamefully light, my feelings depended on my mood at that moment. I usually endeavoured to measure the loss on an imaginary, general scale, that could be consoling.

Because Europe was full of people like me, I came across my countrymen wherever I went: Bosnians, Croats, Serbs . . . Our stories were different but in the end they all came down to the same thing. In truth, I had myself destroyed my 'house'. I had overlooked the fact that 'war and dictatorship are brothers', which Remarque knew. Yes, I had written something I shouldn't have. I did so, I admit, more out of an inability to adapt to a general lie than from the desire to be a hero. I had reached an age when lies were acceptable only in literature, in art, as a legitimate strategy, but no longer in life.

Like my numerous fellow-refugees from my country, I was afraid in the face of the uncertain future in which the only thing that was certain was a passport of little use. Had I been a criminal, perhaps just such a passport would have been valuable, but I was a writer. However, I did not take my 'fate' dramatically. My books were beginning to appear in modest imprints in foreign languages. It was on account of that fact that I had been invited to Portugal to a two-day literary gathering.

Guided by a romantic notion of Lisbon, I asked my hosts to reserve me a cheap hotel room a few days before the beginning of the meeting. It turned out that the hotel was not so cheap. Instead of the small, romantic, decrepit *pensão* (that I had imagined), I ended up in a newish hotel of indifferent appearance which resembled East European ones in every way. The reception area, the little bar and corridors were imbued with the stale smell of cigarette smoke. I arrived on a Friday evening, the literary gathering did not begin until the following Wednesday. At reception there was an envelope with money waiting for me, my fee, left by my considerate hosts. The Rua Castilho was empty, a dirty, windy and damp dusk was gathering.

In the morning I had the impression that I was seeing the city through somewhat dirty, greasy glass. I hardly opened the guidebook and map I had bought in the first newsagent I came to. I let myself be guided by an urban instinct and soon observed with satisfaction that I had come out just where I wanted, at the water, on to the bank of the Tagus river which I first thought was the sea. I sat for a long time in a cafe drinking a morning coffee and watching the faces of the people coming off boats.

Then, as I walked, I wandered into a district with noisy, narrow streets. People were standing outside, talking, quarrelling, shouting to one another and chatting. In front of their blackened shacks, there were small, improvised stalls of vegetables, meat, fish, wine. Around the counters swarms of flies swirled, cats and dogs wound, passers-by, local inhabitants and local madmen milled. I was in Alfama. The hum of noise reaching me from everywhere, the swarms of flies and hot haze made me feel faint. It seemed to me that I was in the very heart of the Mediterranean, extended, admittedly, to the shore of the Atlantic. And, dazed, gasping for breath, I was crawling through one of its ventricles.

I climbed up to the castle of St Jorge in a little open tram on which the passengers were hanging like bunches of grapes. From the castle there was a sumptuous view of the city. The city resembled an over-ripe melon. Even the sky, sliced by thousands of agitated swallows, was yellow.

I returned to the hotel by the route I remembered, through Rossio. In the yellow haze it seemed to me for some reason that I kept seeing people selling lottery tickets. Perhaps they really were all around . . . In my hotel room I fell into a heavy, intoxicating, tropical sleep.

In the evening I climbed up to Bairro Alto. I intended to have dinner in one of the small, cheap restaurants warmly recommended by my guide-book. I stopped in front of the restaurants, pretending to be carefully studying the menus pinned up outside. At one moment, I was overcome by a feeling of sudden, uncontrollable panic. And as I stood, as though rooted to the ground in front of the door of one restaurant, I noticed a young man's face. He was standing in the street leaning against a wall by the door of the next café, surrounded by young people who, like him, were hanging around with nothing to do. He smiled, said something and, although I was nearby, he seemed very far away, like a face on a smudged group photograph. I walked on absently down the road, not really know-ing where I was going.

He was waiting for me at the end of the street. And, as though afraid that I would slip past him, he quickly asked in English whether I had any objection to our having a coffee somewhere, he knew a place nearby. 'It's early for Bairro Alto, life doesn't start here until after midnight,' he added.

We sat in an outdoor café on a square. He asked me where I was from. I answered simply. I usually explain things, add footnotes.

'Aha . . . *Vo-lim-te* . . .?'* said the young man, in an enquiring tone, adding sweetly: 'A woman from your country taught me.'

The young man reminded me of our 'seagulls', young men on the Adriatic coast, who in the sixties used to entertain the first foreign girls who came there, using a repertoire of some fifty words, in ten different languages. He had an unusually pleasant, subdued voice. He apologised for not knowing English, although everything he said sounded simple and therefore appropriate. He took a photograph of a beautiful young blonde out of his wallet.

'That was my fiancée, she's Norwegian . . .' he explained. Then he

_____
*'I love you' (transl.).

told me that his parents lived in Oporto, that they had a house there, that he was alone in Lisbon, that he had only been here a few months, although he was born here, that he had lived all over the world, the longest in Brazil, for a time in Germany, in Norway, of course, that he had a rented flat nearby, that he was trying to settle down here, that he made a living by making jewellery for souvenir shops, and that Lisbon was assuredly the best place in the world.

The young man's simple life story touched me. He had a very fine, sad face, full lips, large, almond-shaped, dark eyes, shiny, black hair that he wore gathered at his nape in a pony-tail, and a boyish figure.

'Fernando Pessoa, our poet . . .' said the young man, not without pride, pointing towards the bronze sculpture of a seated poet.

A damp, sticky dusk was descending on to the square, with its rich, dilapidated facades.

'Would you like me to show you Bairro Alto?' asked the young man agreeably.

As we made our way up the street, I noticed that I was finding it difficult to keep up with his easy step. I stopped for a moment to get my breath. The young man disappeared into a narrow passageway. Then he peered out, gave me a friendly wave and said: 'Where are you? Come this way, there's a short-cut . . .'

And he held out his hand. I hesitated for a moment, but then took it.

I hardly remember anything else. My memory of that night is nightmarish, a series of disjointed images, a rapid, intoxicating night drive. I remember a homosexual behind a bar, his strong, bare arms, port in little glasses, the sound of *fado* which coated the visitors, like dew at dusk, there was a drunken Dutchman, a Polish Portuguese man or a Portuguese Pole who looked like a greyhound, into whose hand my companion thrust some money and received a little lump of hashish in return, then an Englishman, a desperado, and his friend, a local prostitute. I remember the speed and ease with which my companion rolled a joint with one hand . . . I remember a pang of jealousy when a young woman embraced and kissed my companion, then the ever more frequent touch of his hand, tender kisses on my neck, I remember him persuading me to take a taxi and leave before it was too late (why too late?), I remember hot, heavy passion on a bench in Avenida da Liberdade, where we were lit up constantly by passing cars, I remember that he kissed me passionately, moistly, tenderly. I remember the sneering glance of the hotel receptionist, waking up in the night and the pearly line of the young man's almost fluorescent spine, his narrow, boyish backside, his loose hair with a dark sheen. I remember the gleam of my face in the bathroom mirror, my intake of breath at that confrontation, the thought, sharp as a pain, of how much I had aged without even noticing it, then sinking back into sleep as into despair. I remember my hand reaching out in the night, and not daring to touch him, my limp, heavy hand, the morning when he kissed me again, with the same passion, I remember finally his exceptionally straight back in a blue and black checked shirt stopping at the door as though expecting something . . .

'I'll come this evening,' he said without turning round.

After he left I lay in a heavy, hot half-sleep for a long time, and then I finally got up. It occurred to me that I should check the money I had left in the room safe and the wallet in my bag. Everything was there. Yes, I was an old woman, far older than I actually was.

I spent the afternoon in my darkened hotel room watching a Brazilian soap opera on television and, although I did not understand a word, I wept.

My boy did not appear. He was called António.

The following day I punished myself physically exploring Lisbon. I went up Santa Justa in the old city cable car, looked for a long time at the yellowish-blue sky through the long-since splintered cupola of the Carmo monastery, I went to Belém, strolled for a long time round the Jerónimos monastery, walked in the opposite direction to the Gulbenkian Museum. Everywhere I looked for António's fine, sad head.

Towards evening, in my hotel room, I shook myself, held myself on an invisible leash and I did not go to Bairro Alto. I went out late, wandered through the city streets until midnight, meeting beggars, drug-addicts and homeless people. I climbed up Avenida da Liberdade towards the hotel, accompanied by a wind with a sticky, sweetish taste. At one moment, in a passing glance, I saw myself as the heroine of a cheap love story. I was tormented by desire, just that, I was mad with desire to see him once more . . . I rolled round my mouth a sweet whose taste I had forgotten: the taste of humiliation, sweet fever, inner protest and helpless submission. In the hotel I looked enquiringly at the receptionist in the hope that he would stop me and say there was a message for me. The receptionist's sneering look followed me to the lift.

On Tuesday I took a train from Cais do Sodré station and went to Estoril and Cascais. I followed my guidebook obediently, as though that tourist obedience would save me from the desire to see him again. In the evening I broke away from my invisible leash and hurried to Bairro Alto. The old city district was pulsating to the rhythm of my excited heart. I walked through the narrow streets, stopping by the little black taverns. In the dark holes the local people were watching television, playing cards and drinking wine. In one bar, where some older women were sitting, lit by a dull light, my eye was caught by a large oil painting of a young beauty. A dried-up old woman noticed my gaze and, just like a ghost from a nightmare, came towards the door, looked at the picture, and then sighed, nodded her head and pointed to a stout old lady who was staring absently at the television. She was the girl in the portrait. That sorrowful pantomime, that brief lesson on the transience of life, that old woman pointing the way like a grotesque stewardess in the spaceship of life, cut me to the quick like a vague intimation of loss.

An irritable, moist wind reinforced my own irritation. I turned into a bar drawn by the voice of Billie Holiday, sat down at the bar and ordered a port. Billie's spellbinding voice swirled the cigarette smoke-filled air. I felt weak, from the taste of the port in my mouth, from desire. In a bar, where black men were dancing, moving their hips energetically, I drank my second port . . . In a third bar I sat transfixed by the sounds of *fado*, doggedly waiting for António's fine, sad face . . .

At the time I did not know that in looking for António I was looking for the real end of the story. And when I was convinced that I would never see him again, he appeared from somewhere, sat down at my table as though we had arranged to meet, kissed my cheek and said in a subdued voice: 'Let's go . . .'

Descriptions of love scenes, even in the best novels, always verge on the pornographic. What makes love scenes great is not, it seems, the skill of the author's description, but the context, the story. And I did not have one. I had tumbled into the naked formula of the porno genre as into a mousetrap.

António sighed, and we lit post-coital cigarettes. António blew out a puff of smoke and frowned.

'What's the matter?'

He looked at me with his large, slanting, dark eyes and said bitterly: 'The two of us are not equal, that's the matter.'

'How do you mean . . . not equal?' I asked cautiously, convinced that what was coming was a remark about the difference in our ages.

'I'm a man with a problem . . .' António said simply.

To start with, 'the man with a problem' refused to talk, and then, when he began to speak, I hurried after him trying to pick up the threads. His story broke, burst, slipped away and twisted like deceit itself. It turned out that he had to pay the rent on his flat by the following day, and if he did not, his landlord would confiscate his possessions, valuable materials and tools for making jewellery. It turned out that the sum was considerable, that there was no one in Lisbon who could lend him the money. It turned out that he could not borrow from his parents, because they didn't want anything to do with him. It further turned out that his father was a fascist who had fled after the collapse of Salazar's regime (to Brazil? to Germany?) . . . And thank God he had gone, he had abused them all his life, the damn drunk. Although his mother was no better. She had barely waited for his father to leave so as to breathe in her freedom.

'It was terrible to come home and find ashtrays filled with cigarette ends. My mother wasn't a smoker,' he said sadly.

Further it turned out that he had left the house he had acquired by working in Germany to his wife, either German or Norwegian. It turned out that he had found her in bed with another man, that she disgusted him, that he had slammed the door and left his home for ever. From that moment his life had been sliding inexorably downhill.

António demonstrated that 'life sliding inexorably downhill' clearly by turning his thumb downwards.

There is something irresistible about a liar lying in a language he doesn't know. António's sentences were simple, devoid of all sentimentality. Had he been lying in Portuguese, the lie would probably have been obvious. As it was, in his halting English, it struck one as the truth. But, on the other hand, his words concealed a reality I did not know, and therefore I summoned up the assistance of my imagination which came soaked in the moisture of a Brazilian soap opera, the one I had recently watched

146

one afternoon in this same room and wept. And although Portugal is not Brazil, nor life a soap opera, everything somehow merged into one and I said, consoling him: 'Life is unpredictable, António, one moment we are on the losing side, the next we are winning . . .'

The most incredible thing was that, as I pronounced that crass sentence in the dark, I myself believed it and was almost moved by what I had said.

António embraced me and sighed sadly. We kissed lengthily and passionately. The little *fado*-pause with the theme of life slipping inexorably downhill in no way reduced our lust. On the contrary.

In the morning António dressed quickly, started towards the door, then raised his arms, sat down helplessly on the bed beside me and put his beautiful head in his hands.

'What am I going to do?' he asked with despair in his voice.

We went through his case all over again. Friends? He had no friends. He had only been in Lisbon a few months, he had not had time to acquire any. Brothers? Relations? He had brothers, but he wasn't on good terms with them. They would never lend him money. They had hated him all their lives. Postponement? Out of the question, his landlord was threatening him with the police, he'd end up in gaol . . . Earning? There was no way he could earn the money that fast. Yes, there was a way, of course, some gay types had found him an opening stripping in a gay bar, he once did that 'for a laugh', when he'd had a few drinks, he'd enjoyed it, he had nothing against gays, although he wasn't one himself, but he wouldn't even get that money straight away . . . He couldn't see any way out. He'd go to gaol. Naturally, gaol was the rightful end of a life inexorably sliding downhill . . .

António was breaking my heart. Suddenly—whether it was because of my morning amorous weakness and sleepless night, or because of that seductive despair ensconced on my bed—I too broke down. I started to tell him, gasping for breath, that there was a war in my country, that I didn't know where to go and what to do, that I was alone in this world, that I didn't know what was going to happen to me the next day, I was tired of pretending that I felt better than I really did, that I had no protector, no home . . . This was all the truth, which, of course, I would never have interpreted in that way, because that was not how I experienced myself. My truth resembled a nauseating 'soap', and António, who did not know

147

the reality which my words concealed, could not take such a truth as anything other than a lie.

The real truth was nevertheless somewhere else. I sensed that my sudden torrent of words meant just a brief postponement of my irresistible need to save António from his false or real difficulty.

António said nothing. He just embraced me compassionately. I plunged into his embrace and burst into tears. I hadn't wept like that for a long time, I hadn't had a chance. Holding me with one arm, António swiftly unbuttoned his shirt and trousers. He wiped my ever saltier and hotter tears with his lips, for a moment it seemed to me that we were alone in the world, he and I, alike in our woe, then the image flashed into my mind of those ashtrays with cigarette ends in António's mother's room, although she was not a smoker, and then, forgetting everything, I let myself go . . .

Later, still drowsy, I dragged myself out of his arms, went to the safe and took out the envelope containing my fee.

'Take it,' I said.

He had known he would break me. How do I know? By the way he took the money. Like a wealthy man on his way through town, whose wallet with his credit cards and cheque book had been stolen, António thanked me sweetly and promised to return the money by Sunday. He had remembered I was leaving on Sunday.

At the door he stopped. His unusually straight back in its black-and-blue-checked shirt gave the impression that it was expecting something.

'I'll come tonight,' he said, without turning round.

I knew he would not come and that this was the real end of the story. And when he had shut the door, it occurred to me that António was the first lover in my life whom I had ever paid. The image of the old woman from the tavern in Bairro Alto came into my mind, that stewardess, traffic-warden or whatever . . .

In the afternoon I had an official lunch in the hotel with the organisers of the conference. At last I was on sure ground, with 'my own kind'. With relief I forgot about António. Over lunch we talked enthusiastically about books, about Portuguese literature, about the programme of our meeting and the participants. We were joined by P. who had just arrived from the airport and checked into the same hotel. We arranged that a car would come for us the following day, and then our hosts left us.

'How are you?' asked P. after a brief silence, gazing attentively into my face.

'There is no reason why a well thought-out story should resemble real life; life strives with all its might to resemble a well thought-out story,' wrote Isaak Babel.

Of course I had known that P. was going to take part in the literary gathering. I had seen his name among those of the other participants. I had just hoped that, seeing my name on the list, he would drop out . . . Yes, opposite me, as in a life which was striving with all its might to resemble a well thought-out story, sat my former lover, the 'love of my life', the man for whom and with whom I had been 'prepared to die'. Here, within reach, sat my nightmare of many years, a fever of love which had shaken me for too long, my weak point, my wound which had never healed . . .

I think that at that moment I hated him violently. 'I'm fine,' I said with a smile, 'just great, of course.' Then, not knowing why, I added that, if he had nothing else planned, I could take him round Bairro Alto that evening.

He had nothing at all planned.

An acquaintance of mine told me his love story. He had been roughly seventeen when he had fallen in love with a girl of his own age. They were together for some three years, and then the relationship fell apart. She married. He had not seen her since then. The years passed, he did not marry, he often thought of her. And then one day he learned that she had become a widow. The very next day he met her in the street and discovered that she had been living all that time in his immediate neighbourhood. She had a grown-up daughter. They fell in love all over again, with the same intensity, at least that's what my acquaintance said. They spent their first sweet, but difficult days. She accused him of remembering, in his tales of their shared youthful experiences, the experiences he had had with other women.

'That's not true!' she wept. 'What you're describing may have happened, but with some other woman!'

My acquaintance assured her that it was true, that he remembered every detail exactly and that the whole problem was that it was she who had forgotten.

Otherwise, it was all the same, little had changed. Hands retain memories. Only aromas change. Then she had smelled like a young girl, now she smelled like a mature woman.

I had often imagined our meeting. I used to imagine what we would say to each other, if we did meet again one day, how we would behave, whether we would manage to be natural . . .

Now, here we were sitting in a restaurant, with the ironic name *Primavera*, as though it were the most natural thing in the world, chatting about what we were going to order. Neither of us dared pull the string of our shared past . . . I wondered the whole time how much P. remembered, and whether he remembered at all, and how far my memory differed from his. As though guessing what I was thinking about, he tried not to leave the slightest crack for me to break through into the territory of our shared past. He had long since left me my half, taken his own, and now he did not show the slightest desire to join the two halves for a moment.

In fact, P. avoided talking about anything that had any connection with everyday life. He didn't ask me how I really was, where I was, what I was doing. He avoided asking about my former country, about the war, about everything that had happened in the meantime—and a great deal had happened.

P. barricaded himself—that's the right word for it—behind the description of his latest novel. The novel was boring, at that moment more boring than it probably really was. I listened to him and could not believe my ears. I experienced the episode like a kind of grotesque dream. As though P. had landed by parachute from some distant sky, at a table in a Lisbon restaurant, he was guzzling prawns, washing them down with wine and suffocating in the narration of his own novel!

Presumably, P. believed that the story of his novel was a kind of salutary tampon (salutary for me!), sufficiently neutral, and yet intimate territory, which he shared with me. P. evidently considered the narration of his work a form of indirect seduction, which was appropriate for his age and did not commit him to anything.

'Fucking male Scheherazade!' I grumbled to myself. P.'s strategy not only dissolved my hope of opening up a box of memories, but killed any desire in me to do so.

'Where's your heart, P.?,' I murmured to myself, despairingly. I

150

thought of the way P. had deprived me of my right to the drama of memory I had wanted. It was as brutal as a murder. However, it was also P.'s suicide.

To stretch for a little longer the chewing-gum of love, test its elasticity, see whether it had any taste, sniff one's own past, get a little more, tap out a little more, draw out a little more, shake the little strong-box, pick out the last coin, call in one's debts . . . When we returned to the hotel, we went to the same bed, as though it could not be avoided. We had to sniff each other, to see how it was after so many years, did we smell good or bad, could our lips still do it, would our sexual organs still moisten . . . We went to bed out of wantonness, out of greed, because of a right we had acquired, perhaps also because of a tepid tenderness, a momentary piety, for commemorative reasons, we went to bed out of hate, out of curiosity, out of a desire to retain each other in our power, to vanquish once more, to lose once again, to see whether anything was left over, not to hurt one another, in order to hurt one another . . .

It was a slow-motion movement of two bodies which kept stopping to wonder what they were doing. I gave P. and my past artificial respirations, without hope of success. I forced out of him a dutiful respect, punished him, punished myself . . .

And that was all. And my memory, my half, which I had kept like a precious thing in imaginary and real drawers, suddenly lost its value, turned into a bundle of out-of-date notes.

In the morning, he was not in my room, for which I was grateful. I had slept with a corpse, I thought, there's nothing left, there's no more pain, just a little nausea which will soon pass . . .

I was grateful to my hosts that our conference was being held outside Lisbon. We talked about changes in transitional cultures, about the phenomenon of retrograde concepts in national cultures, about the role of the writer, and the latest concept of intellectual commitment. On the Saturday afternoon we said goodbye to our hosts and returned to Lisbon. We were to leave the next morning, P. and I at roughly the same time. We again spent the evening, at my suggestion, in a restaurant in Bairro Alto, with some French colleagues.

There was no sign of António. Only a rose-seller passed down the half-lit street, wearing a dinner jacket and white gloves, with shiny dark hair gathered in a pony tail at his nape. He cut through the dark air in front of him as though he had no weight, and his basket of roses seemed to float in front of him. P. bought me a rose. I had the strong impression that I was receiving it from a cripple.

In the morning there were a couple of hours left before our departure for the airport and I told P. that I was going for a walk. At first he offered to go with me, but then suddenly changed his mind, saying that he would prefer to wait in the hotel lobby.

I set off towards Rossio, the streets were glistening, the wind had dropped, for the first time in these few days. I intended to buy a souvenir cassette of *fado* music and then in a pavement cafe I suddenly caught sight of the person I was actually looking for. He was sitting alone over a coffee. He smiled when he saw me, waved, stood up, kissed me on the cheek, I gave up the idea of buying a souvenir and, as in the happy finale of a love film, we made our way slowly up Avenida da Liberdade, back to my hotel.

On the way António told me that he had paid his rent, that everything was all right, that his mother had come to visit him, and his father had called, they were family after all, and his brother had asked him to be godfather to his newborn child . . . António's story with its exemplary Catholic happy end bored me. He didn't mention the money.

'You'll forget me, won't you?' he said sweetly, aware that I wasn't listening.

In the sharp morning sun, I noticed two tiny lines round his large, almond eyes, the enamel of his teeth slightly yellowed with cigarette smoke . . . I was suddenly overwhelmed by a feeling of warm regret, pity, perhaps. I leaned my cheek against his, we stood for just a moment like that, pressed against one another. There was nothing more to say.

While António and I were standing there, leaning against each other, I caught sight of P. on the other side of the street. And it seemed he had seen us too, but he averted his gaze, pretending not to notice us.

At that moment it occurred to me that here, in Lisbon, life had tried to tell a story, whether it was bad or good was not for me to judge. On the other side of the street, just as in *life which writes novels*, my past was passing by, pretending not to notice me. I reflected about the fact that life had chosen just this place in the secret geography of our lives (mine, P.'s, and, who knows, maybe also António's) to join up dots which would never otherwise have been joined. In this case, life really was trying to outdo the writer.

I thought too about the fact that Lisbon, which I had experienced on the first day, in a hot haze, as a city of lottery-ticket-sellers, was perhaps precisely that. The power of banalities lies in the fact that they are for the most part accurate. Life really is unpredictable, at one moment we are losers, and at the next winners. In Lisbon I had bought an invisible lottery ticket, only I did not yet know the outcome.

I reflected about the fact that António, an amateur, had succeeded in turning our 'porno' episode into a story, whether it was a love story, I didn't know, all I knew was that it was not devoid of tenderness or passion. At the same time P., a professional writer, had reduced our great, passionate and lengthy love story to the level of a pitiful, limp, 'porno' episode. With my help, I admit.

P., whom I knew well, had suddenly become remote from me. António, whom I did not know, had suddenly become close. What is more, it seemed to me that we were equal, were we not both sellers of street tricks, juggling little balls with the speed of the wind, now you see it, now you don't; our skill was the skill of convincing, producing magic which would burst the next moment like a soap bubble. The difference was only that António was better at it. And, for that matter, since we're talking of literature, a better 'writer'. With more heart and more readiness to risk. And, something had been earned. But, although I was worse, I would earn more. That, unfortunately, is the way things go. I had given him my fee, because he had earned it. For his narrative skill, the skill of conviction. Yes, António was my sister, we were the same under the skin, two similar orphans in this world . . .

'No, I won't forget you . . .' I whispered.

'Where have you been?' asked P. gruffly, not looking at me.

From the tone of his voice, I knew I hadn't imagined it: P. really had passed by on the other side of the street, seen us and turned his eyes away pretending not to notice us. That tone was the first intimacy between us all this time, the first crack.

'I went for a walk . . .' The lie was the first intimacy on my part, an outstretched hand, an invitation to a kind of reconciliation.

153

'We should be going . . .' he snapped, his tone apologising for his momentary weakness.

In the taxi, P. sank into silence, and I half-heartedly supported the chatty taxi driver's monologue. In his *gastarbeiter*'s German, the taxi driver outlined his notion of life as work and order. And were it not for those million 'niggers' from Angola, who, incidentally, bred 'like rabbits', were it not for Gypsies, Romanians, Russians, Poles and Yugoslavs, that East European scum which had learned nothing from communism except to avoid work, steal, get involved in petty crime and gorge themselves for nothing on Portuguese bread, life in Portugal would be quite satisfactory . . .

In the hot, dirty taxi, I thought of the way space and time had condensed in this moment, of the fact that at this moment, while the taxi driver was waffling stupidly on and P. keeping steadfastly silent, the eight many-toned points of a collapsed star were hurtling towards Neptune, and in Zagreb my mother was watching a Mexican television serial; in Sarajevo, perhaps at precisely this moment, Hana was running across the road anticipating a sniper's bullet, while in Berlin Kašmir was wandering through Kreuzberg peering into the little, fragrant Turkish shops . . .

And it suddenly occurred to me that in Lisbon I had bought an invisible lottery ticket and won a rare prize, the temporary sense that, in fact, nothing was lost, that therefore there was nothing to regret, that everything existed somewhere, just as we existed, scattered all over the place, that somewhere everything was counted, that somewhere everything was connected . . . In the hot, dirty taxi, I was suddenly overwhelmed by a kind of dumb, inner ode to life . . .

Images mingled in my head and suddenly António's naked back flashed across my mind, stopping for an instant as though expecting something. I saw myself approaching him from behind, passing my tongue over the edges of his shoulder blades, following the path of two small mother-of-pearl scars, one on each shoulder blade, I saw myself moistening with my compassionate saliva the places where, until recently, there had been wings . . .

At the airport, P. and I parted quickly, although there was time before both his and my flights. P. was overcome by a tension I knew well, the neurosis of crossing the border. I left him at a desk where he was forcing the official on duty to check once more that his Portuguese visa was in order . . .

'Everything's all right, besides, you are leaving Portugal now, in any case, aren't you?' the helpless official repeated.

Before passport control I looked round. P. was standing at the desk, still anxiously waving his passport. From that distance, I noticed for the first time that he had aged, that his hair was grey and his face bore the dark imprint of some inner madness.

I did not wave, he would not even have seen me. Besides, there would be more literary gatherings, at least they would still go on, I thought, and left.

PART FIVE

Was ist Kunst?

53. In the Berlin zoo, beside the pool containing the live walrus, there is an unusual display. In a glass case are all the things found in the stomach of Roland the walrus, who died on 21 August 1961. Or to be precise:

a pink cigarette lighter, four ice-lolly sticks (wooden), a metal brooch in the form of a poodle, a beer-bottle opener, a woman's bracelet (probably silver), a hair grip, a wooden pencil, a child's plastic water pistol, a plastic knife, sunglasses, a little chain, a spring (small), a rubber ring, a parachute (child's toy), a steel chain about 18ins in length, four nails (large), a green plastic car, a metal comb, a plastic badge, a small doll, a beer can (Pilsner, half-pint), a box of matches, a baby's shoe, a compass, a small car key, four coins, a knife with a wooden handle, a baby's dummy, a bunch of keys (5), a padlock, a little plastic bag containing needles and thread.

More enchanted than horrified, the visitor stands in front of the unusual display and cannot resist the poetic thought that with time the objects have acquired some subtler, secret connections.

54. Richard's* studio is like a walrus's stomach. Everywhere there are old containers of various sizes and functions: tins, three old, blackened books that look like logs, a globe, forty old chairs with no legs, burned-out light bulbs, a car tyre (large, with a small one beside it), an old, worm-eaten ladder, a well-used mason's spade with an elegant silver sauce spoon grafted on to it, a green wine bottle stuck to the window pane, a round mirror hung on a string from the ceiling, a ball of string reflected in the mirror, birds' nests, street clocks without hands, street signs, a plastic tablecloth with a pattern of dense green ivy, a pile of broken plates of various designs and sizes, a cardboard box with the inscription 'Wings of Fire', empty glass jars, springs, nails, tools . . .

55. Teufelsberg is the biggest hill in Berlin, 115 metres high. Under the grassy surface of the hill pulsate 26 million cubic metres of rubble from

*Richard Wentworth, an English artist. Any similarity between Richard and himself is intended and accidental.

the ruins of Berlin, collected and dragged here after the Second World War. Teufelsberg, Insulaner, Bunkerberg are Berlin's artificial hills which together contain 100 million tons of city ruins.

Teufelsberg is like a walrus that has swallowed too many things. A walrus in a zoo, lying on the grey concrete beside its pool, looks like a concrete mound, an artificial hill.

56. The inside of Richard's car looks just like his studio. Things overflow everywhere: hammers, nails, old containers, bins. Richard drives tensely, he often brakes which makes all the things go mad, they push and shove, trying to get out. The front of Richard's car is stuck all over with little pieces of paper with German words written on them with the articles *der, die, das* heavily underlined. That's how Richard learns German.

'*Was ist Kunst*, Richard?' I ask unsticking from the windscreen in front of me the piece of paper with the German words '*die Kunst*' written on it.

57. Richard bought the plastic tablecloth with the pattern of dense green ivy leaves in a Turkish shop. Then he arranged dozens of little houses, children's models, on the floor like a small village. Then he covered his village with the tablecloth with the dense pattern of ivy leaves. Then he cut holes in the tablecloth. Here and there a roof or a little chimney could be seen poking through the holes.

'What's this?' I ask Richard.

'I don't know, I liked the plastic texture,' he says.

58. The oldest Jewish cemetery in Schönhauser Allee is overgrown with dense ivy. The dark ivy, a devilish climber, winds round the trees, round the monuments, crawls over the broken and overturned gravestones, covers the paths, climbs up the walls of the neighbouring houses.

The gravestones were broken up by the Nazis. Many of the graves have been left open. Some of them were used as temporary shelters by Jews before they were caught and taken off to concentration camps.

The people in the windows of the surrounding houses live ordinary lives. The living and the dead, the past and present live one, inseparable life.

59. Things in Berlin acquire the most various interconnections. Berlin is Teufelsberg, a walrus which has swallowed too many indigestible items. That is why one has to tread carefully in Berlin streets; without thinking, the walker could step on someone's roof. The asphalt is only a thin crust covering human bones. Yellow stars, black swastikas, red hammers and sickles crunch like cockroaches under the walker's feet.

60. Telemachus did not fall into Berlin some thirty years ago from Olympus, but from a village at its foot. Telemachus is a free thinker who makes money for tobacco and wine by playing his *baghlamas* around the Berlin inns.

In the *Terzo Mondo* inn, Telemachus explains to me excitedly that the world is one whole and that all things in this world are connected. For instance, in November 1989, Telemachus had an unusual dream: he saw two crossed axes and himself, Telemachus, sharpening them.

'The object itself, I mean the axe, is not unfamiliar to me. In my younger days I used to earn my living chopping wood for people,' said Telemachus.

The next day, the Berlin Wall collapsed. To begin with Telemachus thought that his dream had provoked the fall of the Berlin Wall. For four years now Telemachus has been straining to summon that dream again and separate the axes.

'I'm afraid it was me who provoked the war in your country,' he said.

61. '*Was ist Kunst?*' I ask a colleague.

'Art is an endeavour to defend the wholeness of the world, the secret connection between all things . . . Only true art can assume a secret connection between the nail on my wife's little finger and the earthquake in Kobe,' says my colleague.

62. Richard made an exhibition entitled 'Travelling without a map'. In the high-ceilinged exhibition hall he arranged slender rakes. The rakes supported plates leaning against the ceiling, face up. The visitors twined in and out of the rakes with protective helmets on their heads taking care not to knock into them and bring down the plates.

'I know, it's an enchanted wood. The plates are like the tops of the trees propping up the sky,' I say.

'Why do you think it's an enchanted wood?' asks Richard.

'Because you have to take care. In every enchanted wood, you have to take care . . .'

63. 'Herr Schroeder! *Was ist Kunst?*' I ask our postman.

'The word itself tells you,' says Herr Schroeder, and with a pencil draws an arrow streaking decisively towards the stamp in the right-hand corner of the envelope. Then he hands me the letter.

64. Richard had placed his plates on the ceiling, propped on thin rakes, because through that act he wished:

a) to increase the level of desire (people would walk round the exhibition craning their necks, staring at the ceiling; the mere physical effort of their bodies and their altered perception would alert them to the existence of other 'worlds');

b) to raise the degree of pleasure (one had to do something silly and out of the ordinary for people to experience pleasure);

c) to break through the walls of the 'prison of dimensions' (we are all shut up in a prison, by the mere fact of dwelling in our bodies, accustomed to certain forms and their dimensions);

d) to use his favourite 'verticals' again (verticals imply stretching, breaking through, striving . . .).

I repeat after Richard the words which I like: 'delight', 'pleasure', 'extension', 'reaching' . . .

'Desire . . .' says Richard, thinking of his plates on the ceiling . . .

'Yes, desire . . .' I say.

65. Richard spends many hours at the Berlin flea-markets. That was where he bought the plates to drag them back to his studio. In his cave, Richard examines his treasure. The plates are all different, they smell different, they have different characters. Plates can be deep, shallow, large, small, they have different functions. They can be broken, whole, rich, poor, cheap and expensive. Plates are like living beings.

Richard is convinced that he is saving his plates from ruin. Richard loves family life. That is why he connects his plates into a family. 'I'm making a family,' he says.

The plates have their own biography. There are French ones, German ones, there is one with a little swastika on the bottom, there are Italian ones (with English landscape designs!), Turkish ones, German ones (from the US zone!), East German ones . . .

'They were so lonely, and now, I think, they are enjoying each other's company . . .'

Richard spent days carefully washing his plates. He even washed the ones he wasn't going to need, even the ones he didn't like, he washed them all . . .

'It's like washing your own body . . . Washing is a kind of intimate inspection. You discover moles, little scars and marks on your skin which you had not noticed before. Washing plates from the flea-markets is a kind of semi-religious ritual. In the course of washing them you become intimate with them . . . Identity is established through looking. They are so full of conversation, so full of different kinds of cooking. I can hear it. They are in collision, these Turkish ones with these French ones, for instance . . .' says Richard about his plates.

'It's as though there's no difference between things and people . . .' I say.

'It seems so. I found a book in the flea-market about censored photographs from the period of the First World War. There were corpses, tidily sorted. The German heap was separated from the French one . . . I won't show you that book.'

66. 'The horse-drawn tram has vanished, and so will the trolley, and some eccentric Berlin writer in the twenties of the twenty-first century, wishing to portray our time, will go to a museum of technological history and locate a hundred-year-old streetcar, yellow, uncouth, with old-fashioned curved seats, and in a museum of old costumes dig up a black, shiny-buttoned conductor's uniform. Then he will go home and compile a description of Berlin's streets in bygone days. Everything, every trifle, will be valuable and meaningful: the conductor's purse, the advertisement over the window, that peculiar jolting motion which our great-grandchildren will perhaps imagine—everything will be ennobled and justified by its age.

'I think that here lies the sense of literary creation: to portray ordinary objects as they will be reflected in the kindly mirrors of future times; to find in the objects around us the fragrant tenderness that only posterity will discern and appreciate in the far-off times when every trifle of our plain everyday life will become exquisite and festive in its own right,' writes Vladimir Nabokov in his story 'A Guide to Berlin'.

67. Richard found forty-four abandoned chairs in the streets of Berlin and showed them at his exhibition.

'They were so tired. I wanted everyone to recognise that they aren't chairs but former chairs. Remembering is actually an act of love,' says Richard.

68. Zoran says: 'That was in Bosnia, at our relatives' place.' The children came home from school and said that they had been learning the Solar System.

'It was winter. I drew the Solar System on a piece of paper. I had always known it well, the Solar System, and the republics and regions of the Socialist Federal Republic of Yugoslavia with their main cities. I loved teaching. Grandfather was sitting in the kitchen as well, he was a hundred years old and he said: "'They taught us all of that in the Austro-Hungarian army as well, that the Earth is round and that it revolves, but they said it was only an hypothesis."'

'The kitchen smelled of milk.

'In that same kitchen there was a television. In that village, in Bosnia, at our relatives' house, television was watched like this: it was turned on at half-past seven, after supper, and watched until half-past eight, when everyone went to bed. It didn't matter what was on, it didn't matter whether a programme had already begun or not yet finished. They all sat in front of the television set and all they saw were faces and all they talked about was who those faces looked like . . .

'"Just look at him, Lord love us, his nose is exactly like our post-man's . . ."'

69. The artist Shimon Attie made an installation entitled *Projected Restoring* with the intention of 'inserting fragments of past life into the visual field of the present'. Slides were projected on to the wall, photographs of Scheunenviertel, the once famous Berlin Jewish quarter. Over the contemporary images, Shimon Attie projected pale photographs of the same places in former times.

The visitor gradually noticed that he was turning from an observer into a voyeur, a witness of a scene in which in the blank windows of an abandoned building in Oraninenburgstrasse the past suddenly came to life. This hologram effect—past life penetrating and eating away the surface of the present like a damp patch—filled the observer with painful disquiet. It suddenly seemed that forgetting was just another form of remembering, just as remembering was just another form of forgetting.

70. '*Was ist Kunst?*' I stopped my Chinese neighbour on the stairs.

'I don't know,' he said. 'I speak English, but not only do I not understand you when you speak English, I don't even understand myself.'

'Oooo,' I say.

'Don't let it worry you. I don't even understand myself in Chinese any more,' said my Chinese neighbour resignedly and carried on up the stairs.

71. Richard's installations resemble a circus in which things perform instead of animals and people. Like an animal tamer or a juggler, Richard trains heavy things to become light.

For instance, having established that the dimensions of a Danish flagpole holder were the same as the dimensions of the leg of a Danish chair, Richard fixed a chair leg into a flagpole holder on a building in Copenhagen. And so a Danish chair was seen flapping in the air, instead of the Danish flag.

Richard forces heavy tables to stand on one leg. Richard places tender light bulbs between enormous metal plates, teaching them not to crush them with their weight. Richard places glass bottles in the most impossible places, where there is the greatest danger that they will fall and break. Richard trains walking sticks not to do what they're made to do. Richard placed one stick on the very edge of a glass surface attached to a wall. The stick didn't fall. Richard teaches heavy containers, leaning on a glass, leaning over to one side, not to fall. Richard makes tin houses and obliges them to hang roof down in the air. Richard adores plates and always puts them in the highest places, supporting them on the slenderest sticks, to see how long they will hold out and whether they will fall. Richard's plates never fall.

Richard expresses love between incompatible materials, marries unconnectable things, he places a rough builder's spade on a soft pillow, dressed in a pillowcase of the finest linen. Richard draws a rough metal mesh under a soft Persian rug, he often caresses cold tin with warm silk . . .

'I'd like to be able to do that . . .' I say.

'I don't know how it's done with words,' says Richard.

72. Like a stray dog, Richard spends days in the streets of Berlin sniffing smells.

'Berlin streets are so full of messages. Berlin is the most attractive rubbish heap in the world. Berlin is the world capital of rubbish. I sense the smell of decay at every corner. Here the whole global digestive process is so terribly and painfully obvious. The flea-markets . . . the Berlin flea-markets are the most intoxicating and most terrible image of an open digestive tract that I have yet seen.'

73. '*Was ist Kunst*?' I ask Sissel.

'I don't know . . . An artistic act is always some sort of alteration in the world,' says Sissel.

74. Richard travels without a map. Richard collects cans which he later builds into great tin surfaces. Afterwards those surfaces resemble maps of the starry sky. He called one such installation *World Soup*, because it was made of soup cans. I gave Richard a present of an old Soviet can of condensed milk which was a gift to me from the Russian minimalist writer Lyova.

As well as cans, Richard collects old light bulbs.

'I don't know why I have this weakness for light bulbs. Incidentally, a light bulb is a very intelligent object,' he says.

'Are there any stupid ones?'

'Certainly,' says Richard.

Richard keeps his light bulbs in net cages, in ordinary string shopping bags, in basketball baskets. Lit with the light of day, the round bulbs jostling in the net look like mysterious space forms . . .

'They look like multiple Audrey Hepburns, they are so fragile and vulnerable . . .' I say.

75. Snježana says: 'On winter evenings, my father would often open the verandah door and look out towards the light bulb which lit up the court-yard from the corner of the building. He was waiting for snow.

'When one of us approached him, he would turn significantly and, to justify standing for so long in the cold and give it sense, he would say: "'It's falltering.'" Or: "'It's not falltering yet.'"

'Often my brother, my mother and I would stand by the open door and wait with him for the first flake of snow to fall past the glowing light bulb. We would cry with pleasure: "'It's falltering! It's falltering!'"

'Later I discovered that the word does not exist and that my father had invented it. But because I don't know what to call the moment when a single snowflake falls through the air announcing imminent snow, today, as I look out of my window into the winter night, I often say: "'It's falltering . . .'"

76. '*Was ist Kunst?*' I ask my neighbour Brigitte.

'I don't know. I always write my poems about something else, so as not to write about the first thing, just as I always paint something else, so as not to paint the first thing,' says Brigitte.

77. Richard says: 'The sadness of Berlin comes from the asphalt.' Richard says: 'The world is confused and full of hazards.' Richard says: 'I only glimpse incidents in the world.' Richard says: 'I have married objects.' Richard says: 'I find rhymes among objects, I seek relatives for objects.' Richard says: 'I test objects, dimensions, their capacity and potential.' Richard says: 'I put one thing on another thing and one thing in another thing.' Richard says: 'Berlin is all so terribly chopped up.' Richard says: 'I'm having a love affair with this city.'

78. Richard has made a book with 117 photographs of Berlin, *Berlin Landmarks*. The book opens with a photograph of a Berlin keyhole (Berlin keyholes are unique, they look like little hooks!), and ends with a photograph of cracked Berlin asphalt. Richard believes that Berlin asphalt behaves in a very particular way.

'Berlin asphalt cracks like nowhere else in the world,' he says.

Richard always has his camera with him. Richard is pursued by the feeling that the city itself, its every detail, is constantly striving to tell its story.

'I can only get rid of that feeling if I focus on fragments, if I steal a picture . . .' says Richard.

Richard's photographs are '35 millimetre thoughts', 'framed thoughts' whose modesty is intended to show that thoughts have no end.

79. 'Berlin is Teufelsberg,' I say, 'madness covered with indifferent grass. Berlin is sodden with the moisture of madness like a sponge. Perhaps that is why the city is so grey and restrained. Madness, however, just like damp, cannot easily be concealed. It will always break out somewhere . . . In the passers-by, in the old woman in her old-fashioned hat and ball gloves, who has forgotten what age and what time it is . . . In the rabbit strolling in the garden of the Café Einstein, and one of the thousand rabbits which lived and multiplied for years in the space between the two walls, and then vanished somewhere . . . Behind the glass cupola on the last storey of Ka-De-We, where over the prawn cocktail and glass of champagne you ordered you can see the plaque on Wittenbergplatz where the names of the German concentration camps are inscribed as a warning. Damp patches everywhere. That's why the asphalt here cracks in a particular way,' I say to Richard.

80. In an Italian restaurant, the waiter, a swarthy Italian, comes up to my table to give me the bill.

'You don't need to struggle with German . . .' he interrupts me in Croatian with a strong Bosnian accent.

'Where are you from?' I ask my countryman brightly.

'From Iran,' he says.

'How come . . . I don't understand . . .'

'I studied in Sarajevo . . .'

'Oh?!'

'But, ssshhhh . . . I'm pretending to be Italian.'

And he sees me to the door.

'Ciao,' he says and winks.

'Ciao,' I say, winking myself in confusion.

81. The invisible fingers of ghosts from Teufelsberg skillfully shuffle people, places and times like a pack of cards. People I once knew, people I know, and those I have yet to meet, flash in Berlin like shooting stars, pass like shadows from some other life, appear for an instant like faces from a nightmarish dream, meet and intersect in me, past, present and future.

So far the following have turned up in Berlin: A. from Moscow, M. from London, D. from Amsterdam, I. from London, A. from Sarajevo, R. from Paris, D. from Zagreb, M. from Manaus, D. from London, J. from Belgrade, D. from Boston, H. from Vienna . . .

82. 'But if you ask me what is the strangest thing that happened to me in Berlin, then it's Frau Hardenberg. Frau Hardenberg was my first German teacher. Sometimes she invited us to her house. Once by mistake I peeped into her bedroom. There was a large board on the wall. On the board, carefully cut out and stuck on, were various kinds of bird, I presume from magazines, such as the *National Geographic*. What was unusual was the fact that all the birds' heads had been cut off. In their place were stuck little photographs of men, portraits taken with a Polaroid camera. I think they were her lovers,' says the sociologist Zlatomir.

83. With our feet on the empty seat in front of us, Richard and I sit under the vast cupola of the planetarium in Prenzlauer Allee. A starry rain falls on us from the sky. And while the tiny artificial stars fall over us I ask quietly: 'What is art, Richard?'

'I don't know. An act which is certainly connected with mastering gravity, but which is not flying,' says Richard.

84. On my desk there is a yellowed photograph. It shows three unknown women bathers. I don't know much about the photograph, just that it was taken at the beginning of the century on the river Pakra. That is a little river that runs not far from the small town where I was born and spent my childhood.

I always carry the photograph around with me, like a little fetish object whose real meaning I do not know. Its matt yellow surface attracts my attention, hypnotically. Sometimes I stare at it for a long time, not thinking about anything. Sometimes I plunge attentively into the reflections of the three bathers mirrored in the water, into their faces which are looking straight at mine, I dive into them as though I were about to solve a mystery, discover a crack, a hidden passage through which I shall slip into a different space, a different time. I compare the position of their arms: all three have folded their arms like wings. The mirror-like surface of the water discloses what their bathing-costumes try to hide: in the water

169

floats a clear reflection of a bared breast. In the right-hand corner are four gourds, an old-fashioned swimming ring. The women are standing up to their waists in the water. Around them hovers an oniric haze full of restrained light. They seem to be expecting something. For some reason I am certain that what they are expecting is not the click of the camera.

85. In the bird house, the *Vogelhaus*, in the section containing various kinds of large parrot, there are no visitors. Illuminated by the artificial light of the glasshouse, I sit on a bench, looking at the largest parrot in the world, *Anodorhychus hyazinthicus*. The splendid bird the colour of blue-bells and I look at each other in silence. I calmly chew bread: with my fingers bent into pincers I break off quite small pieces and put them in my mouth. The blue ara watches me with charming attention.

PART SIX

Group Photograph

finger a worthless souvenir, the only photograph of all of us together. And there, from the left (was it the left?) should have been dark-eyed Nuša, then Doti with her broad face and piercing look, then Ivana with a smile that spread over her face like warm water, then Alma, the colour of copper, beside her the reliable and serious Dinka and I, with a childish face, they say, and a body bequeathed me by the power-hungry genes of my full-breasted foremothers. Nina and Hana weren't there, they hadn't been with us that evening . . .

I place another photograph beside our blank one, this is a photograph I know little about but I always have it with me. The yellowed photograph from the beginning of the century is like a lamp lit in a murky window, a heartening secret gesture with which I draw pictures out of the indifferent whiteness. Intimate rituals with little fetish objects are complex, as are the rituals of conjuring up memories, and they have meaning only for their owner.

Our empty photograph was taken several years ago at a dinner which I want to remember. It is also perfectly possible that it was never taken, it is possible that I have invented it all, that I am projecting on to the indifferent white expanse faces which do not exist and recording something which never occurred.

For all I have in my hand is a blank, reject photograph . . .

I

'And so it was decided, Alfred was brought ina frail young fellow,
delicate, two wings fluttering behind his pale-blue shoulders,
rippling with rosy light like two doves playing in heaven.'

Isaak Babel, *The Sin of Jesus*

We began with a cheese soufflé . . .

We began with a cheese soufflé which Alma had brought.
'Mmmm! . . . This is fantastic . . .' said Doti licking her lips loudly.
'It's divine . . .' said Ivana.
'It hasn't sunk at all . . .' said Dinka.
'Mine always sinks . . .' said Nuša.
'Oh come on . . . what do you mean yours sinks . . .' said Alma.
'I'm sure yours doesn't sink,' I said, reaching for another piece.

And I was sure. For Nuša was a perfectionist. Once she went so far
as to arrange a pink dinner for us. Everything was in russet tones, from the
plates, candles and serviettes to the food itself. I remember it now: red
caviar as the hors d'oeuvre, then rosy prawns, salmon trout cooked in
rosemary and milk as the main course and pale orange crème caramel for
dessert . . . Finally, little balls of coral marzipan, which Nuša had shaped
by hand, were served with a fine imported rosé.

It's true that each of us had something she was good at. If Nuša
excelled at light dishes, Dinka was her opposite. You really ate at her
place. Dinka would serve *kulen,* a hot sausage, and a smaller version
called *kulen's* little sister (we liked those *little sisters* out of female soli-
darity), homemade crackling and sausages, ham, white cheese with pep-
per and wonderful Slavonian desserts which were, quite rightly, short on
flour, but never on eggs, walnuts or poppy seeds.

Whenever she went to Belgrade, Ivana would bring back the local
specialities: cottage cheese and *kajmak.* We ate it all with warm bread
which Ivana baked herself.

And when Hana came on short visits from Sarajevo, she would

always bring a box of Turkish sweetmeats which made us dizzy. Hana's box contained *baklava,* but also the far more exciting version, 'roses', then *urmašice,* dissolving in a sweet syrup of honey and lemon juice, and finally the deconstructionist version of all of that, *kadaif,* crunchy nests of tiny sweet threads with currants nestling in them.

We proclaimed Alma the pasta queen, and as for me, I think it was my salads that the girls liked best.

Only Nina didn't like cooking. The culinary side of life didn't really interest her. She herself ate little, selectively, like a cat.

There was also a masterpiece, an absolutely unique dessert, one that Doti sometimes brought. We called it 'Doti's baskets'. First you had to fashion little pastry baskets (which Doti made by hand, without moulds), then bake them and leave them a day or two in the air, to 'rest'. The baskets were then filled with a special chocolate cream, and a dark red morello cherry placed in the centre. That cherry, that bitter heart of the little sweet bathed in chocolate and edged with crunchy pastry, drove us crazy . . .

Middle age is a battle against cholesterol

We began the dinner with the cheese soufflé, then lingered for some time over chicken baked in orange sauce and sprinkled with almonds, and ended it with Doti's baskets. After the baskets we moved into Dinka's living room and we spread ourselves out like half-dead carp.

'Girls, shall we give the cards a throw?' asked Alma lazily.

Not one of us stirred.

'We could give some thought to the fact that we're eating more and more . . .' sighed Ivana in a half-accusing tone.

It is true that with time our parties had become culinary orgies. But if we were eating more and more, it was a fact that we were also dieting more and more. At the same time we were more excited about the varied dietary possibilities and theoretical arguments than the practice itself. We knew all there was to know about fatty cells, permanently deposited in our bodies, and about the advantages of rice-based diets, banana and milk diets and moon diets, we also knew about the drawbacks of eating meat and dieting with juices. Of course, we were not all equally drawn to this topic. Alma, Nina and Nuša were all ignoramuses in the subject, perhaps because they did not appear to have any fatty cells at all.

'Girls, I think we're all nearing the time of the battle against cholesterol . . .'

We called ourselves girls, although we were long past being that. Doti was right, we were at an age when we should have embarked on a serious battle against cholesterol. To put it more crudely, we were middle-aged.

We were experiencing middle age as a battle against the general disorder of everyday life, which was becoming ever greater, despite all our efforts to reduce it. Our days had suddenly become shorter, or something . . . We were experiencing middle age metaphorically as plugging a hole in a boat, with no thought that one day the boat would sink. On the contrary, we were inspired by the optimistic thought that after all the effort invested in it the boat would not only look new, it really would be new. We were experiencing middle age as the terrorism of the everyday, there was always something that had to be sorted out: the television needed repairing, the washing machine wasn't working properly, your child had tests, your husband had sciatica, you had to write a paper for a forthcoming conference, and the computer had devoured half your text, you had to take your mother to a spa . . . In middle age, everything is still all right, the occasional little wrinkle here, the occasional one there, slightly heavier breathing as we go upstairs, and a larger size when buying clothes, still not the shameful extra-large size, so everything's all right, it's all under control. All right, a slight anxiety, a prick of disagreeable foreboding, a little fear that passes over one's face like a mouse's shadow, but still everything's all right, everything's under control. All right, something needs sticking here, something sewing, something patching, something here needs cleaning, something mending, something needs blocking up, something polishing, something else has to be balanced, but everything else, thank goodness, is more or less in order . . .

'Really, girls, let's have a throw, otherwise I'll fall asleep . . .' said Nuša, beginning to yawn. We had never noticed that before. That Nuša could yawn a dozen times in a row.

We were university girls

We were university girls. Dinka, Alma, Doti and I worked at Zagreb University, Ivana came to Zagreb from one of the Belgrade literary institutes, having first done her postgraduate studies in America, Hana taught in Sarajevo, and Nina at a provincial college.

176

I don't remember exactly when we began our soirées, it could have been about twenty years ago, when we were postgraduates. We would get together once every two or three months, sometimes even more often. We left everything behind us, like a frog's skin: intimacy, husbands, lovers, family life, children, and we appeared before each other weightless, without baggage, in our full glory. We revelled in those evenings as in a hot sauna, we warmed ourselves in the steam we ourselves generated. We talked a lot, flushed like children at a child's birthday party, we gossiped, exchanged trifles, ideas about this and that, argued about films, books, plays, fashion. We exchanged little pieces of advice and as a result we shared the same hairdresser, the same beautician, the same gynaecologist, the same dressmaker . . .

Each of us had her reflection in one of the others, her imagined ideal image, but those pairings were changed and shuffled like a pack of cards. It seems that Doti liked Nuša best as her opposite, Nina seemed to open up only with Alma, Hana was most often in contact with Nina, Alma and Ivana were closer to Dinka than to the rest of us, I was enchanted by Ivana . . .

The only thing we never discussed was politics. Doti had her own political story from long ago. Alma was indifferent to all politics. Nuša cultivated a kind of vague, but hence very chic nostalgia for the days of empire. This nostalgia had its origin in the romantic tale of Nuša's grandfather and grandmother. They had fled from Russia after the revolution and decided to stop in Zagreb. Dinka thought that politics was a profession for fools. In fact we all more or less believed that such an unexciting activity as politics must be a profession for fools and . . . men.

'Come on, Dinka, find the cards, let's throw them . . .' said Alma.

'What do I need with cards, when I know it all already . . .' Nuša commented somewhat bad-temperedly. Her bad temper was caused by overeating rather than life.

We walked ten centimetres above the ground

We lived in a town where the flats were small and the ceilings low; where people were immobile as salamanders, because they were born and died in the same flats; where family histories were remembered and preserved like cheap souvenirs from which the dust was regularly brushed, where even old flags were kept, because one never knew when they might be needed . . . We lived surrounded by inhabitants whose genetic code was clear and simple: how to survive. We lived in a town where people walked slightly sideways (and looked sideways, like rabbits), their cheek always on the alert because you never knew what side a slap might come from. We lived in a town where hatred was cultivated like a house plant (like an ugly, dusty, eternally green rubber plant). We lived in a town of dark corners, where lives were spent quickly, because they were cheap; where hatreds never quite healed over, and loves were lukewarm; where the curtains on windows were always drawn (so that our neighbour shouldn't peer into our dinner plates) and always slightly parted (so that we could keep an eye on theirs). We lived in a town where lives were nothing but brief biographies, and life's turning points just an insignificant touch-up.

Presumably that is why 'we walked ten centimetres above the ground'. In our language that sentence signified a distinction between people. And while the majority endeavoured to keep their feet firmly 'on the ground', we defended our right to those . . . ten centimetres. Being involved with literature helped us for years to maintain a light step. Later we would come down to earth. It would turn out that the force of gravity was after all insurmountable.

'Well, girls, if you're not thinking of throwing any cards tonight, I'll go home . . .' said Doti.

We threw cards

It seems that our 'card-throwing' came from the same desire to overcome the gravity of everyday life. Tarot was a fairy-tale about life, existential obstacles and the ultimate reward, a brightly coloured picture book for adults, in which pleasure was not provoked by the repetition of a familiar story but on the contrary by the possibility of a large number of combinations. Tarot was nothing other than a kind of alternative literature in which the strength of the text depended on the power of the interpreter and the imagination of the reader.

It was Dinka who had introduced the ritual of 'throwing cards' (that's what we called it) into our soirées and it never occurred to us to alter it. Only Hana, when she came to Zagreb, would bring an additional dimension by reading the grounds of black coffee. Hana had a gift for reading people's fates from their palms (that seemed too serious and dangerous to us), and she knew something about oriental fortune-telling with tea (we liked that idea, but we didn't drink tea), she knew how to do it with beans as well (that seemed somehow . . . folkloric).

As far as the 'spiritual' side of life was concerned only Doti was a serious believer. As we're into this kind of topic, Alma used from time to time to go to a psychoanalyst. Nuša had gone in for transcendental meditation for a time, she learned what 'chakra' was, and 'mantra' and then she abandoned it all. As for Ivana, for her in that 'spiritual' sense, even Father Christmas was interesting, the main thing was that it made people happy.

We considered horoscopes vulgar, we had nothing to do with them.

For a time I was enthusiastic about the Russian avant-garde writer Doyvber Levin. Namely, in the thirties Levin, like so many of his contemporaries, had been swallowed by darkness, and with him his novel *The Adventures of Theocritus*. The existence of that novel was confirmed by the memoirs of Levin's surviving contemporaries. So, at that time I tried to talk the girls into taking up spiritualism, defending my proposal as a legitimate method of literary scholarship.

'Just try to imagine what we could learn if we were in touch with Mandelshtam, Pilnyak, Bulgakov, and others, eh?!'

To my great disappointment the girls rejected my proposal with revulsion, as though I had suggested that we should take up haruspication, that is fortune-telling with the fresh liver of a recently slaughtered animal.

We remained true to tarot, even when the incoming tide of New Age moistened even our shores, bringing us new 'spiritual' possibilities.

Dinka was always the one who threw the cards, Alma assisted her in interpreting them, and the rest of us didn't interfere. Dinka always threw the cards in the same, Celtic, manner. Even the cards which she laid out for each of us, the court cards, remained the same for years. What changed were the questions we put to destiny and . . . our passion.

The first, passionate and longest period, when we were interested in questions of love, life and death, or more accurately, just love, was replaced at a certain stage by questions about doctorates (see whether I'll complete my doctorate successfully!), then the interest shifted to family life, children, practical problems . . . Then came a period without questions, a time of some deficiency of imagination, perhaps fear, who can tell, when we invented questions instead of really asking them, just so as to keep the ritual going. It was only Ivana who always asked the same question—

would she have children—and because of her we tried to maintain the same fire. Doti too asked the same question for a long time—would she get a passport—and then the cards, or perhaps just the authorities, finally obliged.

With time we became crude. Dinka didn't try any more. She did it more to entertain us than to tell our fortunes. When the wand card came out, she used to say: 'It's all here in the cards. You'll soon be having it off . . .'

It was all because of that phase . . . that struggle against cholesterol. Before, we used easily to add the pictures, colours, symbols to a reality from which we could expect a lot. Now that reality had become dry, which is perhaps how it had always been, but our imagination too lost its moisture . . . With time we learned that life usually offers the cheaper variant, we no longer had the energy ourselves to illuminate the pictures and words with our own inner glow. Apart from that, we were more inclined to believe the other side than the face, to read the cards in their dark, opposite, reversed meaning than the bright one . . .

'Knock! Knock!' 'Who's there?' 'An angel from heaven!'

'Well? Are we throwing the cards or going home . . .?' said Alma decisively.

'Who shall we do first?' Dinka asked automatically, picking up the cards.

'What more can I ask when it always comes out the same . . .' added Nuša in a tone of resignation.

Just as Dinka was shuffling the cards, at the very moment she was cutting the pack, the power went off.

'Hell . . .!' said Dinka crossly.

'They haven't started cuts again, have they?' whispered Ivana.

Dinka found candles, lit them, and returned to the cards. She shuffled them again.

'So, who'll be first?'

'I will . . .' offered Ivana.

And then just as Dinka was cutting them in two halves and placing the upper half under the lower one, there was a sudden gust of wind, a draught or something through the room and it blew the pack out of her hands. The cards flew around the room.

'What the hell . . .!' shrieked Dinka.

And then the room was bathed in a quite other-worldly blue light.

'Jeeeesus!' screamed Doti and sneezed.

A beautiful young man was standing in the doorway.

He took our breath away. Out of the corner of my eye I noticed that we had all, at the same moment, like soldiers, each made a small movement, a gesture which betrayed instant, unconscious, inner mobilisation. Nuša slightly narrowed her beautiful, dark eyes, Alma flashed a captivating smile, Doti smoothed her hair with her hand, Ivana straightened her shoulders, I drew my stomach in, while Dinka stared at the young man with half-open lips.

'Who are you?' she stuttered.

The young man trembled slightly.

'How did you get in?' gasped Dinka.

'Er . . . through the door . . .' he muttered in a seductive, subdued alto.

'Where have you come from?'

The young man pointed to the ceiling.

'From the Ivićes?'

The young man shook his head.

'From the Turkovices?'

The young man shook his head more vigorously.

'There's no one else upstairs . . .' said Dinka, speaking to us this time.

'Žnidaršić . . .' mumbled the young man, pointing to the ceiling again.

'This guy's fallen out of the sky . . .' said Alma, bursting out laughing.

The young man nodded and smiled sweetly.

At that moment Doti sneezed loudly again.

'Precisely,' said Nuša.

Our visitor is having us on

We discovered that our visitor was called Alfred, that he was an angel who had messed up his immediate task of preventing a certain Božica Žnidaršić from driving her car into a truck in Maksimir Street, which was just round the corner. We learned that after the accident he was desperate, and seeing a window where there was light, the only one in the street, he had suddenly wanted to drop in, and here he was . . .

While the story was completely crazy, our visitor was, on the contrary, a beautiful young man with curly chestnut hair, big almond eyes and full lips the colour of fresh raspberries. The young man had a fine, masculine face and a perfectly built body. He was wearing a light-blue T-shirt, knee-length shorts, blue trainers, gloves which he shoved into his pocket, leather pads on his knees and elbows and . . . a blue skateboard, which he was holding stupidly in his hand. At first glance he didn't look much different from his contemporaries, those solitary young men who come out at night and practise the art of skateboarding in the empty town squares. The only really unusual thing about the young man was the badges he had pinned on his T-shirt. The Yugoslav coat-of-arms, a badge of Tito, the Yugoslav flag, a hammer and sickle. Such badges could no longer be seen even on the formal suits of partisan fighters celebrating the anniversary of one of their offensives.

'Hmm, so you're an angel?' said Dinka, and stopped. As though she didn't know what else to ask.

The young man nodded politely.

'And where are your wings?' asked Nuša ironically. We looked at her, not liking her tone of voice.

'In the hall . . .' said the young man simply. He disappeared for a moment, and then came back with a small bundle, exactly like a cheap folding umbrella. The young man opened the wings, they were dazzlingly white and weightless. They could have been compared to the wings of white imperial peacocks, but the comparison was too feeble.

'What do you want with a skateboard if you've got wings?' asked Nuša in the same insolent, ironic tone.

'Lots of people . . . are allergic to feathers . . .' he said.

'Aaaachooo!' Doti confirmed her presence with a sneeze.

The young man folded his wings and put them back in the hall.

Doti had evidently decided to intervene. With a discreet movement, she took out a little chain with a cross on it, which she had kept tucked into her blouse until then, straightened her hair with the same hand and offered the young man the chocolate baskets.

'Leave him alone! The young man must be hungry . . . Here . . . Help yourself . . .'

The young man didn't appear to notice Doti's signal with the little cross, he was more attracted by the baskets.

'Mmmm . . . Alfred has . . . never been on earth before . . .' mumbled the young man contentedly, reaching for another basket.

'Angel my foot! Just look at him guzzling . . .' whispered Dinka to

Alma. And really, the young man was already reaching for a fifth basket.

'Why do you always talk about yourself in the third person . . .?' Nuša leapt in again.

'Alfred doesn't know . . . what the third person is . . .' the young man replied modestly, taking a seventh basket.

'And do you at least know what those badges on your T-shirt mean?' Nuša attacked like a police inspector.

'Alfred prepared . . .' said the young man.

'This guy's just having us on . . .' whispered Dinka to Alma.

'Maybe he's simply an idiot . . .' whispered Alma to Dinka

Alfred is no faker

It seems that in the meantime we were all recalling something of our general knowledge of angels. Our Alfred really didn't have anything in common with Jan van Eyck's, Memlink's, Botticini's, Doré's, Perugino's, Breughel's, Blake's, Da Vinci's, Raphael's, Dürer's or any other angels . . . Apart from a pair of wings, and even that was questionable, there was nothing about Alfred to prove he was an angel.

'And do you fit on the top of a pin?' Nuša suddenly went on the offensive again. This time we all nodded, approving her question.

'Alfred's not a faker . . .' the young man answered calmly.

Then Ivana took matters into her own hands, went to the kitchen, came back with a jar of flour and emptied it over the floor.

'There,' she said decisively. 'Now walk . . .'

'What . . .?'

'Walk across the flour . . .'

Alfred took a step, two . . .

'Look! There are no tracks!' shrieked Ivana. 'That's proof. Otherworldly creatures, of all kinds, leave no tracks,' she said triumphantly.

'Hmm . . . If he would only show us some miracle, some trick . . .' whispered the still sceptical Alma.

Angels don't know what they're for

Then Alma took on herself the role of judge of angels, and asked sternly: 'Do you have a belly button?'

'A belly button . . . ?'

Alfred lifted up his T-shirt and pulled his trousers down. He definitely had no belly button, but there, stirring and wriggling in the air was his willie.

'Ooooo!' we all sighed in unison. Doti sneezed again. We all moved closer and gazed enchanted at Alfred's willie. If there was anything otherworldly about Alfred it was his willie. Consequently it would be stupid to say that it was the loveliest willie that any of us had ever seen. No, it was something that none of us had ever seen: a divine, large pestle nestling in soft mother-of-pearl fluff which trembled in the air like a humming-bird and emitted a magical bluish light.

'Heavens, child . . .' said Alma in a dark voice.

'Alfred is surprised himself sometimes . . .' said Alfred, looking down.

'And do you know what it's . . . for . . .?' asked Dinka.

'Alfred doesn't know . . . what it's for . . .' said Alfred, pulling up his trousers.

We all stood entranced, overwhelmed by a sudden weariness, perhaps a sense of loss, although we would not have been able to say what that loss consisted of, and who knows how long we would have stood like that had Alfred not caught sight of the pack of cards and said sweetly, 'Alfred throws cards . . .'

The angel throws cards

Alfred picked up the cards, shuffled them and then, instead of throwing them on to the floor as Dinka usually did, he tossed them upwards with a wave of his hand. The cards arranged themselves in the air.

'Ahhhhhh . . .!' we all exclaimed in wonder.

The cards stood still in the air, as though stuck to an invisible vertical piece of glass, or an invisible screen. And we watched them becoming transparent, lit from both sides, like a sumptuous stained-glass window. Alfred arranged the tarot. He seemed to be moving the cards with the help of an invisible computer mouse.

'Uh-uh-huhhh . . .' Alfred sighed.

'What is it? What do they say . . .?' we whispered.

Not paying us any attention, Alfred looked at the cards hanging in the air, mumbled something to himself, sighed, sobbed and clucked like a bushman. He began pouring words around him, as though he were crumbling thousands of fortune cookies in one fist and at the same time reading thousands of paper messages hidden in them.

It was a hypnotic mish-mash of sound. We felt as though we were hearing a sound record of the globe, the sounds of the jungle, the desert, the sea, the steppes and the stars. All kinds of things were mixed up in it and only occasionally could anything be made out. What we were able to understand were quotations from classical works of world literature (many of which, for me at least, had always seemed like messages out of fortune cookies), quotations from the Bible, the Revelation of Saint John ('Behold I stand at the door and knock: if any man hear my voice, and open the door, I will come in to him, and will sup with him, and he with me . . .'), there were messages from the storehouses of famous prophecies, Buddhist wisdom and Taoist commonplaces. Alfred mixed quotations from the Talmud with others from the Koran, and these with New Age messages about the basic truths of life. Quotations from socialist readers ('Whoever labours will not go hungry') were juxtaposed with the teachings of Tibetan mystics. And when we made out in that jumbled rosary of words without beginning or end the line 'In the tunnel black as tar shines the bright five-pointed star', we realised what Alfred meant when he said that he had prepared . . .

Alfred bewitched us. We lost all sense of time, we were quite captivated by his angelic gurgling. Alfred produced words like a magician's silk handkerchiefs from a hat. He pronounced sentences in the rhythm of masters of black rap, interrupting them with sighs which seemed now like a monkey's grunts, now like a bird's chirrup, now like the click of a dolphin . . .

'. . . he that hath an ear, let him hear, ye-ye, for the false side will become the true, the true the false, uuu-huu, the left will become the right, and the right the left, ah-ha, for without are dogs, sorcerers, and whoremongers, iii-hi, murderers, and idolaters, ye-ye, and those that are above will soon come down, i-hiii, and those that are below will rise up, up-up, so, write the things which thou hast seen, ye-ye, for the truth will become a lie, and a lie will be the truth, heh-heh, and the great will be small, and the small will be huge, ah-ha, he that hath an ear let him hear, eh-he, for the ugly will become lovely, and the lovely ugly, uu-hu, and dragons will sprout teeth, and the bones of the dead will rise, iii-hi, they will rise up,

185

up-up, and the spirits of your forefathers will come to claim their due, ah-ha, they picked the cherry tree, hee-hee, without inviting me, hee-hee, one has no fun at all, oh-ho, when one is very small, oh-ho . . .'

'Girls, he's quoting Jovan Jovanović Zmaj!' Doti leapt into Alfred's rosary. And she was right, the last words came from 'The Cherry-Picker'. Doti was clearly offended by the fact that this angel in the middle of Zagreb could think of nothing better than to quote from a Serbian children's poet.

Alfred blushed, embarrassed, and the cards evaporated in the air and piled themselves tidily in a pack by Dinka's feet.

'Now look what you've done! You've interrupted him! And he's been trying to tell us something the whole time . . .' cried Ivana, almost sobbing.

'But he's been talking the whole time,' snapped Nuša.

'God, why are you so stupid all of a sudden? So what if he did quote Zmaj! Can't you see that he's trying to tell us something that concerns us all . . .' said Ivana furiously.

We had never seen Ivana in such an abruptly altered mood. She was on the verge of tears.

'He's not here by chance! He didn't simply fall out of the sky for no reason . . .' she said.

'Maybe we really are stupid,' said Doti in a conciliatory tone, and, like a hen pecking seed, she swiftly kissed the little cross hanging round her neck.

Alfred chooses Ivana

At that moment something unexpected happened, if that is the right expression considering everything that had occurred. Alfred went up to Ivana, tenderly pressed his forehead against hers, as though he were pressing an angelic stamp on to it. As he did this, he placed his hands on Ivana's cheeks, closed his eyes as though he were reading her thoughts, and slowly moved his head, from left to right. Ivana closed her eyes as well. Joined in a tender clinch, Alfred and Ivana swayed back and forth. We watched them open-mouthed, they seemed to be performing some kind of other-worldly dance. We envied Ivana. Doti blushed and lowered her eyes, Dinka watched the scene out of the corner of her eye, Alma chewed her nails, Nuša smiled her special, vulnerable smile.

Alfred began making his seductive bushman sighs . . .

'Mmmmmmmmm . . .' went Alfred.

And then he slowly separated his forehead from Ivana's and looked her straight in the eyes. Ivana smiled a smile that suffused her face like warm water. She even made a small grateful movement like a curtsy.

'And now Alfred has to go . . .' said Alfred seriously.

'But you've only just come . . . !' Doti was genuinely offended.

Group photograph

I too felt a pang at the thought of Alfred leaving. And then, remembering that on my way to Dinka's I had collected my camera from being repaired, I suggested that we took a photograph of all of us together as a souvenir. We put Alfred in the middle. Nuša, Doti, Ivana, Alma, Dinka arranged themselves around him like a bouquet . . . I set it on auto-focus and leapt in myself at the last moment. The camera whirred, clicked and flashed, Alfred nodded, and repeated: 'Now Alfred has to go . . .'

We stood smirking like hotel staff seeing off an important guest.

'Hey, don't forget your wings . . .!' said Doti, handing Alfred the feathery bundle.

And then, as though remembering something, Alfred plucked a few feathers from his wings.

'Alfred says thank you . . .' he said sweetly, bowing slightly, and he handed each of them a feather. Nuša, and Ivana, and Alma, and Dinka, and Doti. And as they took the feathers, they too gave a slight bow.

Then Alfred raised a finger like a conductor's baton and, suddenly, we were all suspended in the air about a foot off the ground. Our heads almost touched the ceiling.

'Jeesuuus . . .' whispered Doti.

Alfred shrugged his shoulders charmingly as though apologising and said: 'Small flats, low ceilings . . .'

'You asked for a trick, well here you are . . .' complained Dinka.

'As long as he doesn't forget to put us down . . .' whispered Doti, clutching her cross.

'If you ask me, I really like being in the air . . .' said Alma.

'Does this make you thinner . . .?' asked Nuša, which I admit had been my first thought as well.

Ivana gazed at the ceiling, she seemed to be in seventh heaven.

And then Alfred put us gently down, smiled, put on his gloves, raised his hand, waved it over his head and . . . vanished! It all happened so fast that we didn't have a chance to be surprised. It was like the TV series *Star Trek*. (There, the characters pronounce phrases like 'Beam me up!' or 'Transmit!' and disappear.) After Alfred's disappearance stardust hovered in the air for a while. We held our breath. It was as though we hadn't believed until that moment that we really were dealing with an angel . . .

And when the last speck of stardust had evaporated, we all yawned simultaneously. Seeing each other with wide open mouths, we all burst out laughing. Then Alma glanced at her watch and said she must go home, Ivana was already picking up her bag, Nuša was putting on her high-heeled shoes, Doti already had her hand on the door handle.

'Hey, why are you in such a rush . . .' I muttered.

But the girls were already leaving, and Dinka did not try to stop us. We dispersed almost as fast as Alfred had disappeared. After everything that had happened, that was actually the strangest thing of all. That we had not stayed to discuss the whole event . . .

A feather as light as oblivion

Before she turned off the light and went to bed, Dinka caught sight of a strange white feather on the table. She smiled, placed the feather on her palm like a firefly, took it with her into the bedroom and laid it carefully on the little bedside table. In the dark, the feather seemed to be glowing and, amused by this thought, she fell asleep.

Nuša came home and went straight to the children's rooms. She softly opened first one door, then the other a crack . . . The boys were sleeping a relaxed, sound sleep. The air in their rooms smelled pungently, of healthy young males.

Nuša went out on to the terrace. She sniffed the warm air and in the darkness surveyed her property. No one can take this from me, she thought suddenly, and then shuddered at this unexpected thought . . .

Nuša went to get her cigarettes. She returned to the terrace, lit a cigarette and in the cellophane wrapping of the cigarette packet caught sight of a little feather tucked into it. She took the feather out, stretched her long, slender arm and looked at it. In the dark-green night the feather seemed to give off an other-worldly glow.

'Strange . . .' whispered Nuša, tucking the feather back into the cellophane wrapper, and went to bed.

Ivana went home holding the little feather in her hand and found her husband in his dressing-gown. He was sitting at the table, not noticing the moths which were billowing like wind into the room through the wide-open door of the terrace. He was watching television, reading a newspaper and munching a sandwich.

'How was it?' he asked, not taking his eyes off the paper.

'Fun, as always,' said Ivana.

Munching, her husband shifted his glance to the television.

'Would you like me to make you something hot to eat?' she asked.

'No, thanks,' he said, turning back to the newspaper.

Ivana went to the kitchen and poured herself a glass of mineral water.

'Would you like some too?'

'What?'

'Water.'

'No, thanks,' said her husband.

Ivana came back with her glass and sat down at the table. The terrace door was wide open, crazed moths fluttered around the room. Her husband was reading the newspaper. Ivana stretched out her hand and tickled her husband's nose with the feather.

'Hey!' snapped her husband, waving his hand as though brushing away a fly.

Ivana looked fixedly at her husband and—without knowing herself what she was doing—she suddenly raised her hand to her lips and thrust the feather into her mouth, rolling it up like a snail. A fluorescent stalk hung out of her mouth . . .

Her husband glanced at Ivana in horror and then covered his mouth with his hand and fled to the bathroom. Ivana meanwhile took her glass of water calmly and with an unusual elegance, and slowly drained it.

When Alma reached home, her husband was already asleep. Alma sat down to look at the newspaper and then, opening it, sneezed. She reached for her handbag and the miraculous feather fell out with the little packet of paper handkerchiefs. Alma first wiped her nose, and then picked up the feather wondering how it came to be in her handbag.

Then Alma undressed and, taking the feather with her, slipped into bed. The moonlight came in through the open window, her husband's warm body was breathing calmly beside her. Holding the feather in her hand, Alma slid it along her husband's skin, noticing with satisfaction that it was still young and smooth, she circled round his nipples, tenderly tickling their tips, then she moved down towards his belly button, then lower still . . . There her husband's cooperative little baton was already waiting impatiently . . .

Although it was late when she reached home, Doti did not feel sleepy. Her mother was sleeping in the living room, her husband in one room, her daughter in another, and so Doti went to the bathroom, the only place in the flat where she wouldn't disturb anyone . . .

She sat on the toilet seat and who knows what she was thinking about, and then her husband burst into the bathroom. He saw Doti sitting on the toilet fingering a strange little white feather. In the dull gleam of the bathroom light Doti saw her husband—a drowsy, sweaty man in a T-shirt and underpants. The meeting was like a sudden discovery, like a blow in the plexus, as though it was only now, after so many years, that they were meeting for the first time. And, gasping, wiping away her tears, Doti burst out laughing. She sat on the toilet for a long time, with the little feather in her hand, choking with laughter . . .

I went home that evening and for some reason went to water the plants on the window sill . . . Suddenly a powerful, irrepressible despair shot through me, like a sharp pain. I lay down, fully dressed, covered myself with the bedclothes and, my gaze fixed on the dark outline of the plants in the window, like petrified bats, I sank into sleep. I dreamed that I did not want to wake up.

In the morning I called each of them in turn

In the morning Alma found a beautiful little feather on the floor by her bed. She picked it up, still wondering where it had come from and put it away in a little ebony box.

In the morning Nuša found an unusual little feather in the cellophane wrapping of her cigarette packet. She folded it up and put it into the locket she wore round her neck.

As she drank her morning coffee, Doti suddenly noticed an unusual lovely white feather in a vase of peacock feathers which her mother had kept on top of the fridge for years. Not herself knowing why she was doing it, Doti took the little feather and stuck it behind the wooden crucifix on the wall.

'It's much better like that,' she said with satisfaction.

In the morning Dinka caught sight of an unusual white feather on her bedside table. She picked it up and put it into a copy of her recently published book *A History of Metaphor*, between pages 104 and 105.

When she woke up, Ivana felt terribly thirsty. Half-asleep, she made her way to the fridge, took out a litre packet of milk and drank the whole thing. She didn't notice her husband leave for work. And Ivana's husband, who was just on his way to work, seeing his sleepy wife thirstily draining the milk, turned pale, and then left the flat, banging the door.

In the morning I called each of them in turn. They remembered nothing at all about the angel.

'Take vitamin B6 and drink lots of orange juice. That's great for hangovers,' Alma advised me.

Then I slipped out to the nearest photo-shop to have my film developed. On the way I bought a paper. When I got home I leafed through it and came across a report that a certain B.Ž., aged thirty-one, had been killed in an accident in Maksimir Street, when her car was in collision with a truck. Our unusual visitor who had mumbled about Bozica Žnidaršić had not been lying. And as for B.Ž. she had evidently had no luck with her guardian angel. So, Alfred was a traffic policeman, one of those guardian angels from cheap popular drawings which are always behind careless drivers, non-swimmers who insist on falling into fast-flowing rivers, suicides, inattentive pedestrians and all kinds of other confused people.

I rushed to the telephone again to tell them of my discovery in connection with B.Ž., but then decided against it. Then it occurred to me to call Nina and Hana, and tell them what had happened last night. But instead I took Alma's advice, found a vitamin B6 tablet and swallowed it with a glass of orange juice . . .

191

Now it was clearer why we had parted the night before without commenting on our visitor. There was nothing to say, the girls had forgotten everything. At the instant of his own disappearance, the angel had wiped away all trace of his presence. However, I had been there too and seen it all with my very own eyes! So it was still unclear why the angel had omitted to touch me with his little feather of oblivion.

II

The young man smiled, raised his hand in its yellow glove, waved it over his head and suddenly vanished. The guard sniffed the air. The air smelled of burned feathers.

> Daniil Kharms, 'The Young Man Who Surprised the Warden'

My Belgrade acquaintance S. T., a psychologist by profession, profoundly disgusted and embittered by everything that was happening, left Belgrade at the beginning of the war with her husband and child to emigrate. After wandering around Europe, she went to America, stopped in the state of Maine, in a small town surrounded by forests, and got a job in a local psychiatric clinic. My acquaintance took only a few things with her, but they included a diary in which she had for years, for professional reasons, recorded her dreams.

Today in snowbound Maine, where, she says, she will stay forever, surrounded by real lunatics, who, she says, soothe her, my acquaintance reads her diary.

'It turns out that I've been dreaming of the horrors of war for years without knowing where those dreams came from. Everything I dreamed happened,' she tells me.

Did my acquaintance dream the horrors of war, which then actually happened or had the horrors of war already occurred some time in the future, and she just dreamed them?

The lords of war like the word 'dream' and its derivatives. They don't dream personal dreams, they make the 'thousand-year dreams' of their nations come true. Do nations really dream? 'Yes,' people say, 'that is what we have dreamed for a whole thousand years. Our dream has become reality.' Perhaps nations choose as their leaders oniromanths, interpreters of dreams, who will then disclose to them what they, the nations, have been dreaming for hundreds of years. In truth, where are the borders between dreamed and real worlds?

Perhaps there are no borders, perhaps both worlds are real, only dreamed reality is more dangerous and 'more real' simply because it has not yet occurred? In his book *Res Gestae*, the historian Ammionus Marcelinus mentions a certain Mercurius, who was known as the 'lord of dreams' because he would sniff around, interrogate people about their dreams, eavesdrop when people were telling each other about their dreams—and inform the emperor about them. Many people lost their lives as a consequence. News of the 'lord of dreams' spread: no one wanted to admit that they had been asleep, let alone dreaming. And the wise regretted that they had not been born at the foot of the Atlas Mountains, for there, says the legend, people never dream.

The lords of war, the lords of dreams . . . The attraction of oniromancy, of every kind of fortune-telling, all reading of the future, is not hidden in the text of the dream but in its interpretation. In that sense any text at all, including a recipe for a cheese soufflé, may be read as a prediction of the future, or, later, as its fulfilment. That is quite clear to fortune-tellers and rulers, emperors and their informers, politicians and psychoanalysts, which is why there are such close links between them.

Alfred does not belong to the same group. The truth of Alfred's reading of the tarot cards, as it turned out later, did not lie so much in the message as in the way it was carried out. Soon after Alfred's visit the surrounding reality would be transformed into chaos (a chaos of quotation, as it happens!), into an inarticulate noise full of sound and fury.

Be that as it may, what is important for our story is that the party when our nocturnal visitor appeared was the last of our gatherings, which we did not know at the time. After that, 'dreamed reality' began to unravel before our eyes.

I do not intend here to wind that terrible reality back into language, transforming it into the story of the local apocalypse, nor to reinforce Alfred's fortune-cookie messages (the story that is!) with images of that terrible reality to prove their validity. At this moment, the reality of which I am speaking is still verifiable. It is enough to go to the dismembered country in the south of Europe and see for oneself. Or at least to look through television film, newspapers and photographs from 1991 to 1995.

That reality is still verifiable, I say. Because soon the minefield will be covered in grass, new houses will spring up on top of the ruins, everything will be grown over, it will disappear and shift once again into dream, story, fortune-tellers' prophecies. Firm borders will be established once again between the existing and dreamed worlds. It is true that there will be people left, witnesses, who will not acknowledge those boundaries, evoking their nightmare experience as proof of what occurred, but few will listen to them, and then with time they too will be covered over with grass.

Before the beginning of the war I dreamed a dream which I still remember. I heard the doorbell of my Zagreb flat ring. I opened the door and rivers of people began to pour into my flat: women, children, men, old people . . . They came into the flat silently, settled themselves, lay on my bed, sat down at my desk, went into my kitchen, opened my fridge, showered in my bathroom, all without a word . . . God, how many of them there are, and how can they all fit into this little space, I wondered. This is my flat, I shouted, how dare you, I protested, I'll call the police, I threatened. The people didn't notice me. I was invisible, they simply did not hear my voice.

Some time later I saw rivers of people crossing the television screen, after a while I began meeting those same or similar people as I travelled through the world. That is to say I no longer live in my Zagreb flat. Nor is my Zagreb flat mine any longer. All I possess now is a suitcase . . .

I do not use my suitcase as a metaphorical substitute for the word 'exile'. The suitcase is in fact my only reality. Even the stamps which have accumulated on the pages of my passport do not convince me sufficiently of the reality of my journeying. Yes, the suitcase is my one fixed point. Everything else is a dream, or perhaps I am a dream dreamed by someone else. It doesn't matter which any more. The suitcase contains some completely senseless things. Including one old, yellowed and another blank, reject photograph.

Our only group photograph. From the photograph gapes whiteness. And there, from the left (was it the left?) should have been dark-eyed Nusa, then Doti with her broad face and piercing look, then Ivana with a smile that spread over her face like warm water, then Alma, the colour of

195

copper, beside her the reliable and always serious Dinka and I, with a childish face, they say, and a body bequeathed me by the power-hungry genes of my full-breasted foremothers. Nina and Hana weren't there, they hadn't been with us that evening . . .

I place another photograph alongside our blank one. The yellowed photograph from the beginning of the century is like a lamp lit in a murky window, a heartening secret gesture with which I draw pictures from the indifferent whiteness . . .

And I think, how is it that, after knowing each other for so many years, I know so little about them . . . With an effort I draw them on to the surface of the picture and, where Nusa's face ought to be an indistinct blur appears, with another just a gesture rises to the surface, with a third just the outline of a face, with a fourth just a smile, with a fifth her whole shape, but quite different, new, certainly not the one I remember . . .

III

The air smelled of burned feathers . . .

Nuša, The Queen of Wands

In 1990, when everything began to seethe, but few believed that it would come to war, Nuša uttered a sentence which sounded quite unreal: 'I believe that every family should give one member for the defence of the homeland,' she said.

In the autumn of 1991 her eighteen-year-old son was among, the first to be sent to the front.

The first time we went to Nuša's house was when her son was born . . .

Lovely Nuša . . . Nuša was the prettiest and most feminine of us all, none of us could compete with her. She was tall, fine-boned, very slender, there was a calm in her bearing and a special lightness in her step. She was fair-skinned, dark-eyed, her face was tinted with a trace of melancholy, like perfect make-up. Around her mouth hovered a readiness for an always ambiguous smile. As though she was not certain whether she was mocking someone or was slightly offended by someone else's invisible mockery.

For a long time Nuša smelled of little babies and children's soap. After the first, she had another boy.

We were also at Nuša's place when she moved into her new house. The house was on a hill, the terrace looked out over a green slope. The whole slope belonged to Nuša. At its foot we could see the first, newly planted tree. That little tree moved us. As though it were bravely protecting Nuša from all evil. As though it guaranteed her a long and harmonious life and, of course, successful completion of her doctorate on Russian symbolism. We didn't throw cards that day, it was unnecessary.

Through her contacts, Nuša managed to get her son back from the front and enrol him at university. However, the boy soon went back to the front of his own accord. They say that he had become war addicted. There are all kinds of addiction . . . They say that her parents died one after the

197

other. Nuša's husband was less and less frequently at home. The fair-skinned Nuša's face darkened.

That green slope became a veritable wood, they say. To start with, Nuša had planted trees on the advice of a landscape gardener. It was from Nuša that we learned of the existence of such a profession. They say that now Nuša drags the seedlings there herself and plants them obsessively. She has learned which trees grow quickest and those are the only ones she plants. They also say that the trees have reached the very edge of the terrace . . .

Incidentally, I made enquiries. Birches are the fastest growing trees.

Alma, The Queen of Pentacles

Alma regularly had the best cards. Perhaps because Alma experienced life itself as a game in which the most important thing, as in every game, was to win and retain the winning position for as long as possible.

In the new times she was prepared to declare that her father, a partisan general, admittedly dead, had been a *murderer*. It was as though she sensed that soon the right side would become the wrong one and wrong would become right.

'And what was he if not a murderer?' she said with conviction and saved her skin.

Once I bought a Croatian newspaper in Berlin and came across her name. There was a petition of tenants seeking the right to buy up state-owned apartments. I knew she would not give up a general's apartment in the centre of town that easily. And why should she? Alma knew that revolutions were never carried out for righteous ideas, but for houses, functions, land, territory . . . And just as her father had been rewarded for his ideological propriety with a large apartment and a house by the sea, so in the new historical times some new *murderer* would try to move into the same apartment in the name of some new propriety.

'Men have no compassion . . .' she once said.

She knew that in fact no one had any compassion and she prepared herself. She applied for and obtained two passports. She bought a flat in a neighbouring, more Western and more secure, new European statelet. She sent her son to a more distant European foreign land, where there was no danger of his being mobilised. She arranged everything, she left nothing

198

to chance. As though she were the only one of us to know precisely where and with whom she was living . . .

It is true that things upset her. It took her a long time to accept that the family of a Croatian soldier returning from the front had moved into her immediate neighbours' flat when they were away on holiday. And her neighbours were out on the street. The people who moved in, the new revolutionaries, did not let them take any of their clothes, let alone anything else. Animal vitality, that is the essence of human nature, everything else is a surplus. What few ideas there are, of one kind or another, it doesn't matter which, just serve as packing, so that human shit should not stink to high heaven. That is why all those who have any brains in their heads change their skin, in dark times such as these they become hard-boned, a new human species, mutants with a reduced heart surface and well-developed eye sockets.

It is true that many things upset her, but it didn't occur to her to play the righteous hero. Besides, she knew better than anyone what happens to heroes. A few years earlier she had attended the unveiling of a statue of her father and the opening of a school named after him in the village where he was born. She put up with the modest ceremony as one endures tedious village events. She need not have gone. Now, only a few years later, the statue has probably been demolished and the school's name (which was her name as well!) changed.

Alma had an unusual beauty. There was something androgynous about her, with her short, shiny hair the colour of copper, her sharp cheekbones, her full, large mouth and broad smile. She was always perfectly turned out. With time the copper colour darkened and became an even more exciting chestnut. She always had two men with her, her husband and a lover. She maintained that the *ménage à trois* was the most natural sexual and emotional environment for a woman. Her early discovery that men had no compassion, combined with the film *Jules et Jim*, had had an effect. She changed lovers approximately every seven years, her husband stayed constant. All Alma's lovers remained confirmed bachelors.

She would not give in. The genes of her forebears, Adriatic pirates, real or invented, would not permit her to give in. She would live like a soldier, do gymnastics regularly, visit a beautician regularly, a psychiatrist from time to time, a dentist and hairdresser regularly, every winter she went skiing, every summer to the sea, every season she would slip over to

Trieste to renew her wardrobe. Armani, Moschino, Mila Schön, Ferragamo, Crisci . . . The elegant Alma would always wear only the most expensive silk stockings and only ever real jewellery.

Alma knew that it was only with the strict control of her heart that she could satisfy her appetite for exclusive things. She considered her involvement with literature one such 'exclusive thing'. She wrote increasingly brilliant literary-theoretical studies. Few people noticed. She was unconcerned. She was reconciled to the fact that the top academic, scholarly, literary and cultural ranks belonged—in war as in peacetime—to men.

In the course of a year spent in Japan, she made contact with the Slavic institute on the island of Hokkaido. Thanks to Alma, the barely connectable Croats and Japanese would be connected in some literary-scholarly project of Alma's.

My imagination adds to this project an infatuated Japanese gentleman, Dr Oshima, a tiny man and a great expert on Russian ornamental prose. The tall, white woman with the pirates' genes would break his Japanese porcelain heart. Dr Oshima would adore Alma passionately in 1994, 1995, 1996, 1997, 1998, 1999, 2000, and maybe even longer.

Nina, The Page of Pentacles

Nina taught Russian literature in a small town on the Adriatic coast. Up in the hills lived mostly Serbs and down on the coast, mostly Croats. In 1991 some of her students fled into the hills, to their own kind. It is perfectly possible that they were involved later in shelling their town. And Nina. She prefers not to talk about it.

In a way I think that Nina moved completely into literature. She wanders through the pages of Bely, Bulgakov and Platonov as over the sea and she does not wish to come into port. She called me several times while I was still in Zagreb . . .

'Do you hear . . .?' she would interrupt the conversation.

I could clearly hear the sound of gunfire through the receiver.

'They're firing again. It seems they haven't fulfilled their quota for today yet,' she said calmly, as though she were talking about rainfall.

'That's your students firing at you . . .' I would try to joke.

Nina laughed quietly, creakily, like an old woman.

'They're idiots firing, not my students.'

'Why don't you leave?'

'Why should I?' she would say in a tone that put a final stop to that question.

Nina could have come back to Zagreb. Her parents lived in Zagreb. I cannot make out why she stayed in the provincial town to share the war fate of her newly acquired fellow citizens. For months she lived without light, water or heat. Instead of simply leaving—slightly-built, slim and unusually lithe, with grey-green eyes and a fine, cat-like head, her hair drawn into a little bun and always dressed in black like a widow—Nina acquired a cat.

'Behemot keeps me warmer than central heating,' she said.

All those months Nina communicated with the world from the bathroom. She would take the telephone into the bathroom, the only safe place in the flat, and lie in the bath wrapped in a sleeping bag. She would put a little table with an ashtray, cigarettes and a drink beside the bath and call everyone in turn, Alma and Doti and Nusa . . .

I shall never know why she decided to stay in a town that was not hers, within reach of her students, some of whom had become soldiers, some of them *ours* and some *theirs,* most of whom were not studying because of the war . . . I can only guess that Nina decided that she ought to stay where life had taken her . . . And then the cat, Behemot, had become accustomed to her, and her next-door neighbour needed her help, and there were other people there . . .

With time, like a clinging plant, she grew into her bath, her wartime daily life, about which she had previously read only in novels, and, after all, her freedom. She didn't have to justify the drink to anyone. And, they say, she drank more and more. They say, when it became easier to travel, she appeared in Zagreb, at a Slavists' conference. And everyone felt uncomfortable. Alma and Dinka and Doti, they were all on her side, no one could say they weren't, but they had somehow inwardly written her off, she was no longer part of the group, and, besides, she was difficult. And it was hard for our foreign colleagues to see her like that.

I sometimes feel like calling her. And then I abandon the idea. Particularly as I don't have her phone number. Although I think that she could tell me something about Hana as well. As long as it was possible, Nina would regularly call Hana in Sarajevo. For some reason I am sure that she has news of her even now . . .

Hana, The Page of Wands

As soon as the war in Bosnia began, Doti called Hana anxiously, learned that she was alive, but she was disturbed by Hana's political blindness, at least that's how Doti formulated it.

'How are you?' asked Doti.

'They're shooting . . .'

'Who's shooting?'

'Everyone . . .' answered the terrified Hana.

'If she still can't say that it's the Serbs who are firing, then I really don't see why I should keep on calling her,' Doti completed her report on Hana.

And for a time Hana was forgotten. And then things got far worse in Sarajevo, the telephone lines were cut, it was no longer possible to go in or out. And then someone connected with Sarajevo remembered Hana, saying that in her younger days she had been a communist, then someone else agreed and said that, in fact, Hana had always been a secret Islamic fundamentalist, then someone else mentioned that Hana's husband, a Serb, was fighting on the side of Sarajevo, and not on that of his people, from the hills. And suddenly Hana was resurrected, and more, she seemed to become closer, now that she was further away. It was as though we were using Hana to stick together the links that had broken between us, as though for a moment Hana's name could open a passage into a time that no longer existed, a time of warm sharing. 'How is Hana?' 'Do you have any news of Hana?' 'We should do something for Hana . . .'

We did things, although at times it seemed that our shared concern for Hana was more important than Hana herself. We sent letters with official stamps, invitations to scholarly meetings at home and abroad, we asked foreign colleagues to help . . . One day Hana's sister appeared briefly in Zagreb, she had been living for some time already with her husband and children as refugees in Prague. We consulted for a long time about how to get Hana and her daughter out of Sarajevo . . .

In February 1993 I received a letter from Hana. I did not reply. That was just when I was leaving Zagreb, when, with a kind of almost suicidal gaiety, I was exchanging my permanent address for future, temporary ones . . .

I hope you will forgive me if I am not in a position to articulate everything one would like to communicate to a friend—outside. I sometimes think I am no longer capable of speaking, let alone writing. Nevertheless, it is incredible how just one friendly gesture can bring you back to life . . . like the meeting with you in Zagreb that my sister told me about.

Please thank everyone for their concern over the papers. We, Sarajevans, look for ways out of Sarajevo like mice and at the same time we know that if we do leave, we shan't achieve anything, apart from saving our skins. When a Sarajevan leaves this town, after everything we have been through, instead of being relieved he feels ashamed. I don't know how to explain this whole tangle of emotions, this mixture of an animal struggle for survival and patriotism, yes, the sort you find in books, which we thought existed only in books . . . I am trying to express something it would be better to say nothing about. But I probably need to feel my own pulse, now that I am in a position to think about leaving. Your invitations have opened some hope of leaving legally and now I can't not think about it. I can't because of Ines. She hasn't poked her nose outside for eleven months now, she sleeps in the pantry, because there isn't a flat which has not been damaged and in which a shell couldn't enter at any moment . . . She's the only girl in our new neighbourhood, she's friends with five little boys. They go together to the fourth, third or fifth floor, for a couple of hours a day, and come in frozen for supper—an American packet to be shared by six people, if there's anything at all . . .

How can I describe the life of an exile in one's own town? In April and May last year we were still in our own house, and then we had to flee. My house is now on the front line. My mother's still there. We get news of her every two months . . . How can I describe a situation in which a person is able to drag himself through all the dangers to within fifty metres of his home, but no further, he can't find out how the people closest to him are doing, he can't cross a bridge he's crossed a thousand times before . . . He can do nothing but carefully observe the windows looking for signs of life . . .

What can I tell you? Behind me are terrible days spent in a shelter in a Zagreb street, hideous scenes of bloodstained Sarajevo streets, behind me are days when I mourned many friends . . . We still live in fear, and we don't know when this dance of death will stop.

In the meantime we have become completely different people. We are accustomed to living from one day to the next. The most important thing is to find food, wood and water. We have gone back to a time when goods were not bought but exchanged. We no longer know what potatoes and onions are, but we know how to make cheese from powdered milk. We make cutlets of rice, we make the famous Bosnian pies, also from rice. We have supplemented Bosnian cooking with recipes the secret of which is to make something out of nothing. We make our own cookers, we have learned to chop wood and make fires. We have cut down all the trees in the avenues and parks, and we're not sorry. We have no electricity, our supplies of candles were long since exhausted. We make oil lamps and improvised lights which work on various sources of power. We can't complain that the time drags. Before now we used to boast that Sarajevo was the meeting-place of different cultures, now we can say that we live here on the border between a complete absence of civilisation and its greatest achievements.

As you see my preoccupations have nothing to do with what I was doing before. I go to the university twice a week, if I manage to get through. All my books are in the occupied territory, I doubt that I shall find any of them if I do go back one day. Just before the war I had a book published, but the entire edition has probably been destroyed. One day I summoned up my courage and went to the Arts faculty which is right on the front line, in the most ruined part of Sarajevo, and managed to take a copy out of my demolished office. By the way, I'm writing poetry now, not theory . . .

There, I've written quite a long letter although I didn't think I would be able to. I hope that you won't find it tiring and too confused. I would like to hear from you as well. Letters mean a lot here. We go to the most impossible places in town to fetch them. The postal blockade has been broken by various brave people, aid workers, people from the Jewish community, Seventh Day Adventists . . . We use foreign journalists as postmen as well, whoever is able to, that is . . .

I hope we shall meet in Zagreb. I would like to come, but for a short time and only if I'm sure I can come back here. There's some hope that this will all end, but life will go on being hellishly difficult here . . . That's why a little break would do me good. Greetings to Nuša, Doti, Alma and Dinka. With love, Hana.

In the autumn of 1993, when I was already abroad, I heard that Hana had managed to get out of Sarajevo and come to Zagreb. But in Zagreb it somehow happened that Doti's flat was too small, and it happened that Alma had some visitors in her flat, and Dinka couldn't have her, and Nuša wasn't in Zagreb at the time. Besides, Nuša had quite a few problems of her own just then. In fact, everyone had problems of their own . . . They were distressed, they telephoned each other, and they were all ready to help, for heaven's sake, how could they not have been ready to help, and they were all very ardent, and they all soon tired of their own ardour, and, in point of fact, no one ever asked them how they were, and Dinka's father had just died, and her mother was ill, and Nuša's son was at the front again . . . And then something had happened with time, or simply with their sense of time, somehow they could not manage to meet, somehow it turned out that they didn't have a free second, and they didn't meet, although Hana, thank goodness, was all right, and she had in any case insisted that she would not stay long, but it was all all right in the end, she stayed with a colleague, one whom they all knew, but never invited. Who can tell why they never included that colleague in anything . . .

I understand that whole story about Hana. What was happening during those months was a terrible betrayal of everything, everyone . . . And it was easy and painless to hide behind that general betrayal and use that to justify one's personal, unimportant one. While some destroyed the house, others massacred the people who lived there, others again dragged out the furniture, others took everything else, yet others looked on with interest, others with disgust, others closed their eyes, others weren't there to see . . . That was how things went.

Abroad I met many journalists who were going to Sarajevo and many Sarajevans who had left and were going back to Sarajevo. I could easily have sent a letter, I could have sent her face cream, a warm scarf and gloves, some money, but, I didn't . . . And I don't know why I didn't do it for her, I did it for others who meant less to me.

My books, photographs, my things are no longer with me. I cross borders lightly, I'm not one of those who pays excess baggage . . . But still, two or three little things have stuck to me and travel everywhere with me. One of them is Hana's letter . . .

Dinka, The Queen of Swords

Who knows whether Dinka who read our destinies in the cards saw anything of all this? I always felt that she knew more about us than we did about her. And while I can easily conjure up in my memory Alma's lively face, Nuša's calm face or Nina's face of a cat, what comes to mind along with Dinka's card, instead of a face, is meaning. Seriousness, reliability, modesty . . .

'That's because I look like a potato, and that's my nature too!' she joked.

Men loved her. I think what they liked most about Dinka was the idea of an independent woman with her own flat. Dinka was a refuge, a shoulder to cry on, a clean bed without commitment or permanence. It wasn't that she was like a potato, of course, but like someone who rejected any suggestion of a lasting tie.

I think that Dinka was petrified of serious ties. Her first husband had died before he was forty, and then her lover, whom we didn't know, had been killed, in a motor accident, they say. Dinka never talked about it. Perhaps a certain dryness about her, the absence of an external sheen, or whatever, was a result of her effort to keep her emotions under control.

She lived in a long-drawn-out relationship with a married man with fine lines and a shiny, round head who brought Dinka a bouquet of fresh roses every day. That's why we remember him, because of those roses. Dinka meant a lot to him. And to us. She was somehow always ready to give advice, and never asked for any herself. That's why we particularly liked meeting at Dinka's. I expect Nuša and Alma still meet there, there's no reason why they shouldn't.

Dinka knows that times are hard and I believe that she is endeavouring to keep things under control. The university is a comforting institution, literature is a comforting occupation. I believe that she notices things, but says nothing. Every day someone removes the name plate of the colleague in the room next to hers. The colleague, with a Serbian name, goes into her room and tells the same story, it's driving him mad, come, see for yourself . . . There's no need. Of course she sees, but she says nothing. She thinks, such are the times, hard, her colleague will survive, his is only a minor misfortune. It's wartime, hundreds of Croatian soldiers are dying from Serbian shells . . . And then she wonders how it would feel if someone kept removing the label with her name and surname from her door . . . And then she tries to think about something else.

Doti, The Knight of Swords

I think that Doti was the only one of us who experienced her life like a story woven for her by destiny with a capital D. The truth, at least as far as our own lives are concerned, is evidently not contained in the facts but in the image we have of ourselves, in the power of our conviction. And on that territory Doti was invincible.

Doti was born in a small place in Slavonia. They say that immediately after the war, the Second World War, her father was killed with pitchforks by furious local people. Her father had fought on the wrong side. Doti had completely eliminated her father from her biography, at least that's how it seemed.

As a little girl Doti fell in love with a handsome, dark-eyed boy, who became and remained her only love. Their family stories were symmetrical too, they say. The boy's father had also been swallowed up by darkness after the war, somewhere in Germany, they say.

In the seventies Doti came to Zagreb with her husband to study philosophy and literature. Doti's defiant Adonis signed something which he shouldn't have done in those days or said something out loud which he shouldn't have said and left the country. Doti followed him and became a political exile. She studied abroad, washed bottles in a factory for a pittance, wrote bitter-sweet patriotic poems and secretly enjoyed the narrative line which Destiny had chosen for her. And while her acquaintances in Zagreb lived their grey 'communist' lives, she passionately loved her husband and above all her beautiful, sad *émigré* story.

Doti gladly identified with the dark media stars of those times, anarchists, terrorists, and all kinds of modern martyrs of state systems. She liked to see herself as a kind of Ulrike Meinhof. As Doti's aesthetic taste tended to change violently, at a given moment she exchanged Ulrike for *Bonnie and Clyde*, a popular film at the time about a pair of American bank robbers. In Doti's film Doti and her Clyde did not rob banks but destroyed the federal socialist republic of Yugoslavia and in the end died, riddled with Yugoslav police bullets with the name of the independent state of Croatia on their lips.

Apart from the touching naivety of Doti's imagination, there is one truly inexplicably naive moment in her biography. Namely, after three years in exile she voluntarily took the bait and returned to Zagreb to receive a prize awarded her by a 'communist' literary jury, for her book of poems. She received the prize but, as soon as they crossed the border, the Yugoslav police confiscated the young couple's passports.

And that was the beginning of the second chapter of Doti's life story, martyrdom.

Doti really did have something of the aura of a political martyr, but this image, attractive at that time, was spoiled by her vitality. And life itself, the joker, gradually devalued the tragic aura of her situation. Doti got a job at the university, bought a flat, gave birth to a fine healthy daughter. Even her husband, Clyde, found a job as a teacher in a secondary school. This last was Doti's strongest proof of communist repression. Doti considered this job in a secondary school a degradation of her husband's great intellectual abilities. It is true that her husband was arrested from time to time, usually when Tito visited Zagreb, but as soon as he left, the police could find no other reason to go on holding their defiant prisoner. Although she would never have admitted it, Doti was a little disappointed by the underhand way the police denied him the right to tragic heroism. We sympathised with Doti, we even envied her a little. We did have passports, but we didn't have a Destiny.

Doti's physical appearance reminded one of the chance fruit of an encounter between a provincial 'auntie' and Attila, divine scourge. Namely, when you first saw Doti you didn't know whether she was about to pick up her needles and calmly knit a pullover or leap on to a horse and subjugate half of some continent. That impression was created less by her Asiatic face than by her hair. It was as though she had forgotten to have her sixties' hair cut. It was long, black hair which she would wave about like a whip and blow off her face like a young girl.

Doti's face was exciting in a special way. It gave the impression of an inner effort, as though she had arranged her face into a permanent expression of kindly apology, like a hotel receptionist, or something. Doti always adopted the same expression and only occasionally would an unintended one escape her control. At such moments Doti would blush without reason, as though she had been caught lying, and quickly pulled the other one on again, like a uniform.

We were able to confirm the fact that Doti had a certain appeal, during a conference at Opatija. We saw a tourist group of Chinese or Korean businessmen set off after her, as though under a spell. Later she told us that these Chinese or Koreans had spent the whole night lurking around the door of her hotel room.

Doti experienced literature as a repertoire of ideas, she was interested in linguistic juxtapositions and literary utopias. She made up for a lack of wide reading through her capacity to speculate.

It is possible that Doti expressed her true nature in a crazy mania for writing letters. She would often leave us letters or written messages, although we all had telephones and although we had all met that day and had a long chat, and although we would meet and have a long chat the following day as well. In these notes she would usually be apologising for something she had said in the course of the conversation, but which she hadn't meant. Her letters were quite incomprehensible, we had no idea what Doti meant and what her epistolary footnotes referred to. There were brighter moments in this mania, however. She would write letters to factories, if she had bought something she wasn't satisfied with, she would immediately write and complain. Unaccustomed to letters from customers, the socialist factories would immediately send Doti substitutes. Thanks to her epistolary passion, Doti reduced her electricity, gas and telephone bills. I believe that the exasperated companies simply threw up their hands and gave in. Of course, Doti corresponded with the authorities asking for passports for herself and her husband. It was only they, the authorities, who remained unmoved by Doti's postal exhibitionism.

I like to think that the third chapter of Doti's life story began with the appearance of Alfred, our nocturnal visitor. It is true that his visit coincided with Doti's discovery of the informer. That is, Doti had discovered that there had been an informer in the house for years. He was her next-door neighbour, a plumber by trade; it was a wholly unexciting tale.

'Spying swine!' said Doti and a hitherto unknown spark appeared in her eyes, announcing the beginning of that new chapter. We were a little confused as to why, with so many really important things going on at the time, she should have got so worked up over an informer, a former one at that, but we put it down to her long-drawn-out police trauma.

And Doti was able to discover the name of her spy because the party which took over power, replacing the previous, communist, authorities, inherited, incidentally, their police files and generously distributed them among their members. And in the meantime Doti's husband had become a member of the party in power, indeed its loyal supporter, propagandist and functionary. Doti herself supported the party wholeheartedly. The party, as the local media confirmed day in and day out, had realised the thousand-year dream of all Croats. Doti's dream too. The only thing that was confusing was that instead of finally calming down because her dream had come true, a previously unknown ferocity became rooted in her.

Ah, Doti . . . Later everything developed at a terribly fast pace, or at least that's how it seemed to us, and now it's hard to follow at all . . . After the episode with the informer Doti reached for a book from her shelves at home and found, just behind Spengler and Kant, two grenades and a revolver. On that occasion we learned—because Doti told us everything— that the generous party in power had given its members not only the names of informers but also weapons. The spirits of their fathers had come to claim their due, just as Alfred, our unusual nocturnal visitor, had announced. At the time, I have to say, I was still more inclined to connect Alfred's messages, which I barely remembered myself, with a longer-term loan which the members of the ruling party received in the form of thirty thousand German marks. 'At last I shall be able to use that money to buy a decent family tomb,' Doti said . . .

Yes, Doti would change. She would come to life, a righteous fire would settle in her, she would not forgive easily, not even the right to a little doubt. People would say that during those months she assiduously assembled secret files on faculty employees, putting little plus or minus signs beside their names. I can only imagine, because I am not in a position to know these things, that plus meant Croat and loyal, minus *non-Croat* and *disloyal,* and two minuses *Serb* and *fifth-columnist.* She did it in defence of the thousand-year dream of all the Croats, in defence of an independent Croatia, in the name of an idea for which she had secretly prepared and suffered all her life. Somewhere over her shoulder peered the shadow of her father, the one who fifty years earlier had wandered onto the wrong side. Yes, Doti would pay back her father's cruel murder, her childhood spent without him, the trick with the passport, the countries to which she had never been, while we all had, she would pay them back for her husband and herself, all the while not abandoning her belief in great and just destiny, the one with the big D.

Ah, Doti . . . She started conspicuously using the pronoun 'we' . . . She exchanged her deep hatred of Yugoslavia and Tito for love of his replica, Tito's general and imitator, the President of the new Croatian state. A merciful amnesia did not let her make the connection. Somewhat later she would see Croatian soldiers off to the front with a smile and her fingers raised in the victory-sign and would hate more fiercely than others that other *barbaric, aggressive, bloodthirsty, Orthodox, Serbo-Bolshevik* side. She would continue to write letters, on her own initiative, this time to many foreign politicians and public figures, she would seek audiences, sometimes she would succeed . . .

Ah, Doti . . . I think that this third chapter was a definitive defence of her own biography. I was to see her, during a short visit to Zagreb, on television. 'I am glad that our victory was clean,' she said into the camera, commenting on one of a series of 'great Croatian victories'. I noticed that she had had her hair cut, she was dressed in a suit, a somewhat too massive gold cross glinted round her neck with a righteous gleam. At one moment a poor television picture, or perhaps just my imagination, produced a hologram effect, and I was suddenly struck by Doti's discordance, her duality . . . For a moment I couldn't decide whether Doti reminded me of a transvestite or an avenging angel.

During that brief visit to Zagreb I learned again of things I already knew: of the forced eviction of hundreds of people from their homes, of the arbitrary rule and police terror of the authorities, those that had finally made the 'thousand-year' dream of their citizens come true, of mass sackings, of greed, insatiability, crime and war profiteering, I learned of houses and villages burned and their inhabitants turned out by force . . . I learned also some details which I did not know before. I learned, for instance, that during those years some thousand people had committed suicide, mostly Croatian soldiers, those who had ensured the 'clean victory', and pensioners, who would perhaps have carried on living but they had nothing to live on . . .

I learned also, of course, of Doti's newly achieved honours. Doti had joined the right side, because she could not possibly have joined the wrong one, and quite naturally became the point of reference of cultural-political life (it wasn't possible to separate the two), a member of this and that, editor of this and that . . . The staunch Doti would take up, in addition to her own, her husband's banner, when at a given moment he stumbled and dropped it. That is, the new authorities had sent Doti's husband, as a diplomat, to the same country where his father had been swallowed by darkness fifty years before. His father's spirit settled in him as Doti's had in her. He began to drink, to sniff around like a well-trained police dog, and in the end, they say, everyone got fed up with him, he was replaced, sent back, they were afraid he might one day start giving them trouble. Yes, Doti defended their shared biography.

Sometimes I feel that Doti's true nature could be read from all those prolific letters she wrote in the course of her life, apologising for this and that, asking for this and that . . . There is an anecdote that in the hard Soviet times some hard-up Russian kept having the same nightmare dream, that Stalin summoned him to a meeting at seven o'clock in the morning, and he didn't wake up until eight and then tried frantically to find an excuse for his lateness. Now it seems to me that the permanently apologetic expression on Doti's face, Doti's crazy mania for writing letters to all and sundry, and even Doti's involvement in literature, was all a kind of indirect excuse for being an hour late. What and whom she was afraid of I shall never know.

I learned, however, that in the secret faculty accounts of loyalty to the new Croatian state I was given a minus, perhaps even two. Doti's minuses. It was Doti, I believe, who had liked me best.

I was to think of Doti one day in Berlin. News about her reached me in a letter from friends, out of the letter slid a newspaper interview with a large photograph of Doti. In the interview Doti spoke of her new book, something about literature as destiny or perhaps the other way round, then she accused Western postmodernism of amorality, demanding a restoration of moral principles into the nation's life and culture—she used the firmly adopted pronoun 'we'. 'We are creating a new, moral postmodernity. That is the priority and responsibility of our intellectuals,' she said and then she mentioned me, indeed my name was printed in large letters in the title of the interview. Doti accused me of amorality, that postmodern kind, and ended her interview with an ambiguous statement. 'The Berlin Wall has been destroyed, but a new one has been built, in our hearts,' she said. Knowing Doti, I sense that the message about the Berlin Wall was actually meant for me. Covering herself first with her holy 'we', Doti was executing me, publicly this time.

I was surprised by her face in the newspaper photograph. It was somehow smooth and calm. She had evidently put on weight, there were the little suit and the cross and the silk blouse, but everything seemed finally to have settled into place. Her expression and her face at last coincided, yes, Doti had at last connected with herself. As I looked at her newspaper portrait, I almost envied her. It was the face of someone who no longer had nightmare dreams. Instead of that poor Russian who kept dreaming he was late for a meeting with Stalin, Doti reminded one more of Stalin dreaming about the person who was late.

Ivana, The Empress

That evening, when she went home and swallowed the feather, Ivana may not have known that, according to many ancient beliefs, women who swallow a fly or a moth become pregnant. In the Balkans there is a moth known as a 'witch'. According to popular belief, a woman touched by a 'witch' will conceive. What happens with feathers I don't know, but exactly nine months after that evening, at the age of thirty-eight, Ivana gave birth to a son.

Some ten years earlier, Ivana, from Belgrade, met a man from Zagreb, fell in love with him, left her job in a literary institute and a half-finished doctoral thesis, her parents and friends, and moved to Zagreb.

Ivana had a large heart. With Ivana everyday life, every outing to the cinema, shopping, every little trip to a café seemed like a celebration. She had that rare talent. She devoured books, she had an acute literary taste, she was an excellent chess player, she learned languages easily, she was eloquent, she mastered the computer in a flash, she even learned to drive in a matter of days when it became necessary, although she had always been a little afraid of cars.

At a given moment she wanted children. The first time she spent four months lying down and miscarried, the second time she made it to five months and then miscarried. Her pregnancies were like a kind of girl's camp. Ivana would lie with her feet up on the sofa in the living room, with heaps of books scattered around her, I would have to keep going to the kitchen and bringing things to eat according to Ivana's instructions; we ate, spread crumbs everywhere, laughed, often without real reason, chatted for hours on end, about this and that . . . With each of Ivana's pregnancies I myself put on several pounds. During those months—because of her hopes or her hormones, or both—the air around Ivana was light, intoxicating and keen, like champagne. And Ivana herself fizzed and overflowed like champagne . . .

Finally Ivana gave birth to an exceptionally beautiful little boy. Life seemed intoxicating and bright even when she came out of the house to find her car (with a Belgrade number plate) covered with spit, even when she found anonymous messages in her postbox . . . 'Serbian whore. Go home!'

Ivana changed her Belgrade number plate for a Zagreb one. Life seemed bright even when she went to Belgrade and found her car covered with spit, even when she found anonymous messages in her postbox . . . 'Croatian whore. Go home!'

Ivana left Zagreb and went to Belgrade with her child at the beginning of September 1991 when the inhabitants of Zagreb moved into their cellars and shelters for fear of possible bombing. Soon all links between

213

Zagreb and Belgrade, four hundred kilometres apart, were severed. Ivana called her husband via Sarajevo. At that time people were getting the better of the system, they learned the right number to call to be able to go on phoning one another. Ivana's husband began disappearing more and more frequently for a few days at a time, not telling anyone where he was going. He travelled by interminable, smelly buses through Hungary to Belgrade. Ivana travelled by those same sad, half-secret buses, with her child, from Belgrade to Zagreb. The buses, where the drivers set the timetable and the fare, were full of unhappy people dragging their modest belongings, travelling like lost souls, not really knowing where they were going. At the border posts, the Serbian and Croatian ones, border officials with grim faces humiliated the passengers, at the Hungarian frontier the Hungarian officials stamped their passports compassionately . . .

For some time Ivana had not been afraid of anything. The only thing she feared was that her son might have an attack of panic-stricken terror, in the bus, in front of other people. She was afraid she might not have the strength to restrain his frantic little body. However, as though he sensed her fears, the little boy calmly closed his eyes, shutting out the outside world like too bright a light. Or he put his hands over his ears if the noise of that world was too harsh.

Ivana was not afraid of anything else. She accepted humiliation, she crossed frontiers, came and went, reconciled quarrelling worlds, towns and people, placing bandages on other people's wounds. She passed through hatred easily, as through water . . . They said there was something wrong with the child. Coming into the world at a time when people were destroying everything in front of them—towns, people, memory—the little boy remembered everything, in his own way admittedly. It was as though the world was for him a long, disconnected, meaningless, catalogue of numbers, letters, signs and words, which was after all perhaps what it was . . . Coming into the world at a time when his mother tongue, the one he was just about to learn, had been forcibly divided into three, the child speedily mastered all three variants with indifference, in his own way admittedly. Nevertheless the words he pronounced most clearly were in a language that was not his own, if he had one that was his own—he spoke them in English, a language Ivana taught him in play. At a time when the word 'identity' resounded everywhere like the holy word of God, and people were killing one another with divine ease in its name, the little boy steadfastly refused to learn the pronoun 'I'. He experienced him-self—if that was what was going on—in the third person, pronouncing his name only when he wanted . . .

It is not that there was something wrong with the boy. There was something wrong with the world, and that is why, from the moment he was born, the boy wanted persistently to get off. Ivana knew that it was not possible to get off the globe and so she did her best to put it right, she smoothed its rough edges, warmed the world with her own breath, adorned it like an angel's nest, tried to persuade her son to be born again. That must be why she has been laughing a special laugh for some time now, driving away evil spirits maybe . . . It is true that she sometimes breaks down, and then she runs into the bathroom and turns on all the taps. The water drowns out her sobs.

Ivana does not remember what it has been left to me to remember. Otherwise, I believe she would make the connection. Her son sometimes comes up to her, presses his forehead against hers, as though he were ten-derly pressing an imprint on to it, he places his plump little hands on her cheeks, sways his head from left to right. Ivana copies the rhythm, quite enchanted. Their foreheads joined, their eyes closed, they sway. From the outside they seem to be performing an other-worldly dance. The child ten-derly mumbles, in a voice at times guttural, almost like a bird's, at times unnaturally deep . . .

'Mmma-ma, ma-ma . . .'

And then he lets go of her face, moves his forehead away and goes off into his corner, occupied with something else. Then Ivana rushes into the bathroom and turns on all the taps.

Me, The Fool

What about me? It seems that the whole story is shaped by one detail which I am revealing at the end. That is, the angel left me out and omitted to give me a feather, intentionally or by chance, who knows. Be that as it may, the angel bequeathed them a feather and complete oblivion, but to me he gave tattered remembrance. It was as though he did not know that it ought to have been the other way round. He should have left them the memory, and me a feather and complete oblivion. Oblivion from which one day—stretching up on tiptoe to recall—I would be able to begin to invent reality. Because the invention of reality is the job of real literature.

Yes, it was not just my film that was wiped out by Alfred's angelic flash of light, it was also their memory. The girls would remember absolutely nothing. It was only with Nina that I was able, one night, much later, to talk about it.

'Hm, I don't know what to say, you know yourself that I'm an expert on evil demonic forces,' said Nina, an expert on Bulgakov, lying tipsy in her bath, warmed by her sleeping bag and her cat Behemot.

Perhaps that is how it was, and perhaps it was different. Perhaps invisible, incorporeal and anonymous angels long to leave an imprint and reflection, to have someone describe them. If that's how it is, then our Alfred certainly could not have counted on appearing to a Gabriel García Márquez. He had appeared to me. And something else: the phrase 'behind God's back' or 'where God said goodnight' is used to describe places forgotten by God. The first assumption is that He would not send angels or at least not angels of substance to places where He had decided to say 'goodnight'.

Perhaps that is how it was, and perhaps it was different, who can tell . . . Angels were invented by grown-up people, to make life more bearable. Writers are grown-up people, who like inventing things. That's why I gave them an angel. A little something to make life more bearable . . . And I know it has turned out feeble, but . . . an angel's only as good as his writer. Still, just in case, I have left each of them a little feather so that real angels can find them in that terrible 'divine darkness'.

Yes, the world has grown dark, and they themselves seem to have grown dark. Bit by bit they are being swallowed by their rooms, their heads droop like house plants, they are quieter, more preoccupied, sadder, less resistant, they absorb the smoke of time as the window curtains do, they grow into their house, furniture, family memories, they are woken increasingly often at night by an uncomfortable foreboding, they have let themselves go, with the years the force of gravity has become increasingly weighty, so they try to slide along without too much resistance, life must go on, the world is not pleasant, but they try to forget that, and increasingly often they succeed, yes, they are quieter, they are quietening down, new people are coming, louder ones, emerging from nineteenth-century lumber-rooms, young commissars at the end of the twentieth century, sometimes they wonder whether they are not in fact in a time machine which is going backwards, only they have failed to notice it, besides, who can tell any longer what is backwards and what forwards, these times too will pass, as everything will pass, and perhaps they will meet again, in some new time, which they will recognise as a time which was once and now is and will not be again, yes, the worlds have divided, and only one thing is true, and that is that no one is the same any more . . .

No one is the same any more, I myself have changed. I am quieter, sadder, more preoccupied, less resistant. My life has changed: I live in other cities and other countries, there are other people around me. Even my climatic preferences have changed. From the moment when Alfred fell from the sky and returned there just as speedily, I, uprooted daughter of the Adriatic sea, have developed a passion for snow.

When it snows I go outside and gaze enchanted at the sky. I seem to attract snowflakes like a magnet, I drink in the snowy moisture like merciful oblivion. I feel my body—the one bequeathed me by the power-hungry genes of my full-breasted foremothers—becoming lighter. And, suddenly, I wave my arms energetically and see the glass dome above me misting over . . . Feathers fall over me, a white feathery snowstorm enfolds me, envelops me . . .

PART SEVEN

Wo bin ich?

86. 'Berlin is hard to describe,' wrote Viktor Shklovsky long ago.

'That's because in Berlin there's more of what there's not than what there is,' says Bojana.

'That's because Berlin is a non-place,' says Richard.

87. Berlin is a museum-city. In Berlin buses you can see the oldest and wiriest old ladies in the world. They don't die because they have already died once.

'All of us here are museum exhibits . . .' says Zoran.

88. Berlin is an archaeological find. Layers of time pile one over the other, the scars heal with difficulty, the seams are visible. It's as though some invisible, confused archaeologist had been leaving the wrong labels everywhere: it is often hard to say what came first, and what later.

'That's because Berlin is a before-and-after place,' says Richard.

89. Berlin is a city of museums. There are many museums in Berlin: the Sugar Museum, the Hairstyle Museum, the Toy Bear Museum and the Museum of Unconditional Surrender. Or, more accurately: *Muzey istorii bezogovorochnoy kapitulatsii fashistskoy Germanii v voyne 1941–1945*. The museum with perhaps the longest name in the world is in Karlshorst, in the building where German capitulation was signed during the night between 8 and 9 May 1945.

That is the part of Berlin where the former Soviet barracks and living quarters for the former Soviet soldiers are. It's all former, but there are still people living there. Some thirty thousand, they say. Through broken windows one can see that many flats have already been abandoned, with strips of wallpaper peeling off the walls like lichen. In front of the blocks of flats are huge rusty containers. They say that these containers hold the possessions of the Russian soldiers which they will take with them when they go home. Furniture, television sets, fridges. At night thieves rob the containers.

At the entrance, beside the little guardhouse, stands a soldier, a child, scarcely eighteen years old. He wears a fur hat which is too big for him, he smokes, smiles broadly, displaying yellowed teeth. He's from Moldavia, he says. He's only been here for eight months. He's going home in August. The soldier smokes, he doesn't know what to do with his hands, a museum exhibit. A former soldier guards a former barracks.

Thieves, small-time ones, rob containers at night. The big-time ones are penetrating previously impenetrable parts of the city. They say that Kantstrasse is in the hands of the Russian mafia.

90. It's quiet in the museum, there are no visitors. Through the half-open door of the museum office an old lady can be seen. She is sitting on a chair, her arms hugging her own stomach like a cushion, asleep.

In the museum forecourt there is an enormous sculpture of Lenin. The musty exhibition rooms contain three thousand documents: maps, photographs, flags, pictures, sketches of battles, posters, a large, dusty model of Berlin with the street names written in Russian . . . From the walls Cyrillic slogans threaten: 'The Motherland summons you!'; 'The military commissar is the father and soul of his unit'; 'Contempt of death must be spread among the masses and victory thus assured.'

The old woman has woken up. She stands in the corner, smoothing her hair with her hand, watching me with sleepy eyes. The museum is the property of the former Soviet Union. What will they do with the museum? I wonder. Put it in a container, and take it home.

91. In the Berlin flea-markets, people, a museum race, sell things which have gone out of use. Turks, Poles, Russians, Gypsies, former American soldiers, ex-Yugoslavs offer moth-eaten rabbit fur, old medals, steam-irons, iron weighing-scales with lead weights, ancient radios, gramophone records . . .

A man with a blue military helmet, my countryman, sells cassettes. Beside him on a wooden chair is a cassette player. Folk songs whine, the sounds circle round the seller like dying flies and expire.

92. In some places the Wall still stands, thin and dry as Jewish matzos. Here and there, as in the courtyard of the Europe-Center, the piece of wall has been put under museum glass. Visitors to the shopping centre stop in

front of the glass-covered piece with interest, as though they were seeing it for the first time.

93. With our feet on the empty seats in front of us, Richard and I sit under the cupola of the planetarium on Prenzlauer Allee. Starry rain falls over us from the sky. And as the artificial stars fall on us, I say: 'Everything's muddled up, Richard . . . I write about one thing in order to write about something else, just as I recall something that never happened in order to remember what did happen. It's all somehow going in the wrong direction . . .'

'Just keep going. This is Berlin, the wrong direction is the right direction here,' Richard consoles me.

94. By the Brandenburg Gate one can buy souvenirs of the age: a little piece of Wall in a plastic box, hammers and sickles, red stars, old Soviet medals. This small-scale trade is no longer carried out by Russian *émigrés* but by Pakistanis. Pakistanis selling souvenirs at the place where the Wall stood until a short time ago are the metaphoric heart of the end of an epoch.

A left-over Russian offers me little busts of Lenin.

He winks at me, saying: 'Come on, buy a Daddy . . .'

95. 'We are the children of Bouvard and Pécuchet, that's why we're over-loaded with facts, so pointless, just occasionally cheerful . . .' says a colleague.

96. The sky over Berlin cannot be described. Sometimes it seems that the city—wrapped in a dark-blue sky held up by a golden girl with wings—is imitating the aesthetic of the glass ball. Sometimes I have the impression that I am walking upside down, in a glass ball turned on its head. Berlin grows in the clouds. I sense this by the reflections which flash in window panes, on the surface of water, in someone's eye. Drawn by the golden goddess, like insects drawn by street lights, Berlin is being built by confused angels, from the top down.

97. There is a café in the basement of the Museum of Unconditional Surrender. In the café are a counter, some tables and chairs. On the counter

is a television set and behind it a willowy blonde waitress, Russian. On a small table are Russian souvenirs: *matryoshkas,* a samovar, wooden spoons, a white goat-hair shawl.

'They're cheaper here than in Moscow,' explains the charming waitress in Russian.

The café is visited by my countrymen, Yugoslav refugees living in the surrounding buildings. You can get coffee brewed in Georgian *džezvas,* exactly like 'our', 'Turkish' coffee. Russian advertisements rotate on the television: for Moscow fitness centres, for English language lessons . . . An elderly Bela Akhmadulina, a Russian poet, appears on the screen to advertise a set of English-language cassettes. Bela has the unambiguous stamp of capitulation on her face.

Black-haired, drained, with dark, sunken faces, my countrymen play chess and cards.

'They come every day and stay for hours . . .' the waitress sighs compassionately.

98. Jochen Gerz, a German artist, secretly constructed an unusual monument with a group of students over a period of three years. Having discovered that 2146 Jewish graves in Germany had been destroyed, Gerz and the students stole paving stones from the main square in Saarbrücken. Gerz and the students inscribed the name and number of a vanished Jewish grave on the bottom of each stone, and then put them back in their place. The main square in Saarbrücken acquired a new name: The Square of the Invisible Monument.

99. The Museum of Unconditional Surrender was closed in the summer of 1994, when several tens of thousands of left-over Russian soldiers left Berlin. A little later an exhibition of 'Russians in Berlin' was opened at 75 Prenzlauer Allee. In the little basement room an invisible projector showed slides of Berlin buildings before and after the arrival of the Russians. At the entrance to the room hung long accusing strips of paper. The paper strips listed the names of all the Berlin streets destroyed by the Russians. What I remembered from the Museum of Unconditional Surrender was a heavy, stale, sweetish smell. The smell here was identical.

100. Katarina Kolin was born in 1922 in the Yugoslav village of Srpski Miletići into a family of poor German *volksdeutscher*. In 1939 she travelled to Germany and found a job in a munitions factory in the town of Dudenstadt. There she met a worker named Fikret Murić. Katarina and Fikret fell in love. Since at that time their relationship was 'racially' unacceptable, Fikret was gaoled by the local authorities and Katarina was sent back to Yugoslavia. Katarina returned to her home town, but she soon ran away. She went back to Fikret. Soon afterwards, she gave birth to a daughter, Ajša.

At the end of the war, Fikret and Katarina set off with their child to Bosnia. As Katarina was German and Fikret had 'worked for the occupier', they ended up instead in a camp for Germans in Zemun. By a whim of fortune they managed to get out and in November 1945 they reached the Bosnian town of Brčko. Katarina learned the language. The locals called her 'Katica Švabica' (Katie the Jerry). She worked at all the hardest jobs. She gave birth to two more children. Fearing at a certain moment that, when the time came, she would be buried apart from Fikret, she converted to Islam and became Fatima Murić.

Now Katarina is back in Germany for the third time. She lives with her Fikret in a refugee *heim* in East Berlin. Her daughter Ajša lives in Belgrade, one son is in Canada, the other in Munich. Katarina Kolin, Fatima Murić or Katica Švabica has only one wish: to return to her Brčko.

I heard the story of Katica Švabica, just as it is reported here, from Kašmir R.

101. Kašmir R. is a young man from Brčko, a law graduate and a refugee. Kašmir's father was recently murdered by Chetniks. Kašmir's girlfriend Nermina hanged herself in the psychiatric wing of a German hospital on the day before she was to be discharged. Kašmir lives in the refugee *heim* with his mother.

Kašmir spends his time in the streets of Berlin, mostly in Kreuzberg. In the small, aromatic Turkish shops, he feels closer to Brčko. On Saturdays and Sundays Kašmir visits the Berlin flea-markets. There he meets 'our folk'.

Kašmir's mother likes the flea-markets too. She crochets a few little mats, and on Sundays takes a chair to Fehrbelliner Platz. There she pretends to sell, but in fact she is on the lookout to meet 'our folk'.

Sometimes she takes people back to her little refugee room, makes them coffee, bakes Bosnian pies, asks them where they're from and how they are getting on.

Kašmir's mother was arrested for selling her little mats without a licence. Kašmir paid the fine. He was not able to explain to the German police that his mother went to the flea-market in order to meet up with her 'own people', to talk, to make herself feel better, and not in order to sell anything.

'She's at it again . . . crocheting . . .' says Kašmir.

102. In Berlin everyone is lonely and no one has any time.

Sissel calls.

'Do you have some time?' she asks.

'No, I don't,' I say.

'What are you doing?' she asks.

'I'm writing down other people's biographies, and then I stick the little pieces of paper with the biographies on to pebbles . . .'

'What do you stick them with?' the artist asks me.

'With glue.'

'Hmm . . . Interesting project,' she says.

'It's not a project.'

'What is it then?'

'I don't know . . .'

103. At the exhibition 'The Art of Memory', one of the exhibits is a project by the artist Horst Hoheisel, entitled *Denk-Stein-Sammlung* which was made by children in Kassel. Each of the children was asked to research the biography of one Jew who perished in a concentration camp. Then the children wrote out their short biographies on pieces of paper. They would fold the papers, stick them on to pebbles with glue or wrap them round the pebbles. Then the 'memory stones' were placed in little railway trucks, models of the ones in which the Jews were taken away to the concentration camps.

104. On the corner of my street is the Dresdener Bank, a bus-stop and a block of flats. As I wait for the bus, I amuse myself by reading the names of the tenants listed at the entrance. None of them is German, they are all

'our folk'. Bećirević, Hadjiselimović, Karabeg, Demirović . . . I often read these names to myself, learning them by heart, for no reason whatever.

On the corner, leaning against the wall of the Dresdener Bank, an old Bosnian man squats in his slippers, smoking. He blows little smoke rings out into the Berlin air.

105. In Wedding, beside an enormous building site which you have to skirt, in a place which is almost impossible to find, is the Berlin office for asylum-seekers, exiles, *émigrés,* various kinds of applicants for German residence permits. They gather early in the morning and wait in line. The office does not open until 7 a.m., but they arrive long before that. When the door opens, one by one the applicants are given green numbers. With these numbers they hurry off down the long corridor looking for the waiting room designated by their number.

The floors of the waiting rooms are covered in grey linoleum, the walls are painted a yellowish colour. The walls are bare, apart from red signs proclaiming *Rauchen verboten.* Plastic seats, as in a cinema, face a door above which is a display panel showing a succession of numbers. The applicants compare their numbers with the ones on the display panel and enter when their turn comes. In the room behind a glass screen sits an official. He takes the applicant's passport. Then he gets up and disappears among numerous shelves on which there are files. Having looked through the file, he hands the applicant a number. The applicant goes back to the waiting room and waits for his number to appear on the display panel.

The appearance of the number is accompanied by a gong. Gongs sound from all the waiting rooms, it is all reminiscent of a deserted provincial airport. If it should happen that the waiting rooms are empty, the applicant will see plastic seats leaning against the wall and then on the wall, above each seat, the imprint of a head, like a halo ringed by a circle of yellowish dirt. Under the neon light, with the dark Berlin morning sky in the windows, with their cold grey linoleum and their gongs, the empty rooms with their imprints of heads on the yellow-painted walls seem deathly and terrifying.

106. A refugee from Zenica, who now lives in Berlin, left his flat in a hurry with a few essential items. When he reached the street, he remembered that he should have taken some family photographs with him. He

went back, but the door was already bolted, and some other people were in the flat.

'I'd just like my photographs . . .' he said.

'We live here now,' said the people from inside, without opening the door.

107. 'There are two categories of refugees: those who have photographs and those who have none,' said a Bosnian, a refugee.

108. 'Waking up in the morning in a train that has stopped, facing the sea which you can sense; the polished cobbles on Dusan's Bridge in Skopje, where as a five-year-old I first noticed that I had a shadow; skiing with my father on Jahorina outside Sarajevo; a May night on the north Dalmatian island of Silba with its abundant Mediterranean plants; a boy killing fish with stones in lake Prespa in Macedonia; a three-day lightning adolescent love-affair in Vrsar; military service in Rijeka, in Trsat; a little railway station on the Zagreb—Belgrade line whose name I have forgotten, with a waiting room out of Menzel's film *Closely Observed Trains* (the solitude there was as thick as oil); school trips to the waterfalls on the river Krka in Hercegovina; a muddy stream in the suburbs of Zenica in Bosnia, beside which I walked to a school named after 'The Dietrich Sisters', with my shoelaces undone, because I didn't yet know how to tie them; a heap of cockroaches in a hotel room in the Slavonian town of Osijek and sleeping with the light on; Džiajić's goal against England at the European football championship in Italy in 1968; travelling by the narrow-gauge railway from Sarajevo to Nikšić in Montenegro; the reception for Djurdja Bjedov on the quay in Split after she won the gold medal in Mexico; the early concerts of the Bosnian group Bijelo Dugme in a New Belgrade sports hall; the source of the Una river; singing the national anthem before inter-republican matches (a choir of a hundred thousand people); the abandoned synagogue in Subotica; every shot of the basketball star Kresimir Ćosić; drowning in the Vardar (four years old, my first brush with death); an avenue of trees as dark as a tunnel, in Pula, and a summer shower over that avenue; the feet of the statue of Grgur of Nin; the silence and shadowy emptiness of the streets of Ohrid in the heat of an August day; an electric shock as a child, peeing by the gutter of a deserted house in a village near Nikšić; waiting as a pioneer to greet the President on his

return from Asian and African non-aligned countries; the first Czech-made *Jolan* electric bass-guitar; sleeping in a tent in the Karst mountains of Hercegovina and travelling slowly from Mostar, down the Neretva valley, to Dubrovnik; news of the earthquake in Skopje; the check shirt I received as aid from Mexico (or was it Venezuela?); a tramp on lake Matko singing to a squeaking oriental instrument: "What'll we have for our teas: potatoes, bread and some cheese . . . " '

'Those are all cold, melancholy, objective images (or more precisely: verbal photographs) from a past life in a former country which it will never again be possible to connect into a whole,' writes Mihajlo P. in a letter.

109. 'I'm more and more convinced that we are all museum exhibits . . .' says Zoran.

110. The Berlin flea-markets resemble the slit stomach of Roland the walrus who swallowed too many indigestible objects. The Berlin flea-markets resemble the Teufelberg with its long-hidden contents spilling out. The Berlin flea-markets are open museums of everyday life, past and present. In Berlin flea-markets times and ideologies are reconciled, swastikas mix with red stars, everything can be bought for a few marks. In the Berlin flea-markets surviving uniforms with different insignia are heaped together harmoniously, their owners long since dead. They rub together, and their only enemies are moths.

In Berlin flea-markets east trades with west, north with south, Pakistanis, Turks, Poles, Gypsies, ex-Yugoslavs, Germans, Russians, Vietnamese, Kurds, Ukrainians all sell souvenirs of a vanished daily life at the flea-market, that rubbish heap of time. There one can buy things which nobody needs: other people's family albums, a watch that doesn't work, a broken flower vase . . . A modern commercial invention, 'kinder-eggs', chocolate eggs with a smaller, plastic egg inside, and in it the tiny parts of little plastic models which have to be put together—those collections of little plastic models fetch a very high price.

111. At the Berlin flea-markets one can buy a photograph album for a mark or two. The albums lie in heaps. Some of them have photographs spilling out of them, some are worn, some empty, some quite new. I come

across an album belonging to a lonely, elderly woman who used to go on modest journeys and who evidently liked having her photograph taken as a memento. I look at a photograph of a large, ageing woman with the Eiffel Tower behind her. Under the photograph she has written in a neat hand: 'Me in front of the amazing Eiffel Tower, that symbol of beautiful Paris, 21 april 1993.'

That's the last photograph in the album.

112. Christian Marclay lined a whole exhibition hall with photographs of the same size. The photographs were pinned to the wall face down. From their backs one could see that they were old, on some of them the photographer's stamp could be made out, on some a dedication could be read. Rust-coloured patches penetrated the yellowing paper. It looked as though the walls had been colonised by some unusual plant. Just pinned to the wall, a little deformed with age, the photographs breathed a very exciting life.

113. The Turk sits in the cab of his truck surveying his territory: a scattered heap of old books, records, albums, photographs . . . The seller of dead souls sits silently, smoking. When he's asked for a price he holds up his fingers: one, two, three marks . . .

Things last longer than people. Albums outlive their owners. A prolonged life hides in an old coat, in a senseless object which meant something to someone and which will again mean something to someone else. That is how souls migrate.

Here refugees from Bosnia meet. They enquire after souls: who is from where, does anyone know what's become of so and so, where is such and such now . . . They exchange news. They gather according to their towns and villages. Along the way they buy some small thing which will help their little refugee room look like home.

Here, in Gustav-Meyer Allee, on Saturdays and Sundays, the country that is no more, Bosnia, draws its map once again in the air, with its towns, villages, rivers and mountains. The map glimmers briefly and then disappears like a soap bubble.

114. At a Berlin flea-market, I leaf through an album. It had belonged, I presume, to a Bavarian, a German soldier, of an order and rank I couldn't

make out. The photographs show the owner of the album and his wife of modest appearance. Most of the photographs are landscapes. There are a few peaceful photographs of Prague (war tourism), and then a mass of equally peaceful photographs of Bavarian villages. Two seasons dominate the album: summer and winter. Our photographer's approach is often 'artistic'. He particularly likes to take pictures of landscapes through natural frames: a window, an open door, a tunnel. He is unusually attracted to heights, snowy mountain tops bathed in sunlight, views down into valleys and lakes. There are no children, parents, other people, in the photographs. The photographs date from the Second World War and immediately after the war. The album exudes emptiness and a striking absence of life. The owner of the album evidently wanted to see his biography as an aesthetic collage of snowy mountain tops bathed in sunlight.

115. Jane, a black American, who likes Berlin and knows everything there is to know about Europeans, bought some old photographs at a Berlin flea-market, had them tidily framed, hung them on the wall and now explains animatedly . . . 'These are my great-grandmother and great-grandfather, this is my grandfather, this is my grandmother, those are my parents, and these are my aunts . . .'

'There isn't a single black person,' I observe.

'How malicious you are . . .' laughs Jane, shaking her head. With its mass of tiny plaits her hair reminds one of spaghetti.

116. In schizophrenic Berlin there are two cities in constant conflict: one which wants to forget and the other which wants to remember. In Grosse Hamburger Strasse the French artist Christian Boltanski set up an installation which is the trademark of that other Berlin. The installation is called *The Missing House.*

There is a house missing from Grosse Hamburger Strasse, it was destroyed during the Second World War. On the side walls of the neighbouring houses, in the places where the flats had been, Boltanski has fixed name plates with the names and occupations of the former occupants. Most of the former occupants were Jews killed by the Nazis.

Christian Boltanski is one of the greatest archivists, biographers and reconstructors of anonymous human lives at the end of this century. His installations—rows of cardboard boxes roughly tied together with string containing the photographs and souvenirs of anonymous people, these endless archives of ordinary mortals resembling cardboard children's coffins—are in fact nothing other than the Berlin flea-market put in order. So human rubbish recycled into an art exhibit achieves the right to prolonged life, to an ironic eternity.

117. '*Bitte schön*! Jackeee, hosee! Long brieeefs, short brieeefs! *Bitte schön*!' shouts a Gypsy woman in Gustav-Meyer Allee. I stop beside a jumbled heap of clothes. She peers attentively at me.

'Are you one of us . . .?' she asks cautiously.

'Yes, I'm one of us,' I say.

'Where are you from?'

'Zagreb.'

The Gypsy's face broadens into a smile.

'Hey, she's a Croat!' she shouts.

'Where from?' asks a Gypsy man.

'Zagreb . . .'

'Oh, from Zagreb! We used to go there . . . It's all flat round there, do you know where it is?'

'Yes.'

'And whereabouts did you live?'

'In the centre . . .'

'We're from Bosnia, Bjeljina . . . And now we're here . . . Which *heim* are you in?' asks the man.

'Hey, she's one of us . . .' the Gypsy woman calls to a passer-by. He stops.

'Where from?'

'Zagreb.'

'I'm from Zenica . . .' he says.

Quite a large group begins to form. We are all caught up in an unexpected warmth, as though we were at a child's birthday party. We chat, enquire, joyfully repeat the names of towns and villages. They're all Bosnian. I'm the only one from Zagreb. I conceal the fact that I am not a refugee. A light, thick rain falls over us. We smile for no reason, almost lovingly, we gaze into each other's faces, sniff each other, wag our tails joyfully . . . And then we are overcome by sudden sadness, we shift our feet, shrug our shoulders, nod our heads . . .

The Gypsy woman shakes her head and sighs: 'Oh, stupid people . . .! Oh, stupid people . . .!'

118. One corner of the Deutsches Historisches Museum is devoted to things. There, under glass, are Babysan baby food; brightly coloured plastic shopping bags *(Einkaufsbeutel);* a white plastic basket for seasonings; a man's suit made of *rundstrick* material, with a Prasent 20 label, manufactured in 1969; a Narva light bulb; a Komet blender; metal plates with golden numbers which were awarded to the tidiest houses in East Berlin (*Goldener Hausnummer*); souvenirs of Vietnam made out of fragments of American aeroplanes; blue pioneer scarves and caps; plates inscribed *Heute keine Ware*; a child's toy, *Sandmännchen im Helikopter*, made in 1972 according to a popular television series; a faithful model of a typical three-bedroomed flat in a typical DDR apartment-block (with a miniature poster of *Lady and the Tramp* hanging on the children's bedroom wall!).

'I fed Saša on Babysan when he was a baby,' says Mira, moved.

'We had the Tramp at home . . .' says Zoran.

In another corner objects from West Germany in the fifties are displayed. A 'modern' kitchen; posters for Coca-Cola and bubble-gum; a Wurlitzer brand juke-box; a home cocktail-bar; a Volkswagen car; a Phillips television set; a popular children's toy, Mecki-Puppe; a dress with the names of airlines and airports printed on it, a design manufactured in 1951.

'We had the very same kitchen at home,' says Mira.

'We'll never have a museum like this,' says Zoran.

'How could we when the country has disappeared,' says Mira.

'That's why we're all walking museum pieces . . .' says Zoran.

'But if the country has disappeared, then so has collective memory. If the objects that surrounded us have disappeared, then so has memory of the everyday life that we lived. And besides, memory of the former country is tacitly forbidden. And when the ban is one day lifted, everyone will forget . . . There'll be nothing left to remember,' I say.

'Then everyone will remember something that never existed . . .' says Mira.

'I remember everything,' says Zoran.

'What?' I ask.

'Gavrilović meat pâté,' he says.

'I remember as well,' says Mira.

'What?' I ask.

'The first Yugoslav washing powder, Plavi Radion!'

'I remember as well,' I say.

'What?'

'The first Yugoslav television programme, *Studio Uno* with Mike Bongiorno and the Kessler sisters!'

'There, that's what I've been telling you all along. We're all just walking museum exhibits . . .' says Zoran.

119. Zoran says: 'I grew up in an apartment building for officers' families. Our flat was 42 square metres. How can I explain what a "'mezzanine'" is? You stand between flats 13 and 14 for instance, and then you go up some steps and you're on the floor where flats 15 and 16 are. Simo Solomun and Adam Starčević. Flats 13 and 14 look out over the courtyard at the back, while flats 15 and 16 face the same way as ours. A quite, quite different kind of people live in the flats facing the courtyard, from those in the flats on our side . . .

'As for flats 17 and 18! They're on the courtyard side, but above us. That is, half above us. Do you see? The flats half touch. From our bathroom we can hear perfectly clearly when someone is practising the piano in flat 18. The feet of their piano end roughly at the level of the plastic handle on our toilet.

'Once my mother lent my velvet jacket to the woman from flat 18 for their younger son when he needed it for a concert, but later they didn't want to lend us their military encyclopaedia when my brother needed it . . .

'I still can't understand how they managed to get the piano up there. They couldn't possibly have carried it through the corridors, up the narrow stairs . . .

'It was in that corridor that my best friend's father killed himself. He jumped into the space between the stairs, from the top, when he was on his way to visit his relations who were called Ratković . . .

'I think someone once said that they got the piano in from outside with a crane . . .

'Ratković, the son, went to the same school as me, but he wasn't in the same class, since he was learning English and I had Russian. He lived directly above our neighbour with the piano, that is on the very highest floor. He used often to sit on the balustrade of their balcony, when his parents were at work, with his legs dangling over space. He called to us to look at him when we were in the courtyard, on the frame for beating carpets, pulling ourselves up by our arms . . .

'I encountered love much earlier. I loved a boy whose name I won't tell you, who sat on the bench beside me. He had enormous black eyes, long eyelashes, wonderful long legs and somehow specially shaped thighs. I used to press my legs firmly against the wooden seat trying to make them a little broader, with thin, reddish veins. The other thing that was attractive about him was the fact that his father had died.'

120. At the exit from the U-Bahn on Adenauer Platz stands a Bosnian woman in the traditional baggy trousers, who evidently does not know which way to go.

'Where am I . . .?' she asks helplessly.

121. In the Berlin restaurant I Due Emigranti on Belzigerstrasse, the visitor can see an enormous oil-painted triptych on the wall, which would appear to represent a short biography of the restaurant owner. On the left-hand panel there is a little coastal village (looking out to sea), in the centre panel are two men in a boat with suitcases (they are both wearing caps). The third panel, on the right, is a painting of a surreal cityscape, after the manner of De Chirico. If the visitor takes a closer look, he will see the year, 1989. It is only after lengthy examination that it is possible to make out in the deserted city the broken top of the Kaiser-Wilhelm Gedachtniskirche, the Kurfürstendamm U-Bahn and a dissolving piece of the Berlin Wall. On one side of the Wall among illegible graffiti only one can be read: *Napoli.*

If the visitor is himself an exile, he will be stunned by the impression that the third, Berlin, section of the painting, however amateur, has hit on something that he himself recognises, without being able to articulate it. Instead of the expected end, which ought to be a painting of the Italian restaurant in Berlin, this powerful triptych-biography ends in hallucination.

122. An exile feels that the state of exile has the structure of a dream. All at once, as in a dream, faces appear which he had forgotten, or perhaps had

never met, places which he is undoubtedly seeing for the first time, but he feels that he knows them from somewhere. The dream is a magnetic field which attracts images from the past, present and future. The exile suddenly sees in reality faces, events and images drawn by the magnetic field of dream; suddenly it seems as though his biography was written long before it was to be fulfilled, that his exile is therefore not the result of external circumstances, nor his choice, but a jumble of coordinates which fate had long ago sketched out for him. Caught up in this seductive and terrifying thought, the exile begins to decipher signs, crosses and knots and all at once it seems as though he were beginning to read in it all a secret harmony, the round logic of symbols.

123. With my feet on the empty seat in front of me, I sit under the enormous dome of the planetarium on Prenzlauer Allee. A starry rain falls over me from the dome.

'*Wo bin ich?*' I ask.

124. Berlin is a mutant city. Berlin has its Western and its Eastern face. Sometimes the Western one appears in East Berlin, and the Eastern one in West Berlin. The face of Berlin is criss-crossed by the hologram reflections of some other cities. If I go to Kreuzberg I shall arrive in a corner of Istanbul, if I travel by S-Bahn to the edges of Berlin, I can be sure I shall reach the outskirts of Moscow. That is why the hundreds of transvestites who pour out on to the streets of Berlin on one day in June each year, are the real and at the same time the metaphorical face of its mutation.

At dusk rose-sellers swarm through the city, dark Tamils with round childish faces and moist eyes. In the half-lit streets and cafes of Scheunenviertel young people perform the post-apocalypse. White Jamaicans with their hair woven into innumerable tiny plaits pass through streets thick with the shadows of vanished lives, like angels. In smoke-filled taverns on Oraninenstrasse, Turks listen to Turkish music and play cards. On Kottbusser Tor a spiteful wind licks posters where the profiles of Marx, Lenin and Mao Tse Tung hang side by side. In front of a dazzlingly lit BMW shop on Ku'damn bare-chested young Germans take each others' photographs as mementos. In Kurfürstenstrasse, not far from the Café Einstein, a prostitute, a Polish woman, walks nervously up and down. An American Jew, a writer and homosexual, looks through the bars for male prostitutes and settles on a young Croat from Zagreb, who had turned up in Berlin escaping the draft. Alaga, a toothless Gypsy from the Dubrava district of Zagreb, tinkles awkwardly on a child's synthesizer in front of the Europa-Center. At the Berlin Zoo station a young man with a sunken face sits on the asphalt baring the stump of his leg and begging. The coins thrown by passers-by thud dully on to a piece of dirty cardboard with *Ich bin aus Bosnien* written on it.

125. At number 13 Tuentzienstrasse, on the fourth floor, there is a JOOP women's fitness centre. Dr Jürgen Joop is the powerful proprietor of a fitness-chain. The huge windows of the studio, beside which are arranged a succession of exercise machines, face the street and look on to the Europa-Center and the Kaiser-Wilhelm Gedächtniskirche, which the Berliners call a 'soul silo'. On top of the Europa-Center the three-pronged, metal Mercedes star slowly revolves.

In this city the fitness centre is my healing temple, the price of soothing is cheap, I come here more and more frequently. I stand on the moving steps, the only exercise machine I use, and direct my gaze towards the three-pronged Mercedes star. One-two. One-two. Standing on the spot I climb stairs which lead nowhere.

Female samurai come here, strong, slender, young women with perfect muscles, smooth, set jaws and inscrutable expressions, so different from me. One-two, one-two. We march in a row, we, moving dolls, each determines her own rhythm. The three-pronged metal star revolves slowly, its rotation puts me into an hypnotic half-sleep. The metal goddess like a laser strokes the rough scars of the city, reconciles times and the different sides of the world, the past and the present, West and East . . .

I hear my heart beating in the darkness. Pit-pat, pit-pat, pit-pat . . . I feel touched, as though there were a lost mouse inside it, beating in fright against the walls. Somewhere far behind me the landscape of my deranged country is ever paler, here, in front of me, are steps that lead nowhere.

If I look up, I shall see the metal three-pronged star, if I look down, I shall see Alaga, the toothless Gypsy from the Dubrava district of Zagreb sitting on a folding chair in front of the Europa-Center awkwardly tinkling on a child's synthesizer.

One-two. One-two. I bow to my angel of appeasement, the three-pronged star against the empty sky, I pay physical homage to the indifferent lord Joop. Sometimes I think that I ought to leave but I calmly refrain. I don't know where I should go if I left this glass bowl. Besides, my feet are tired, as though they were stuck to the steps . . . And so, my jaw set and with an inscrutable expression I dutifully climb the steps as I stand on one spot . . .

Through the glass I see the broken tower of the Kaiser-Wilhelm Memorial Church. And there is no one who could possibly see me. Apart from the large Russian magpies which have settled for a moment on the tower. The Berliners say that they appear every winter. They migrate here, to warmer climes . . .

1991–1996.